Snow on High Ground

SNOW ON
HIGH GROUND

Raymond Sawkins

HARCOURT, BRACE & WORLD, INC.

New York

Contents

For M.S.

1
A Man Called Bernstein

'He was not the kind of man to take his own life and I don't believe he ever had an affair with that woman.'

'You think it was an accident then, Mrs Roberts?'

'No, Mr Snow, my husband was murdered.'

Snow sat back in his chair and studied the woman sitting opposite him. He wished she had put on the light so he could see her more clearly.

The hot dusk of the Indian summer crept in through the open window. The first day of October, but it was more like an evening in July.

Even in the semi-darkness of the small London flat she made a striking impression. About twenty-five years old, she was very small and slim in her sleeveless dress. Her face expressed a frozen determination.

She was slightly foreign in appearance, her long dark hair falling straight down from the top of her narrow head. She had a broad mouth and a pointed chin, suggesting unusual will-power. Her large tragic eyes held his gaze steadily.

'Are you English?' he asked.

'No, Belgian. I came over from Brussels as an *au pair* girl when I was eighteen. Soon afterwards I met David and we were married. He spoke no French and my English was quite primitive. He used to laugh at some of the things I said.'

Her eyes glared and her lips tightened with the effort

I

of self-control. Snow moved slightly in his chair. He wished he had never come. It was going to be quite hopeless.

'Mrs Roberts, I shall have to ask you questions. Some of them will be painful. Are you sure you want to go on with this?'

'Yes.' A single word, expressing ruthless purpose.

'You suggest your husband was murdered. But you must face the fact that the coroner's jury investigated the whole case thoroughly and brought in a verdict of suicide.'

'They accepted the evidence put before them. It was a formality.'

'What else could they do?'

'Nothing. But I have a personal interest in the matter.'

'I must warn you again I shall have to ask some unpleasant questions.'

'Never mind that. When you have experienced so much pain the mind refuses to take in any more. So I am immune.'

She gave him a defiant look, with the same steady glare of the huge eyes. Snow began to sense a certain atmosphere. He told himself he had better be careful. He spoke quite unemotionally.

'Your husband was supposed to be having an affair with a Mrs Warner, an Australian visitor to London. You went to the inquest. I have read the report. Now, Mrs Warner admitted she was having an affair with your husband. She says she became tired of him and told him to leave her alone. When she refused point-blank to continue being his mistress he threw himself out of a window in her flat. She was in the room when it happened, Mrs Roberts.'

'I know all that. I saw her give evidence. She is a liar.'

'It's not uncommon for a wife to be unaware her husband has a mistress.' He spoke gently.

'I know that too. I am not a child. I knew my husband well, Mr Snow. If he had been seeking amusement elsewhere I would have known. I would have faced the fact. I am capable of things like that.'

Snow leaned forward. He looked straight at her.

'Which factor carries most weight with you – your belief in your husband or your conviction that Mrs Warner is a liar?'

'My feeling that Mrs Warner is lying.'

Snow sat back again. It was not the answer he had expected, not at all. He tried again.

'I gather he spent quite a few evenings working late at his office, according to your evidence?'

'Yes, he did. He was a free-lance accountant. Gradually he was building up his own business. He worked very hard.'

'Mrs Warner said he was not at his office. She said he was with her. Did you ever visit him in the evening when he was working late?'

'No. I had to stay with the children.'

'Then he had the opportunity?'

Snow shifted in his chair restlessly. What was the good of all this? If only he could make her see the verdict was correct she might one day begin to build her life again. Murder! A fantastic idea. She began talking again.

'I know Mrs Warner was lying. Lying about everything.'

'How can you know?'

'Mr Snow, when they told me what had happened I refused to believe it. But later, before the inquest, I started to wonder if I was wrong. After all, we had been married seven years and men like a change. By the time I went to the inquest I had half forced myself to believe it must be true, although I had noticed no difference in David at all. I was curious to see Mrs Warner. I had got to the stage of wondering what sort of woman David had found. Then I saw and heard her.'

She paused, picked up Snow's empty cup and poured more coffee. He noticed her hand held the pot quite steadily. He had almost hoped to see it shake. Her iron self-control was beginning to affect him.

Passing him the cup, she crossed one leg over the other, rested her bare arms on her chair and stared straight at him, almost like a prosecuting counsel.

'Mrs Warner was lying in her teeth. She was playing a part. I am quite sure of it. And if she was lying none of it happened the way she said it did.'

'This is only your personal opinion. Even if it wasn't suicide it could have been an accident. Perhaps Mrs Warner preferred to tell the story the way she did.'

A ridiculous idea, thought Snow. But he was still feeling his way, trying to throw her off balance.

'An accident? I wondered about that too. I went to a friend who is an insurance actuary and asked him whether it was likely. He looked it up in the statistics. Very few people die by falling from windows accidentally. You should know that, Mr Snow. An ex-superintendent of police.'

Snow did know. He had once checked the statistics himself. What surprised him was that Mrs Roberts should have thought of checking them.

'In any case,' she went on, 'it's the wrong sort of window. Nobody could fall out of it by accident.'

'How do you know?'

'Because I've seen it. After the inquest I visited Mrs Warner at her flat.'

Snow just looked at her. He had a feeling of being out of his depth. She never took her eyes off him. He found it disconcerting.

'Why on earth did you go and see her?'

'To make sure she was lying.'

'That must have been an uncomfortable interview.'

'It was, for Mrs Warner.'

'What did you say to her?'

'I asked her to prove that she had been my husband's mistress.'

'How did you expect her to do that?'

'I told her that if she and David had been lovers she must know he had an identification mark on his body. I asked her what it was. She couldn't tell me. She pretended to be upset.'

'What was the mark?'

'A crescent-shaped scar on his abdomen. If they had been doing what she said they had she must have seen it.'

'She would hardly have liked to talk about it, to you of all people.'

'I told her if she could prove she was telling the truth I would stop bothering her, but if she didn't she would never hear the last of me. She just pretended to be more upset.'

'Most women would be upset, confronted by the wife in such circumstances.'

'Not Mrs Warner. She's as hard as nails. But she was frightened to death of something.'

'Of you, perhaps?'

For the first time Mrs Roberts smiled. Her face lit up briefly and then the smile faded.

'I don't think so. I'm quite small. Mrs Warner is six inches taller than I am. When I left the flat I was quite convinced her whole evidence was a pack of lies. Then there was the electric razor. She made a bad mistake there.'

'Electric razor?'

'Yes. At one stage Mrs Warner did try to convince me David visited her by showing me some pyjamas. She said they were his. She was quite willing to show me those but she didn't know about the crescent-shaped scar. Then she took me into the bathroom and produced an electric razor. She said when he was there he shaved with it. David did once have an electric razor. It's over there in that drawer. I bought it for his Christmas present. He used it for a week and then went back to the old type. The electric one didn't give him a close enough shave.'

Snow leaned forward and produced his cigarette-case.

'Not for me, thank you, Mr Snow. But you go ahead.'

Snow lit his cigarette and sat back again, thinking. It was getting darker now. A heavy sultry atmosphere filled the air, like the gathering of a storm. His hands were moist. It was going to be another hot night.

Mrs Roberts got up and switched on the light. Snow saw the room clearly for the first time.

A few pieces of old-fashioned furniture, undoubtedly second-hand, were placed methodically. The room had a neat, well-cared-for look. A round table by his chair gleamed with polish, reflecting the lamp-shade above it. He could hear the wall clock ticking off the seconds, time slipping away unnoticed. He looked back at Mrs Roberts.

'Did you notice anything else at Mrs Warner's flat?'

It was something to say while he struggled with his thoughts, trying to think of some way he could persuade her to accept the coroner's verdict. There was nothing to her suspicions. If all these ideas had been aired at the inquest they would have made no difference. They were just little things, intangible things.

6

'No, not at her flat. But I noticed something after I had left it.'

'What was that?'

'Someone was watching her flat from the attic window at the top of the house opposite. A man behind a curtain.'

'Probably just a neighbour looking out.'

'He had a pair of field-glasses.'

'A peeping Tom. Heaven knows there are enough of them.'

'He was still there half an hour later.'

'How do you know that?' His favourite question.

'I walked down the street, waited a while and then took a taxi. I told the driver to go slowly. When we passed Mrs Warner's flat the man in the attic was still watching her window. Doesn't that seem strange? You're a detective, Mr Snow, or you were. How much do you need to make you realize something is terribly wrong?'

She gave him a vehement glare. Her hands gripped the arms of her chair fiercely.

Snow leaned forward. His voice was sympathetic.

'Mrs Nelson asked me to come and see you because she said you needed help. What exactly did you hope I would do?'

'I was told you had retired from the police when you were very young. I can see that's true.' She smiled at Snow and paused.

'I also heard that sometimes you are willing to undertake investigations. I want you to investigate my husband's death. I want you to go and see Mrs Warner. If you agree with me that she is lying, I want you to find out what really happened to David. The police refuse to do any more. Will you help me?'

She leaned forward, her mouth firmer than ever. As she

did so her hand knocked Snow's cigarette-case off the table. She bent forward quickly and slowly picked it up.

Snow watched her. As she leant down close to him he could see down the inside of the front of her dress, which revealed the upper mounds of two firm white breasts. He was startled for a moment. He felt sure she was deliberately exposing herself to his gaze.

She straightened up, handed him the case and looked steadily at him, her eyes without expression.

'I must tell you, Mrs Roberts, that nothing you have said would have made any difference to the verdict.'

'I'm not just asking for myself. I have two children. One a girl, five years old. The boy is four. It's his birthday today. What am I to tell them one day when they ask me what happened to their father?'

Snow made no reply.

'I only ask you to see Mrs Warner, to judge for yourself. I asked Mrs Nelson what your fee would be and she gave me an idea of the advance amount. Here is a cheque.'

Snow looked at the cheque she held out to him without taking it.

'That's a considerable sum of money. You will need every penny now.'

'You are wrong. I am quite well off. David had very large insurance policies. I know there will be expenses on top of the fee. I can easily afford it.'

'Are you sure those policies are valid? Remember, the verdict was suicide.'

'I've already checked with my solicitor. The policies were taken out several years ago, and the verdict was suicide while the balance of his mind was disturbed, so it's all right.'

Her mouth tightened again as she said the last words. Snow gave up. Her sheer intelligence and grim de-

8

termination defeated him. And after all, it was just possible that . . .

'Very well. I will go and see Mrs Warner. I may visit her tonight, if she's in. No, keep the cheque for the time being. And you must realize that if after seeing her I still think the verdict is correct, then there will be nothing more I can do about it.'

He felt his tone was brusque, almost unfriendly. His manner was completely unintentional, but he wanted to get out of the flat. Heaven knows what she might persuade him to do next if he gave her half a chance.

'Now, Mr Snow. I've written her address on this piece of paper. Here is a recent photo of David. And a letter of introduction to show you are acting on my behalf.'

'You were very confident you could persuade me.'

'I was quite determined to do so.'

Snow looked at the photograph. It was a head-and-shoulders portrait of a serious-faced man wearing horn-rimmed glasses. The mouth was obstinate, the expression persistent. He would be in his early thirties, in fact about Snow's age.

'Mrs Roberts, do you know anything about Mrs Warner's background?'

'She's Australian and a director of a public relations company called Pacific Promotions. They're quite large, I believe, and have offices in Sydney. Mrs Warner has been over here on business for about five months.'

'What is your impression of her as a person?'

'She's very attractive. About forty, I would imagine, although I'm bad at guessing people's ages. The only person she cares about is herself. When I saw her she wasn't wearing a wedding ring. She dresses expensively, in the latest fashion. She's a chain-smoker and when she's nervous she has a habit of fiddling with her right

9

ear-ring. Her accent's a bit odd. She sounds Australian when you first hear her speak, but I got the impression she might really be German.'

Snow smiled. 'You should have been a detective yourself. I'll go and see her but I don't promise anything.'

He rose to go. When she stood beside him she was almost tiny. As she walked with him to the door, Snow noticed an accounts ledger on a table.

'Is that your husband's?'

'Yes. He not only worked late at the office. He brought work home too.'

'You said he worked free-lance. Who were the last people he worked for?'

'He had just finished a financial report for the Checkers-Chase Group of companies. I think that was the name. He made a recommendation that they should be merged with some other company.'

'Who gave him the job?'

'I'm not sure. But he mentioned the name of a man on the phone several times when he was making some inquiries.'

'What sort of inquiries?'

'I wasn't really listening. I'm afraid I've no idea.'

'Can you remember the name of the man?'

'I'm sorry. It's completely gone.'

'It probably doesn't matter. Good night.'

She opened the door and he walked out on to the landing. As he started down the stairs she watched him descending, a serious look on her face. He was just turning the corner to go down the next flight when she called out to him.

'Mr Snow, I've remembered the name. A man called Bernstein.'

2
The Woman from Australia

'Good evening, Mrs Warner. My name is Snow. Mrs Roberts was going to come and see you again, but I thought it best to come myself.'

'I've said all I want to say to Mrs Roberts. I'm not going to discuss the matter any further.' Mrs Warner spoke with complete indifference.

'Then by seeing me you can prevent her coming again.'

'I don't know that I'm willing to see anyone. In any case it's rather late.'

'If you leave it to the morning, Mrs Roberts may have gone to the police. She might even go tonight.'

'I don't understand. I thought it was all finished with. I suppose you'd better come in for a moment. I can't give you long.'

Snow walked into a small hall. Closing the door, Mrs Warner led the way into a large living-room. She sat down in a high-backed chair and left him standing. Taking a cigarette out of a box on a round table she lit it and casually crossed her long legs. Snow sat down in a twin arm-chair and watched her without speaking. The foot of her crossed leg started to move round as though trying to escape the shoe.

She was an elegant woman of about forty. Her mass of auburn hair was carefully coiled and set. She had strong-boned features and her shrewd eyes glanced across at Snow thoughtfully.

Her green dress, belted at the waist, was splashed with streaks of golden rain. As she shifted in her chair her figure stirred against the cloth. A silent minute passed. Then she could stand it no longer.

'Tell me, Mr Snow, just what is this all about?'

There was a suggestion of a smile in her eyes now, as though she was prepared to be friendly, on certain conditions.

'Mrs Warner, how many times have you seen Mrs Roberts?'

'Once. That was quite enough.' She twisted her full lips.

'Naturally you didn't like her?'

'Not naturally. It's possible to have an affair with a woman's husband and still like the woman. I've seen it happen. But I didn't like Mrs Roberts.'

'Why not?'

'For a woman who has just lost her husband she asked some extraordinary questions. Hardly decent, really.'

'She thinks you were lying. She is quite convinced her husband never committed suicide.'

'It could hardly have been an accident.'

Mrs Warner's eyes glanced automatically across towards the uncurtained window.

'Not an accident, Mrs Warner. She believes her husband was murdered.'

There was a pause, complete silence inside the room. The double window was closed in spite of the heat. Snow was suddenly aware he could hear no clock ticking. He looked around. It had the appearance of a room Mrs Warner had just moved into, no time to unpack yet. Or perhaps . . .

'Mr Snow, I feel like a drink. What would you like? Gin and something? Sherry? Whisky?'

'I'll have a small whisky.'

Mrs Warner stood up. She was about Snow's height. Without a trace of self-consciousness she looked down at herself and slowly smoothed her dress over her thighs, glancing at Snow. Her right hand started to fiddle with her ear-ring. Then she walked across the room and disappeared through a swing door.

As the door closed behind her Snow stood up and wandered over to a half-open door in the same wall as the swing door. Inside he caught a glimpse of a large double bed. Just beyond the door stood a family of pigskin suitcases. Against one wall he could see a dressing-table. The glass-topped surfaces were bare. There were no brushes, not a single bottle, in sight.

He wandered over to the window. It was a tall double window which opened outwards. The window-sill was quite high. Then he heard the sweep of the swing door again.

Mrs Warner had come back, carrying a full glass in each hand. As she walked her dress rustled faintly in the silence. She put the glasses on a table between the two arm-chairs, sat down and arranged herself again. Picking up her own glass she drank half the contents.

'Mr Snow, are you a friend of Mrs Roberts?'

'Yes, that's why I'm here.'

'I see.'

The thoughtful look returned as she watched him over the rim of her glass.

Snow walked towards her, picked up his own glass and sipped it, still standing. He spoke in a matter-of-fact tone.

'How long had you known Roberts before he went out of that window?'

'About three months. I find all this rather distressing.'

13

'You look remarkably self-controlled.'

'I can't do anything about David. When I can't do anything about a problem I stop worrying. Life's too short.'

'It was very short for Roberts. Had he threatened to commit suicide before he went out of that window?'

'I do wish you'd stop repeating that phrase. Yes, he talked of taking his life several times. I never took him seriously.'

She put her drink on the table and started stroking the calf of her crossed leg, watching Snow as she spoke.

'I really can't help you or Mrs Roberts. No one can. It's all over. She must face up to it.'

She was still stroking her leg. A wave of hair fell over the side of her face. It gave her a wilful look. Snow was staring down at her. He had a feeling he was getting nowhere.

He walked back to the window and gazed at a doorway let into the inner wall. It joined the front wall a few feet away from the window. A new brass rail projected from the top of the door-frame.

'Where does this door lead to?'

A slight hesitation. 'It's to the fire escape.'

'Why was there a curtain over it?'

'Was there? I'm sure I don't know.'

'You can see the scratches where the curtain rings have dragged along the rail.'

'There hasn't been one there ever since I rented the place. I suppose it was there originally to stop the draught.'

'And yet these scratches are very recent. The rail is quite new. It must have been a heavy curtain.'

Mrs Warner stood up, a look of hostility on her face.

'I don't think I'm going to answer any more questions. In fact I'm going to bed. I'll have to ask you to leave.'

Snow unfastened the catch and pushed the windows wide open into the night. Warm air drifted into the room. He put one leg over the window-sill and sat astride it, his feet clear of the floor. Below it was a sheer drop to the distant pavement.

Mrs Warner started to walk slowly towards him, her face stretched and rigid.

'Mr Snow. For God's sake.'

'It would be unlucky if I slipped, wouldn't it? Unlucky for you. They'd never believe you a second time.'

She stood quite still, like a statue. Snow smiled.

'Perhaps he was trying to frighten you and slipped? By the way, do you know who lives opposite, on the attic floor?'

She was trembling with terror, unable to speak.

Snow lifted his leg back over the sill and closed the windows. He looked across at the house opposite. Behind the attic window the curtains were almost closed, but there was a gap between them. The room was in darkness.

He turned and began to move towards Mrs Warner.

'Do you know a man called Bernstein?' It was a shot in the dark.

She retreated slowly before his advance. Twice she opened her mouth to speak and twice the words were still-born, as though she had lost her voice. At the third attempt words came, high-pitched and shrill.

'Get out. Do you hear me? Get out. If you don't go I'll call the police.'

'There's the phone. I'll wait for them.'

She exploded into hysterical rage, her eyes wild with fear and fury.

'Get out. You'll wish you'd never come near me. I'll . . .'

15

Snow walked quickly out of the room, crossed the hall, opened the door and left the flat, closing the door behind him. Standing still for a moment, he looked up and down the deserted corridor. It was a very quiet block of flats, almost as though only Mrs Warner lived there.

As he went towards the lift he saw the staircase, changed his mind and ran down the steps. On his way to the ground floor he met no one. The lobby was empty. A uniform cap lay on the hall porter's desk. He walked out into the street.

His shirt was sticking to his back. His feet felt too big for his shoes. The street was full of still, warm air, like a putrescent haze filtering off a swamp.

When he was walking along the street he glanced at the old house facing Mrs Warner's flat. On each floor the curtains were drawn and there were no lights anywhere.

At the end of the block he turned left down a side road. A mews courtyard ran along the back of the flats. Looking up he saw a fire escape running down the side of the flats. The last flight led into the mews courtyard, which was open to the road.

He walked on until he reached a main street. Fluorescent lamps flared in the sticky darkness. A vehicle cruised round a corner and crawled towards him.

'Taxi!'

The cab pulled into the kerb. The driver looked at Snow without speaking.

'I want you to drive round the block and pull up near the entrance to Garfield Court. Out of sight if you can, but I must be able to see the main entrance. There'll be a decent tip in it for you.'

The driver said nothing, flicked over his meter flag and waited while Snow got inside.

He drove round the block and parked at the right-hand

kerb behind a stationary van. Snow could see the entrance to the block of flats a dozen yards away.

'What's it all about?' asked the driver.

'I'm expecting a woman to leave soon. If she does I want you to follow her.'

'It's your money.'

The driver took off his jacket, hung it on a hook, lit a cigarette and gazed into the night.

Half an hour later another taxi drew up at the entrance. The driver climbed out and disappeared inside the block of flats. After a few minutes he appeared again, carrying three suitcases. Behind him followed a woman, carrying a fourth case.

'There she is. Don't lose her.'

The driver said nothing. As the other taxi moved away Snow's taxi followed.

Twenty minutes later they were speeding along in light traffic when Snow's driver spoke over his shoulder.

'It's London Airport.'

'Be careful. Don't lose her.'

'Pound to a penny. It's London Airport.'

Snow's taxi was close behind Mrs Warner's when it turned into the airport. He sat quite still and watched her get out, pay her driver and summon a porter.

As she went inside the building Snow paid his own driver and followed her. Overhead a plane droned in a circle, its coloured lights winking on and off in the Prussian-blue sky.

Inside the reception hall Snow paused. Passengers with luggage were standing against a counter. He watched Mrs Warner join them. Going behind a bookstall, he prepared to wait.

Time slipped away into the night. The passengers stirred irritably, looked at their watches, walked up and down. Mrs Warner still stood by the counter, her passport in her hand.

Suddenly the speaker-system clicked. An impersonal voice relayed a message, like a recording-system repeated scores of times each day.

B.O.A.C. Flight BA 165 departing for Rome and Cairo. All passengers please assemble in the Final Departure Lounge.

Snow picked up a timetable from a rack and studied it for a moment. There were connexions for Australia from Cairo on the following day.

The group of passengers were moving away from the counter in a weary straggle. Snow watched Mrs Warner's back grow smaller and smaller, trailing down the long corridor towards Australia.

Five months in London. A man dies. A young wife with two children is widowed. And an auburn-haired woman from the other side of the world walks away with her luggage and her secrets.

The large reception hall was deserted now. Snow was alone, except for one person.

On the far side of the hall someone was sitting in a chair next to a rubber-plant. Snow frowned. There was something odd about the seated man. He sat quite motionless, legs apart, hands resting on fat knees, gazing at nothing, almost as though at home in his own lounge.

Snow began to walk slowly down the hall, his footsteps echoing like the swing of a pendulum. He veered slightly to pass close to the man in the chair. As he reached the chair he glanced down.

The occupant was a small fat man dressed in a foreign suit, possibly German or Austrian. He was wearing a soft broad-brimmed hat. Snow had an impression of a large round face with a short thick nose. It was impossible to see the eyes under the hat. He seemed to be

18

asleep. There was no sign of movement as Snow walked on.

At the far end of the hall stood a row of telephone-boxes. All the doors were open. Snow went inside the first one, closed the door and dialled a number.

'Jonathan? Snow here. Sorry to phone you so late. . . . Yes, I know you keep all hours. Look, I want you to find out something . . . The Checkers-Chase Group of companies . . . you've heard of them? Good. Can you find out who controls them? They may have been taken over recently. . . . And another thing, an Australian firm called Pacific Promotions, based in Sydney probably. . . . Find out who controls them too. . . . No, I'm at London Airport . . . I'm just going home. . . . I'll ring you in the morning at your office. . . . No, I haven't been anywhere. . . .'

He put the phone down and looked along the hall. The chair by the rubber-plant was empty.

The phone was ringing when Snow arrived back at his flat. He hurried inside, expecting the bell to stop just as he reached it.

'Snow speaking.'

'Jonathan Slope here. Look, Snow, I've done a bit of homework on those queries you phoned about. I was going to leave it till the morning but I never sleep these hot nights anyway. I looked up the Checkers-Chase outfit in my library. . . . It's a bit odd. . . . What's that? No, wait till I've finished, old man. I've managed to trace back the controlling interest to a firm in Barcelona of all places. The Industria Colonia. It was quite a trail. I've been through four holding companies already to get to Barcelona – two Dutch, a Belgian and a French. Now I

19

want to find out who controls this Spanish company. I'll have to wait till I get to the office.'

'You said something was a bit odd. You're a stockbroker. What's odd about it?'

'Well, just that I keep thinking I'm at the end of the line and I find the company I'm checking on really belongs to someone else hundreds of miles away in another country. Of course, there's a lot of that sort of thing nowadays. Cuts down on taxes.'

'But you said it was odd.'

'Yes, I did, didn't I? Just an idea. You develop a nose for these things. The pattern of shareholdings is a bit queer, difficult to unravel. Almost as though it was meant to confuse chaps like me trying to find out what was going on. I'll get some of my people on to it tomorrow morning.'

'How long will it take?'

'No idea. It's beginning to look a bit complicated. What's all this about?'

'I don't really know myself. What about the Australian company?'

'Pacific Promotions? That one was easier. Still a bit tricky, but I got there. Pacific Promotions is controlled by International Publicity Services, Inc., of San Francisco, a subsidiary of the Ikolon Corporation.'

'Ikolon? What's that?'

'I thought you'd have heard of it. A huge German company owned by Bernstein.'

'Bernstein? You mean *the* Bernstein?'

'That's right. Josef Bernstein. The one and only. Ikolon controls the Atlantic Tobacco Trust. It's one of the richest companies in the world. The Tobacco Trust, I mean. So that gives you an idea of what Ikolon must be worth. Mind you, it's difficult to find out how much

Bernstein does control. A good deal more than he lets on, I should say. Bit of a man of mystery.'

'Can you give me a brief picture of Bernstein?'

'Not really. He doesn't come over here much. Spends most of his time in Europe and the States. In a way he's an international financier, but he's a good deal more than that. One of those wizards who spring up once in a hundred years.'

'What nationality is he?'

'No idea. Sounds silly, but that's the sort of person he is. Runs about all over the place but his background's obscure. He cropped up just after the war. Meteoric rise and all that.'

'Have you any idea where Bernstein is now?'

'Oddly enough, I can tell you exactly where he is. I read a gossip item in the evening paper. He's in Frankfurt – Frankfurt-am-Main, the West German one. There's another in the east.'

'Yes, I know. You're quite sure he's over there now?'

'Absolutely. In fact he's holding some reception or other tomorrow night. No, not tomorrow night. Friday night. I gather Frankfurt is one of his H.Q.s, although he nips about all over the shop.'

'Look, Jonathan, you'd better let me phone you next. I may be going into Europe. I'll phone you when I can.'

'You'll be flying, of course?'

Snow heard Slope's dry chuckle.

'No, I shan't. You know how much I dislike flying. I shall use the Channel ferry and then go on by train. It's better than hanging around in some fogbound airport.'

'Can I write you somewhere?'

'I don't know where I'll be.'

'You're a bit of a man of mystery yourself.'

'I simply can't be sure of my immediate movements.

21

By the way, I'm willing to spend a little money to find out who controls Checkers.'

'Don't worry about that. I'm enjoying myself. I'll get to the bottom of it. Have a good trip.'

Snow replaced the receiver and sat down in a chair. He lit a cigarette and watched the smoke rising, not really seeing it. He sat for several minutes, frowning, until he had finished his cigarette. Then he picked up the phone and dialled a number.

'Is that Mrs Roberts? Snow here. I hope I haven't got you up?'

'That's all right. I can't sleep this hot weather. What have you found out?'

Her voice sounded surprisingly fresh for so late at night.

'Not a great deal. But I've decided to check a stage further. You'll have to leave it to me for the moment. I just wanted to let you know I was going on with it.'

'Have you seen Mrs Warner yet?'

'Yes, earlier this evening.'

'You agree she was lying?'

'It's difficult to be sure, but there was something strange about her.'

'Strange? In what way?'

'Well, when I arrived I implied you'd found something to go to the police with and she let me into her flat far too easily. Then her reactions weren't right. I said things which should have provoked indignation and she just changed the subject. Thirdly, she's scared stiff of something or someone.'

'You see, I was right.'

'Now don't be too sure. There may be nothing in it.'

'But there's enough to make you feel it's worth investigating. When shall I see you again?'

'I'm not sure. It may be a while before I get in touch with you again.'

'Are you going somewhere?'

'Yes, into Europe. To Germany.'

'David flew to Germany a month ago. I forgot to tell you when you were here.'

'Whereabouts in Germany?'

'Frankfurt. He was away several days. Then he flew back from Zürich.'

'Can you remember the exact date?'

'Yes, I can. He took the morning plane to Frankfurt on September 1.'

'This could be important. Where did he stay in Frankfurt?'

'It was a big hotel. Sounded like a sausage.'

'The Frankfurter Hof?'

'Yes. That was it.'

'Who did he go to see?'

'I don't know. He didn't say anything when he got back.'

'Was he in the habit of going abroad?'

'No. It was his first trip in five years.'

'Why did he go on to Zürich?'

'I'm sorry. He never said.' A pause. 'I may go and see Mrs Warner again while you're away.'

'You can't. She took the night plane to Cairo this evening. She'll be off to Sydney tomorrow.'

'That's strange.'

'Not necessarily. Now you'd better get some sleep. Good night.'

Snow put down the phone, went into his bedroom and began to pack a suitcase. It was nearly full when he opened a drawer, took out a ·38 Special Smith & Wesson Centennial revolver and slipped it under a suit.

3

Sapphire Express

The boat for Ostend left Dover at noon in a blaze of sunshine.

Snow was on deck as the harbour wall slid away astern, the gap widening until the boat became a single entity once more, resuming the independence only the sea could give, like a decision taken beyond the point of recall.

It was too late to turn back now. Snow had a feeling of nostalgia as the vessel slipped between the outer walls into the open sea, as though leaving behind something which might never be the same again.

He stood alone by the rail, wondering where his wife was now. Probably she was still with Charles Nessler. The last time he left Dover she had been by his side.

He watched the cliffs assume their stern shape, stretching farther and farther along the coast until they became just another land.

Rapping his hand twice on the wooden rail, he turned away, walked down to the main deck and along the companionway to the restaurant.

It was lunch-time. The large room extended the full width of the Belgian boat. Snow chose a table near the cashier's desk and sat down with his back to the wall. Now he could see everyone easily.

Half the tables were empty. There was a feeling of relaxation, the next stage in a Channel crossing. England was forgotten. Passengers were beginning to settle down, grasping the layout of the boat, looking around at their companions on the floating island.

No one familiar was in sight, which always seemed odd to Snow, considering the number of times he had made the trip. So far he had never even met an acquaintance on the steamers. He experienced a pleasant relief to find himself alone. Now for the menu.

He went through the dishes described in Flemish, French, English and German. Not the soup. Soup took away the appetite before the main course. He decided on a small whisky and some grilled sole.

He was becoming accustomed to the motion of the boat. In fact it was hardly noticeable, a slow gentle rocking, as though the vessel swayed in a mechanical cradle.

Beyond the windows the horizon quietly rose and dipped. The empty sea reflected afternoon sunlight. Four hours to Ostend. There would be no hurry over the meal. He had all the time in the world.

Snow revelled in the sensation of peace, sipping his whisky, glancing round the room. There was the usual mixture of nationalities, talking in hushed voices, giving the impression they discussed secrets.

A tall silver-haired Englishman exchanged the odd word with a girl. She answered briefly. Probably his daughter, thought Snow, although she was rather young for a daughter. Several pairs of Belgian men occupied tables for four by themselves. They looked like businessmen on their way back from London as they talked quietly to each other, never glancing round at all. Snow guessed the crossing was as familiar to them as the commuter's train home in the evening.

And then there was the little man all by himself.

He was sitting three tables away from Snow, eating

absentmindedly, a bottle of white wine in front of his plate. About fifty years old, there was something aristocratic in his appearance. He had a large beaked nose and his soulful eyes gazed vaguely from underneath deep curved eyelids. A man from the Teutonic north, thought Snow, possibly German or Austrian. He went back to his sole.

Four Englishmen sat at another table, talking continually, absorbed in each other's company. Between the engine vibrations snatches of their conversation drifted across to Snow.

' . . . the Book Fair . . . we reach Frankfurt at 10 tonight . . . must see what the Japanese have . . . Sir Stanley said . . . my first trip, you know. . . . Really? They let you off the boat first to catch the Sapphire . . . like a Grand Hotel on wheels . . .'

The afternoon dissolved gradually. When he had finished his leisurely lunch, Snow left the restaurant and wandered round the boat. After checking the position of his bag and brief-case he found the special Sapphire disembarkation point.

He was beginning to recognize passengers by sight. This was the third stage, mid-Channel. He might have been on the boat a whole week. It was a different world from the landsman's, the tilt of the deck beneath his feet, a new way of walking to counter the motion, the endless sea under a blazing sun.

On the open deck people sagged in deck-chairs, watching the sea, lulled into a pleasant daze, half awake, half asleep. It seemed the lazy afternoon might go on for ever.

Down below there was a little activity at the purser's office, a query over tickets, changing pounds into other currencies. Someone had lost a camera.

Snow completed his tour of the boat. He went inside a lounge on the lower deck and sat down in a leather armchair. His watch registered 2.30 p.m., another hour and a half to go. He closed his eyes and fell asleep.

He was woken by the ship's tannoy system broadcasting a message in Flemish, English, French and German. In a fuddled way it struck him that the traveller was directed by unseen announcers.

Passengers holding seat reservations . . . Sapphire Express . . . will disembark first . . .

He stood up and went along to the first-class bar at the front of the boat, where people were clustered together at the circular window. On the open deck below another huddle of passengers stood in silence, gazing ahead.

The sea was like blue glass. Several miles away to the right was a suggestion of sandy beaches. Straight ahead in the distance lay a smudge of a town. Ostend.

It was impossible to see the harbour yet, let alone the entrance by the jetty. Snow looked at his watch. There was at least another half-hour before landing. The crowd would stay there until the boat was close inshore. There was something hopeful about the port in the faint distance. It was the edge of a new continent. Perhaps life would begin all over again.

Snow started wandering round the deck, stretching his legs, until the tannoy renewed its crackle. It was time to make for the disembarkation point.

Near the enormous stone jetty the boat appeared to become confused in its movements, swinging round in a slow circle, until it was impossible to be sure which way it was facing. Sirens snorted. Then the vessel began steaming steadily backwards, past a huge jetty wall lined with tiny figures waving at the passengers.

Only a handful of people stood at the Sapphire point,

27

holding their special coloured tickets, clutching luggage, ready to rush ashore. There was a hint of importance about the little group, a privileged class, to be let off as soon as the boat docked, even ahead of the other first-class passengers.

The gang-plank was down. Snow walked across it, following the others along the quayside. No one glanced back at the boat. They hustled towards the Customs shed, their feet slapping the bare cement floor. Snow showed his passport and walked through the turnstile.

Customs officers stood behind their counters, waiting for the main invasion. As he walked out of the shed into the station, a porter guided him towards a ticket barrier. Behind it the train was waiting.

Snow paused at the barrier and looked at the Sapphire Express, one of the Trans-European Expresses, the most luxurious trains in the world. Even when stationary the gleaming coaches suggested velocity on wheels.

Half-way along the platform Snow found his coach number and climbed aboard. Thick carpets softened the corridors. A steward took his coat and bags. His compartment was a small room furnished with rich upholstery.

When the steward had gone Snow looked at the numbered plaques behind the seats. Only his seat was reserved. At this time of year he might keep the compartment to himself all the way to Frankfurt. Since he was a small boy he had always loved trains.

He got out again and strolled towards the end of the platform. A giant diesel was linked to the head of the express, its motor ticking like a clock moving towards zero hour.

Walking back, he climbed into the dining-coach and sat down in an arm-chair at a table for two. Warm sunlight radiated through the window. The dining-coach was less than half full.

A uniformed hostess came to take his order. She spoke in stilted English, her manner polite and correct, like an air hostess.

She had just come back with coffee and an open sandwich when the train started to move. There was no whistle, no warning, just instant movement. The platform vanished past the open window to be replaced by iron track. The Sapphire was heading for Germany.

He had finished his snack when a girl carrying a flash-bulb camera walked into the coach. She said something to the four Englishmen sharing a table farther down the car. They laughed and began talking to each other in a self-conscious way. A flash-bulb flared. Then she walked down the coach towards Snow.

'Would you mind, sir? I am taking pictures for railway publicity. If you give me your address we will send you some prints.'

'All right, go ahead. I don't want any prints.'

He had hardly finished speaking before she aimed the camera at him like a gun. There was another explosion.

'Thank you, sir.' She went off into the next coach.

Snow paid his bill and began to walk along the train. The express was travelling at high speed through Belgium. Inside the coaches there was hardly any sensation of movement.

Reaching his compartment, Snow opened the door and sat down. The corner seat facing him was now occupied. Someone was hidden behind the *Frankfurter Allgemeine Zeitung*. As Snow picked up his book the newspaper was lowered.

Facing him sat the little man with heavy eyelids he had seen on the boat. They looked at each other. The little man began talking in English with a heavy Teutonic accent.

'I believe I saw you on the boat. I am Dr Zimmermann.'

'In the restaurant, wasn't it?'

Snow's manner was not encouraging. He held his book open in his hand.

'*Ja.* We were taking lunch. Are you going to Frankfurt too?'

'Yes.'

'There are several Englishmen on the train. I understand they are going to the *Buchmesse.*'

He waited for a reply but Snow remained silent, watching Zimmermann.

'Always in Frankfurt we have the shows. Now it's the *Buchmesse.* Next the Motor Show. And so on and so on. We live on the fairs.'

Zimmermann laughed vaguely, not entirely at ease, but determined not to give up.

'Do you visit England often?' asked Snow.

'Only occasionally. Not so often as I would like. My work takes me there.'

'What work is that?'

'I export German wines to several countries, including Britain.'

'Isn't this a strange time of the year to be going to England? In your business, I mean.'

Zimmermann looked at Snow sharply.

'You are in the trade?'

'No, but I know something about the seasonal movements of wine exporters.'

'I am just entering the British market, making contacts. Always everything takes so much time to get started. The English are very cautious.'

The train was slowing down. It glided to a halt. Snow looked out of the window. Ghent, half-way to Brussels. The express was moving again after a one-minute stop. Settling back in his seat he looked across at the little man who was all attention, obviously waiting for Snow to speak.

'What part of Germany do you come from, Dr Zimmermann?'

'From the East. Like so many of my countrymen, mine is a troubled history. You are visiting Germany on business?'

'You could call it that. Tell me, Dr Zimmermann, do you live in Frankfurt?'

'Well, yes and no. Since the war I have always lived in hotels. They give me a feeling of security. You never know when you may have to move on, at a moment's notice. You in England do not know what it means when the world collapses around you. Your house is gone. Every mark you possess vanishes overnight. No, I shall never buy a house again.'

Zimmermann relaxed back in his seat. His hand cradled his lean aristocratic face. He gazed out of the window, sad eyes seeing something far away and long ago.

Snow went back to his book, a signal for more conversation. Rousing himself, Zimmermann leaned forward and placed a long sensitive hand on Snow's knee.

'You must forgive me, but one never quite forgets.'

Snow sighed inwardly, closed his book and waited. The sadness had disappeared from Zimmermann's face. His eyelids were drawn back, giving the impression of a hawk poised to pounce. His hand rested on Snow's leg clenched like a claw.

'They once asked me to kill a man. I was in a hotel bedroom overlooking a street corner. Any car entering the

31

town that way had to slow down almost to a stop to get round the corner. I had a telescopic rifle. I heard the car coming a long way off. It was early in the morning, just after dawn. It carried an S.S. leader in the back. I can see him now in the 'scope. The car not only slowed down. It stopped. The engine gave out on the bend. I had him in the 'scope for a full minute while they tried to start the car again. I couldn't pull the trigger. And then the car was gone.'

His eyes shone fiercely, lost in the recollection. Beads of moisture gathered on his forehead. Leaning back in his seat he took out a silk handkerchief and mopped his head. Then he spoke four more words, almost in a whisper.

'It still worries me.'

'When was this?'

'Nineteen-forty-four. Berlin. At the time of the Plot.'

'Who asked you to shoot him?'

'Some people I knew.'

Zimmermann waved his hand vaguely. The hawk-like look faded away. He smiled.

'Why does it still worry you?' asked Snow.

'Because I didn't shoot. An act of cowardice. It happens.'

'You'd feel better if you'd pulled the trigger?'

'I don't think so. If I had done I wouldn't be here now. The only way out of the hotel was the front entrance. The fire escape had gone in an air raid. There were three guards in the car. You see?'

Snow smiled and nodded, opened his book again and started to read. The little doctor sank back in a dream-like state. He clasped his hands and gazed at the compartment ceiling.

The express swept on, closer and closer to the German border.

Brussels Midi. A scatter of people lounged about on the platform.

Brussels Nord. Passengers left the train, a few got on.

Liége. Beyond the window sprawled a grimy shabby city, the last stop before the border.

Snow was half asleep when the tannoy system squeaked and gibbered. A girl's voice, calm, impersonal, disembodied, transmitted the message in German, French and English.

Dinner is now being served in the dining-car. Will passengers please take their seats for dinner.

Zimmermann sat up, alert again.

'I should be happy if you would join me for dinner. Eating alone is a dreary process.'

'Certainly. After you.'

Zimmermann started walking along the carpeted corridor. Snow followed just behind him. Beyond the windows hilly wooded country slipped away behind the train. The Sapphire was moving at tremendous speed but inside the coach it was almost like walking along a pavement.

Snow stopped suddenly.

'I've left my cigarettes behind. I'll join you in the dining-car.'

He turned and walked swiftly back to the compartment.

After a last glance down the corridor, he reached up to the rack above Zimmermann's seat. The suitcase was very heavy. He placed it on the seat and tested the catches. They were locked. Taking out a bunch of keys he experimented until one turned the lock. The catches sprang up.

Inside the case a magazine lay on top of a neatly folded suit. He lifted up the suit carefully and held it for a moment, looking at what lay beneath it.

33

On top of another suit lay the tortoiseshell-coloured stock of a ·22 A.R. 7 collapsible rifle, a 4 x 18 telescopic sight and a yellow package of 50 rounds ·22 hollow point ammunition.

He put the suit back, placed the magazine on top. closed the case, locked it and lifted it back on the rack. Shutting the door behind him, he walked rapidly along the corridor towards the dining-car. . . .

Herbesthal. The frontier town looked like the gateway to the grave. Passport Control and Customs officials came aboard and strolled through the train.

Aachen. The express was inside Germany now. It was early evening, the light fading in the west.

Cologne. The tannoy was announcing the approaching station just before arrival. After a two-minute stop the Sapphire moved off into the darkness, accelerating.

The train was travelling at a fantastic pace now. It swayed slightly as it raced on, a few miles east of the right bank of the Rhine, heading deep into the continent.

Snow and Zimmermann were back inside their compartment, facing each other in silence, like two chess players without a board. As the fatigue of the long journey took hold, an atmosphere of weariness filled the compartment. Snow was apparently asleep. Zimmermann gazed at the ceiling, hands clasped, his face expressionless.

As the tannoy announced the imminent arrival of the train at Wiesbaden, Snow happened to open his eyes. Someone went past the compartment, walking in the opposite direction.

There was something familiar about the figure. What was it? The hat! Snow remembered the fat man sitting slumped in a chair at London Airport.

He got up, slid the doors apart and walked down the corridor. The fat man had disappeared.

He walked faster, opening the automatic doors with a touch of his finger. Another empty corridor stretched ahead. As he passed each compartment he glanced inside. The train was almost empty now. Several compartments were completely unoccupied.

He must be nearing the end coach now. The train was slowing down. A long concrete platform skimmed past below the windows. Then the train stopped.

Snow pulled down a window and leaned out. The station sign was at right-angles to the train. It was impossible to read it without leaning out.

Wiesbaden Hbf.

An endless platform of concrete stretched away in both directions. Nearby was a huge clock, the red second-hand turning like a rocket count-down. 9.30 p.m.

Then a figure climbed down from the end of the last coach, a squat figure wearing a soft wide-brimmed hat. The man walked slowly away in the opposite direction until he reached a staircase leading underground, *Ausgang*.

There was never a glance back as he began to descend. The hat disappeared below the level of the top step.

Snow stayed watching until the train moved off, picking up speed with every revolution of the wheels. Closing the window he walked back to his compartment.

Zimmermann was sitting in exactly the same position. As Snow entered he swivelled his eyes without moving his head.

'We have just time for a drink before Frankfurt. Will you join me?'

'No, thank you.'

Zimmermann leaned forward as Snow sat down.

'Have you accommodation in Frankfurt? If not you could join me.'

35

'That's all right. I have a room.' A complete lie.

'Without accommodation it would be impossible to get anything within twenty miles of Frankfurt. The Book Fair, you know. These publishers reserve their rooms a year ahead. In fact for the next Fair while they are still here.'

'Well in that case it's a good job I booked in advance.'

Silence returned to the compartment. The two men might never have spoken to each other.

The train made a final spurt down the track, past an oil refinery. It was a strange sight, a blaze of fluorescence behind a wire fence, a network of pipes and silver spheres, like a space colony on the moon.

Speeding along an avenue carved through a forest, it emerged from the trees and rumbled across the Main River bridge, straight on into the lights of Frankfurt. The city closed in on both sides, slab buildings pin-pointed with lights, dark needle spires.

The Sapphire suddenly lost speed, quietly slipped inside the steel and glass cavern of the Hauptbahnhof, and stopped.

The two men got up without speaking, adjusting themselves to the lack of movement, put on their coats, lifted down their luggage and walked along the corridor. At the end of the coach they clambered down the steep steps on to the platform and paused.

The station was vast, the roof high enough to house airships. At the end the wall was covered with neon signs.

As they walked along together Zimmermann glanced at Snow.

'This incredible Indian summer we are having. Months and months of it. Nothing but sunshine. It's all over Europe, they say.'

36

Snow made no reply.

'I'm taking a taxi. Can I give you a lift?'

Zimmermann was puffing slightly to keep up with Snow's long strides.

'No, thank you. I've been here before. I'll manage.'

'It's made the journey go quickly. Having someone to talk to, I mean.'

'It always does.'

They passed through the ticket barrier into the huge concourse. People were standing around with a lost look. An enormous clock registered 10 p.m. Dead on time.

For no reason at all a phrase flashed into Snow's mind. It is better to travel than to arrive. . . .

4
The Tip of the Iceberg

The following morning in Frankfurt the sun blazed down out of a pale hot sky. By eleven o'clock the warmth had penetrated inside the buildings.

Snow walked along the hotel corridor looking at room numbers. The atmosphere was stuffy, like the interior of a greenhouse.

He reached No. 41 and knocked on the door. It was opened almost at once by a coloured maid.

'Good morning. My name is Snow. The reception desk phoned to say I was coming up.'

'*Entrez s'il vous plaît, monsieur.*'

Snow walked into a palatial room. Tapestries covered the walls, the ornate ceiling was decorated with plaster scrolls. On the floor pieces of antique furniture stood like islands in a sea of rich carpet.

At the end of the room was a deep bay window flanked by red velvet curtains. A woman sat inside the bay behind a large mahogany desk, apparently absorbed in her writing.

When Snow had almost reached the desk she stood up, pen in hand. With a gesture she indicated a chair in front of the desk and sat down again.

Snow settled himself in the chair, placed his hands on the arms and stared at the woman facing him.

A tall woman, her dark hair was parted in the centre. She had a long face and a Roman nose. There was something imperial in her manner. Her large, almost black eyes returned his stare calmly, her thick lips pressed firmly together. It was impossible to guess her age or nationality. She was possibly forty, perhaps Slavic. She began speaking English in a business-like voice with a trace of an unknown accent.

'I am Mme Savigny. Can I help you? I can only give you a moment, Mr Snow.'

'I have come to see Mr Bernstein.'

'A lot of people would like to see Mr Bernstein. He is a very busy man. What is it you wished to see him about?'

'What I have to see him about is a personal matter.'

'You can tell me all about it, Mr Snow. I have Mr Bernstein's complete confidence.'

'But then you'd have to have mine as well.'

Mme Savigny looked at Snow for a moment, a hint of annoyance in her dark eyes. Then she picked up her pen and began writing. She continued writing as she spoke.

'I know all about Mr Bernstein's affairs. In fact I deal with many of them. I shall have to ask you to be more explicit. I may be able to help you.'

'To see Mr Bernstein?'

'I should say that is most unlikely.'

She referred to a red notebook and then resumed her writing. Snow watched her for a moment. There was no sound in the huge room except for the scratch of her pen. Her white face expressed an air of disdain, of complete concentration, almost as though she were alone in the room.

There was a sudden change in Snow's manner, an abruptness in his tone of voice.

'Then I shall have no alternative but to take up the matter with the *Kriminalpolizei*.'

39

'What matter are you referring to, Mr Snow?'

This time Mme Savigny had looked up as she spoke, but she began writing again.

'The Checkers-Chase Group of companies, in London.'

There was a minute pause in the writing, half-way along a downstroke, then a resumption at the same even pace.

'The Checkers-Chase Group no longer exists, Mr Snow.'

'It existed a month ago.'

'Yes, but it was merged with the Ikolon Corporation yesterday. It no longer has a separate identity.'

'Then Mr Bernstein controlled the Checkers Group?'

'I'm afraid I don't know who you are, Mr Snow. Did you have some connexion with the Checkers Group?'

'I'm investigating the strange circumstances surrounding the death of David Roberts.'

Mme Savigny had put her pen down now. She looked calmly across the desk at Snow.

'Who is Mr Roberts?'

'If you really know anything about Mr Bernstein's affairs you must know Roberts was the accountant who produced a financial report on the Checkers Group.'

Snow's manner was growing more aggressive. His expression was unpleasant.

'Mr Bernstein owns so many companies. . . . The Checkers was a very small concern . . . hardly more than a post office . . . just a convenient vehicle for very small transactions . . . Mr Bernstein was probably hardly aware of its existence. . . . You say this Mr Roberts has died?'

'He fell out of a third-floor window. When they found him he had a broken neck.'

'Tragic, I'm sure, but nothing strange, surely?'

'It may well be a matter for the *Kriminalpolizei*.'

40

'But the verdict was suicide.'

'I congratulate you on the sudden return of your memory.'

Snow spoke almost brutally. He shifted in his chair as though he had decided to leave. Glancing deliberately at his watch, he conveyed a suggestion that his patience was exhausted.

'Mr Snow, there is a reception at the Kaiserhof at Wiesbaden this evening. Mr Bernstein will be attending it himself. I doubt if you will be able to meet him but I will be there. If you would like to come along we could talk a little more.'

Mme Savigny opened a drawer and took out a gilt-edged invitation card.

'What is your full name, please?'

'John Snow.'

She wrote rapidly and handed him the card.

'Seven o'clock. There will be a lot of people there but I will make a point of seeing you. In fact I shall look forward to seeing you again.'

'Might I ask what your position is?'

'Certainly. I am Mr Bernstein's private secretary. . . . Please do not think me discourteous . . . but this reception tonight . . . entirely my responsibility . . . a large affair . . . you can imagine what is involved . . . a thousand and one things.'

Snow stood up as Mme Savigny walked round the desk and stopped very close to him. She was exactly his height. He detected a faint drift of perfume, like the scent of a rare rose.

'Mr Snow, are you a rich man?'

She spoke very softly, almost a whisper. Her eyes, enormous at close quarters, waited for his reply.

'No, Mme Savigny, I am not a rich man.'

Snow looked straight at her with no particular expression.

'You must excuse me now. Céleste will show you out. *Auf Wiedersehen.*'

The door of Mme Savigny's apartment closed behind Snow. He stood for a moment in the wide carpeted corridor, absorbing the discreet silence, the luxurious atmosphere. He was on the second floor of the Frankfurter Hof, the most expensive hotel in an expensive city.

It was a place of character, the most important address in town. Businessmen who could hardly afford the bill made a point of staying there. It created a good impression. They emphasized it in conversation.

'You'd better come and have dinner. I'm at the Frankfurter Hof. . . . I always stay there: the service is good.'

Snow walked down the staircase until he reached the ground floor. From the vast reception hall avenues led off on all sides. More tapestries covered the walls.

Guests sat half-submerged in deep arm-chairs, reading papers, chatting, waiting. Everywhere was a constant bustle of activity. Uniformed porters hurried past carrying expensive luggage. The reception desk was in a frenzy, people arriving, people departing.

'I am sorry, *mein Herr* . . . no accommodation at all . . . quite impossible . . . . Cancellations? Most unlikely . . . a waiting list already . . . the *Buchmesse*, you see. . . . Somewhere else? . . . Very difficult to say. It is like this all over Frankfurt. . . . Can I help you, *mein Herr?*'

'Yes, you can.'

Snow spoke in German. He produced Mrs Roberts's letter of introduction, holding it in his hand. His manner was confidential.

'I have just seen Mme Savigny. You know her?'

42

'*Ja, ja.* But of course. Mr Bernstein's secretary. They have a permanent suite here.'

The desk clerk's attitude was attentive. The magic name had been spoken.

'We are trying to find out if a Mr David Roberts from London stayed here on the night of September 1st. An insurance matter. Incidentally, here is a letter from Mrs Roberts whom I represent.'

'Certainly, *mein Herr*. Only a moment.'

The clerk turned away and then immediately turned back again.

'Did you say September 1st?'

'Yes.'

'I am afraid that will be difficult. Most unfortunate. Our registration records for that day were stolen. Extraordinary! Never before in the history of the Frankfurter Hof has such a thing happened.'

'Stolen? What do you mean?'

'All our records for that night were taken. A very strange affair. It happened at 3 a.m. on the morning of the following day. Organized like a bank raid and the only thing missing was the registration record.'

'Organized like a bank raid? I don't understand.'

The clerk's eyes gleamed. He waved away a fat woman with synthetic blond hair to another receptionist.

'There were two receptionists on duty and the doorman. A man arrived at the entrance and told the doorman a woman had fainted in the street. They went round the corner and the doorman was knocked unconscious and left in an alley. Then another man came downstairs and told one of the receptionists he had found a woman unconscious in the corridor on the first floor. Neither receptionist even knew that the doorman had left his post. Then the receptionist went upstairs with this man and he

43

was knocked out too. The same man came downstairs again and attacked the other receptionist. When the doorman staggered in from the street the bandits had gone – and so had the records.'

'Did the police ever trace these men?'

'No. They found nothing.'

'Well, let's try another method. Here is a photo of Roberts. Can you remember whether this man ever stayed here?'

The clerk glanced at the photograph.

'So many people stay with us. How can we remember them all?'

'Have you anyone on the staff who has an exceptional memory for faces?'

'*Ach!* That is an idea. Walther the doorman. He always remembers everyone, even years later. There he is. Walther!'

The doorman marched across the hall, erect as a Prussian. The clerk pushed the photograph across the counter.

'Walther, this gentleman is making certain inquiries. Has this man ever stayed with us?'

The doorman picked up the print and studied it at arm's length. He glanced at Snow for a moment, as though he himself was taking a photograph. Then he looked at the print again and handed it back to Snow.

'*Ja.* This gentleman stayed with us. About a month ago it would be. It was only for a short period, possibly just one night. He asked me how to get to the Henninger Tower.'

Snow looked at the clerk sceptically.

'You must have thousands of people staying here every year?'

'That is true, but Walther has an amazing memory. People make bets with him when they come again that he

44

won't be able to remember when they were last here. He always wins.'

Snow looked at Walther.

'That bit about the Henninger Tower. How on earth do you remember that?'

'Because of the tip. The gentleman was in a hurry. He only had high-denomination notes in his wallet. So for a tip he gave me a cigar, a good cigar.'

'What was his name?'

'I never knew that, but I remember he was British.'

'I haven't got a good cigar so take this instead.'

'*Danke.*'

Walther slipped the note inside his pocket and marched back to his door.

'He makes a fortune out of his memory,' whispered the clerk. 'People like to be remembered.' He pocketed the note Snow handed him.

At that moment Snow heard a familiar voice behind him in the hall. A woman's voice was issuing orders in staccato German. He looked round cautiously.

Near the main entrance stood Mme Savigny, dressed in a black coat. She pulled a black glove on to her hand as she talked to a uniformed chauffeur. Snow watched them walk out into the street and followed them.

·He was just in time to see the chauffeur getting into the driver's seat of a large black Mercedes. He waved furiously at a taxi cruising past. Swerving over to the hotel entrance, it pulled up with a shriek of brakes.

Walther opened the door and Snow jumped inside. He waited until Walther turned away before giving instructions. He was almost too late.

'Follow that Mercedes, the big black one pulling into the traffic. Don't lose it, but don't let them see us.'

The taxi jerked forward. Snow saved himself by

stiffening his legs. The driver was a professional maniac. He began to spin and weave through the traffic, lurching sideways, braking, hurtling forward again.

An iron juggernaut appeard from nowhere, loomed above the taxi. Snow heard the clang of a tram bell as the taxi made a break-neck swing to the left and then right again. The tram plunged past the rear of the taxi, missing it by inches.

A straight road lay ahead between walls of department stores. There were streams of traffic everywhere, speeding along with Teutonic urgency.

The taxi roared ahead, overtaking, passing and overtaking again. They were approaching a road junction, a whirlpool of cars, a confusion of trams. There was no way through. The driver accelerated, twisting and turning.

Snow sat quietly in the back, very still, his legs tense, waiting for the shambles.

Suddenly the taxi emerged from the wall of buildings and drove on to a huge bridge across a river. On the opposite bank rose a skyline of old houses. Mme Savigny had crossed the Main into the ancient suburb of Sachsenhausen.

The water was busily choppy. In mid-river a long barge train moved downstream, heading for the Rhine. The barges were low in the water, laden with standards of timber.

Leaving the bridge behind, the driver picked up more speed as he drove down a long straight road. There was less traffic now, so fewer swerves. It became one headlong dash.

The street began to climb steeply uphill. In the distance Mme Savigny's Mercedes raced to the summit.

Just beyond the hilltop a curious building rose sheer

into the sky. A slim square tower, with walls of blank concrete, was crowned with a windowed column, like the nose of a huge periscope. Snow recognized the Henninger Tower, built on the profits of beer, surmounted with a revolving restaurant.

He leaned forward anxiously, peering over the driver's shoulders. Mme Savigny's Mercedes had vanished over the ridge. He felt sure they had lost her.

The taxi reached the top of the hill. There it was! The Mercedes stood parked at the base of the Tower.

Snow rapped on the window. The taxi slowed down and then stopped with a jolt.

'I'll get out here and walk up to the Tower. Here's your fare and something for your trouble.'

'*Danke*. I can wait for you?'

'Yes, you can. When I've reached the Tower, take the cab half-way up this road, turn it round and wait for me. I've no idea how long I'll be.'

'I'll wait. You'd never get a taxi round here.'

'I know that.'

'The Mercedes. It is Herr Bernstein's car.'

'How do you know?'

'Every driver in Frankfurt knows that car. The chauffeur is even madder than we are.'

Snow walked up the little side road. He was glad to get outside the taxi. The sunshine was very hot now. As usual all the windows had been closed. This passion of the Germans for airlessness!

Before he went inside Snow looked up. The side of the Tower stretched above him like a cliff wall. At the top the observation lounge peered down at him over the concrete rim. He walked in through the doorway.

He found himself inside a small neat lobby. A girl sat behind a ticket counter. It was rather like entering a cinema.

47

He bought a ticket and walked over to the waiting lift. The attendant closed the doors. There was a second's pause and then a feeling of being fired out of a vertical gun as the lift shot skywards like a shell. Snow had an expectation of going through the roof.

When the doors opened again he walked out to a small landing. Opposite him a circular staircase led up to the observation platform. To the side a doorway opened into a restaurant. He walked to the entrance and peered in.

The outer wall was a curve of glass window. Beyond and below lay the city, sparkling in blue haze, flattened out, a patchwork of buildings stretching an immense distance.

Mme Savigny was sitting alone at a window table, her back to Snow. The restaurant was almost empty. Snow walked quietly to a table behind a pillar and sat down out of sight. When the waiter came he asked for coffee.

He was swallowing his first cup when he heard the lift doors open. Footsteps like the tread of a mechanical doll crossed the landing. Someone entered the restaurant and stood near the door. Snow looked up casually.

The mechanical doll was tall, thin and very Teutonic. He stood quite still, his hands inside the pockets of a fawn raincoat, staring at Snow. His lifeless eyes seemed to register nothing.

When Snow caught his gaze the thin man looked away. For a moment he stared round the restaurant, as though not sure where he was. Then he took off his hat, walked over to Mme Savigny's table, said something to her and sat down.

The restaurant completed one 360-degree revolution each hour but Snow could detect no sign of movement. While he drank three cups of coffee he heard nothing

48

from Mme Savigny's table except snatches of trivial conversation in German. Sometimes they lifted their voices, almost as though for his benefit. The rest of the time they chatted quietly.

Snow thought they would probably be leaving soon. When they did so Mme Savigny would walk straight past his table. It was just possible she had not seen him.

Beckoning to the waiter, he paid his bill and walked back to the landing. He thought for a moment and then pressed the lift bell. They would hear the lift doors and assume he had gone down.

He went swiftly up the spiral staircase. At the top of the steps he was faced with a heavy metal door. Pushing it open he stepped out on to a terrace and held the door against the spring to close it silently.

He looked at his watch. Give them fifteen minutes. They would either be gone or else . . .

To kill time, he began to stroll round the deserted platform. The outer wall was low but metal bars projected upward from it. To climb over would require a certain effort.

The circular sweep of the city seemed far away. It gave him a disembodied feeling, like being in a plane, all links with earth severed.

At one point he stopped and looked down. He had always feared great heights. The sensation of giddiness began, his legs turning to rubber.

Placing his hands on the railing, he forced himself to gaze down. The giddiness receded and then vanished. He was almost enjoying himself. He watched a toy car crawl along a ruler-straight highway. Recalling the street plan of the city he tried to match it with the view below.

Suddenly he lost interest in the panorama. He had heard nothing, not even the opening of the door, although he had been waiting for it. But he knew he was no longer alone on the platform, four hundred feet above Frankfurt. He thought for a moment. If he was right he had completed one circuit of the Tower. The door must be immediately behind him.

Abruptly he swung on his heel. He was right. The door was there, but so was the doorman.

The tall, thin German in a fawn raincoat was standing perfectly still, hands inside his pockets, staring at Snow.

For a moment Snow waited, one hand on the railing, the other by his side. He would never reach his gun in time. At this hour of the day the platform was probably deserted for long periods. No one inside the restaurant would hear a shot. Something must be done, quickly.

He dropped his hand off the rail and began to walk towards the German very slowly, carefully keeping his hands away from his pockets. As he walked his eyes never left the thin man's incredibly steady gaze. He was very close now.

The thin man stood motionless. Snow's right hand moved up to the door handle like a slow-motion film. He told himself there was all the time in the world.

His hand felt the handle, grasped it, turned it. He started to pull the door outwards. It was half-open now. Suddenly Snow stepped forward, his shoe grinding down on the thin man's instep with cruel force. The German gasped and stepped back, his eyes blazing with fury and pain.

Dashing through the doorway, Snow slammed it shut behind him and ran down the steps. At the bottom he pressed the lift button, took his revolver out of his shoulder holster, slipped it inside his pocket and kept his hand on it.

There was no sound from above. He tiptoed across to

the restaurant. Mme Savigny had gone. There were no more customers. Even the waiter had disappeared.

As soon as the lift doors opened Snow stepped inside. He watched the staircase until the doors closed and the lift began its descent. It was a breath-taking drop, almost like falling off the platform. The attendant yawned and gazed at his control panel.

Down in the lobby the ticket girl was eating an apple. Snow hurried out into the sunlight. The pavement seemed very solid as he walked down the hill to his waiting taxi. There was no sign of Mme Savigny's Mercedes.

His taxi was exactly half-way down the hill, pointing towards Frankfurt. The driver sat slumped in his seat, his cap pulled over his eyes. He was fast asleep.

As Snow arrived the driver woke up, straightened his cap and jerked a thumb upwards.

'Dramatic, isn't it? I take my girl there on Saturdays. We'll be up top tomorrow night. First of all a drink, then a stroll round the platform. You can't beat it. Funny thing, some people don't like it up there.'

It was dark outside the Kaiserhof at Wiesbaden. Inside the huge building Snow stood at the top of the flight of steps in the main hall. A jostle of people in evening clothes were standing in the hall below, crowding up the wide staircase, wandering in and out of the reception room. The hall was vast, supported by alabaster pillars, illuminated with chandeliers suspended from the high ceiling.

From his vantage point Snow studied the swarm of people, grim-faced women in flowing dresses, their plump arms and necks shrouded in jewels, tiaras in their hair, furs across their shoulders; fat men straining in dress suits, flesh bulging over their collars, thrusting against their waistlines.

There was a babble of conversation. 'I hear that Krupp . . . The Americans will co-operate . . . this foreign labour is expensive to train. . . . We shall spend a month in Morocco . . . the Egyptians take so long to . . .'

Below him milled the cream of German society, ship-owners from Hamburg, steel men from the Ruhr, bankers from Frankfurt, the German miracle in human form, fat with success.

He saw occasional glances towards the entrance, men checking their watches, waiting for something to happen.

He turned to a German with a long cigar standing next to him.

'What are they all waiting for?'

'He'll be here shortly, then we can have a drink . . . this heat . . . He's expected any moment now . . . we'll be able to see his car coming from here.'

'Who?'

'Bernstein, of course. The reception is in his honour. Probably organized by him, but it all comes to the same thing.'

From where he stood Snow could see lanterns lighting the avenue which ran straight through the park outside up to the hotel entrance. On the horizon there was a blur of trees near the main gate, a quarter of a mile away.

A series of sunken gardens, spotlighted with green lamps, ran parallel to the main avenue. German motorcycle police stood by their machines at intervals along the avenue.

It was another hot evening. Inside the hall the temperature was sub-tropical. People were getting restless, starting to cough in the cigar-smoke haze. Foreheads were mopped with silk handkerchiefs. Women examined their make-up in compact mirrors.

Suddenly there was a buzz of conversation, louder than before. People crowded out of the reception room and massed at the head of the staircase, leaning on the balconies overlooking the steps. A mob pressed in on either side of Snow, gazing down the stairs, across the entrance hall to the avenue beyond.

The motor-cycle police lifted their arms, one after another, passing the signal down the line. In the distance a car approached, headlights beaming down the avenue.

The hubbub of voices increased.

'He's coming now . . . the police are signalling . . . that's his car . . . can you see him properly?'

The car turned the avenue corner and pulled up in front of the entrance. The headlights were switched off. Nothing happened for a moment.

Then a man in uniform dashed forward and opened the rear door. A tall man walked out of the hotel entrance and waited.

Someone was getting out of the car, still a distance away. A single figure in evening clothes walked up to the entrance to be greeted by the tall man.

'The tall one's the mayor.' The German with the long cigar nudged Snow in the ribs.

The two men came inside the entrance hall. The guest who had just arrived was smoking a cigarette in a very long holder. He took it out of his mouth and paused to look up the staircase. Then he began to ascend it slowly.

Mme Savigny, imperial in a long black evening gown, appeared from nowhere and joined the man with the cigarette-holder. He was quite close now. People from the lower hall crowded round from all sides. He had some difficulty moving up the steps.

Snow could see him clearly now. Small and slim, his dark hair was brushed well back over his head. His features were sharp and animated. Snow's first impression was of a relaxed man, possessed of enormous vitality.

He kept bobbing his head, a perpetual smile on his face, somehow noticing everyone, acknowledging it all with a simple courtesy. There was not a trace of arrogance. Listening attentively, he hardly spoke as he walked up the staircase. It was not at all what Snow had expected.

Then something curious happened. Bernstein was almost level with Snow when Mme Savigny said something to him. Bernstein looked to his right, listening to a stocky man walking beside him. But as he listened he was looking over the stocky man's shoulder, gazing directly at Snow with a penetrating glance.

For a moment the two men looked at each other across the crowd.

Then the procession moved higher up the stairs, reached the top and made its way to the reception room, lost in the swirling mass of people. This was Snow's first momentary encounter with Josef Bernstein.

5
Bibi

For a change Bernstein was talking to one person. His companion was a tall slim girl wearing a midnight blue dress which reached her ankles. Her hair was jet black, parted in the middle. She stood rather boldly, hands clasped behind her back. Every slight movement revealed the beauty of her body, her full breasts, her slim waist, the slope of her thighs.

Bernstein was talking non-stop, emphasizing points with waves and jabs of his cigarette-holder. He appeared to be telling her a funny story. The girl was shaking with laughter, her body vibrating and rippling with merriment. She seemed unaware there was anyone else in the room except Bernstein. Her eyes never left his, a genuine absorption in all he was saying.

Snow looked around. A middle-aged German woman stood next to him, a glass of champagne in her hand.

'Excuse me,' said Snow, 'but I think I recognize that girl talking to Bernstein. Do you know who she is?'

The woman glanced across the room. Her lips tightened.

'You mean the girl in the blue dress?'

'Yes.'

'That's Bibi Decker. A friend of Bernstein's.'

She gave the word 'friend' a certain emphasis and turned her back on Snow.

He watched the couple still talking animatedly.

Gradually he edged his way through the crowd closer to them. Bibi Decker's face was pink with amusement. She kept interrupting Bernstein with a few words. He nodded, smiled agreement and started talking again.

Snow was very close to them when Bernstein suddenly stopped talking, gave a little salute with his cigarette-holder, turned away and was swallowed up inside the pack of people.

Snow was now immediately behind the girl. When she turned round she bumped into him. She smiled instinctively, began to move past him and then paused, staring at him with one eyebrow raised. It gave her a comical look.

'I don't think I shall ever meet him!'

Snow lifted his hands in mock defeat.

'Meet who?'

'Mr Bernstein.'

She was still gazing straight at Snow, rather mischievously, like a cat prepared to play with the mouse. There was no hint of reserve, just frank appraisal.

'Mr Bernstein is a very busy man. So many people would like to see Mr Bernstein.'

Her mimicry of Mme Savigny was astonishingly clever and not a little malicious.

'Yes, I saw her this morning.' Snow smiled. 'As a great concession she said I could talk to her again this evening, but not to Mr Bernstein. Incidentally, I'm John Snow.'

'Your German is very good – for an Englishman.' A wicked smile. 'But then so is my English, so we will converse in English. I'm Bibi Decker. Just Bibi will do.'

She was openly flirting with him now. She managed to give the impression the evening had begun with Snow's arrival.

56

'Well, what shall we do about Mr Bernstein?' asked Snow.

'You shall meet him now.'

She linked her arm with Snow's. As they made their way through the crowd he felt her right breast press against his arm. No embarrassment, it seemed quite natural, as though they had known each other for years.

'Mr Snow, you remind me of no one I have ever met.'

She glanced at him sideways, peeping round her long black hair.

'That makes me an original person.'

'I collect original people. There he is. Over there.'

Bernstein was talking animatedly to a group of people, waving his holder, eyes sparkling, full of life. Bibi waited until he had noticed her and turned round.

'Josef, you must meet my friend Mr Snow. An original Englishman.'

Bernstein looked straight at Snow, his manner pleasant, immediately interested. He gave no sign he had ever seen Snow before. His smile broadened and he began talking at once in excellent English.

'Mr Snow. How fortunate you are . . . a friend of Bibi's. She has a weakness for Englishmen. . . . I cannot imagine why . . . doubtless because I have not the privilege. . . . We must have a chat and some champagne, just the three of us. There is a small ante-room . . . all these people . . . quite overwhelming . . . follow me.'

They made their way to the side of the room, almost like struggling through a street mob, Bernstein leading, with a word here, a word there, as he passed people.

'Frau Gerhard . . . how lovely you are looking this evening. . . . We shall meet tomorrow, *Herr Doktor*. . . . Don't forget the party in Munich, Renato. It would be

boring without you. . . . Yes, I may be in Rome in No-
vember, Janos. If so, we shall see you. . . .'

Eventually they reached the side of the room. They
followed Bernstein through a doorway into a much
smaller room. He closed the door behind them and ges-
tured towards a long table surrounded with chairs.

'This heat! . . . Snow, we must have champagne. Without it we shall feel tired. On these occasions the problem
is to keep going . . . people think I never tire . . . it is
simply that I don't show it: it is the outward impression
which counts, all through life.'

Bibi sat down at the head of the table, put her head between her hands, her elbows on the table, like a small
girl, and took occasional sips from the glass of champagne
Bernstein put in front of her.

Bernstein sat half-way down one side of the table, facing Snow. He nodded, drank half his glass, his eyes fixed
on Snow over the rim. He said nothing and the momentary silence emphasized his extraordinary capacity for
talking endlessly.

'Mr Snow speaks excellent German,' remarked Bibi.
She was tracing imaginary pictures with her finger on the
polished table.

'German! A language for psychiatrists!' Bernstein
brandished his cigarette-holder. 'English is the universal
language today, thanks to the Americans.'

'How many languages do you speak?' asked Snow.

'Seven. I can get by in English, French, German,
Italian, Swedish, Russian and Polish.'

Bibi laughed.

'Don't believe a word he says, Mr Snow. He speaks
them all fluently. He could be mistaken for any one of
those nationalities, if he wished.' She sipped some more
champagne.

Snow pushed his glass aside and leaned across the table. He spoke very deliberately.

'Mr Bernstein, it is a serious matter I wish to discuss with you. Would it be better if I came to your office?'

'The worst possible place to discuss anything! . . . The telephones . . . they never stop . . . a horde of people waiting to descend on me, rather like a dentist with appointments all day long. . . . Mme Savigny reminding me that So-and-So has been waiting for two hours. . . . Sometimes I think I shall run away from it all. Here, tonight, now, Mr Snow, is the ideal moment. I have locked the door. We have ample reserves of champagne. I am at your service.'

'Mr Bernstein, I am investigating the death of a man called David Roberts. He was the accountant who produced a financial report on the Checkers-Chase Group of companies in London.'

'Checkers . . . Checkers . . . Checkers . . . a very small organization, Mr Snow. Checkers-Chase Group of companies . . . sounds enormous. . . . Very odd things, names. . . . I control Ben Davis, Inc. . . might be a drugstore in Little Rock . . . actually it is capitalized at $80 million. . . . I was very sorry to hear about Mr Roberts. Why did he do it?'

'You've heard that he jumped out of a third-floor window, then?'

'Yes, indeed. A tragic affair. I met him twice when I was in London. A very able man. I should have given him more work. I might well have made him my chief accountant in Britain. He had a very astute mind.'

'You only met him twice, you say?'

'Yes, and then only for about an hour on each occasion. Once when I originally gave him the job and once when he handed me the report recommending we close

59

down Checkers and amalgamate it. Duplication of over-heads . . . that sort of thing.'

'Have you any idea why he should suddenly decide to take his own life?'

'I heard something about a woman. I don't know the details. Are you a policeman, Mr Snow?'

The question was quite offhand. Bernstein was smiling, finishing off his champagne.

'Yes, at one time I was a policeman.'

Bernstein jumped up, fetched another bottle and poured champagne into the glasses. He glanced at Bibi. She shook her head. Her glass was still almost full.

During the conversation she sat quite still, watching Snow, the faintest suggestion of a smile on her lips. Once Bernstein looked down the table at her, glanced across at Snow and smiled. As much as to say: 'She's getting interested, Snow. Better watch out!'

Bernstein slid the bottle back inside the ice bucket on the sideboard and returned to his chair.

'Mr Snow, where does this woman come into it?'

'Roberts fell from a window in her flat. She's Australian. She says he was having an affair with her and when she insisted on breaking it off he went to pieces and jumped out of the window. She says she saw him do it. The coroner's verdict was suicide.'

'Then why are you investigating his death?'

'Because his wife asked me to do so. She refuses to be-lieve her husband had an affair with this woman. She is quite convinced he would never have killed himself. There are two children, four and five years old. One day she will have to tell them what happened to their father. She isn't looking forward to telling them he committed suicide because the woman he was having an affair with threw him out.'

'Poor woman. What a tragedy.'

Bernstein fitted a cigarette into his holder and lit it with a gold lighter. As an afterthought he pushed the cigarette-box over to Snow. The gaiety had vanished from his face. He seemed genuinely moved as he thought about the unknown woman in London.

'What do you want me to do, Mr Snow?'

'I'd like to see the report he wrote on the Checkers-Chase Group for one thing.'

'Certainly, certainly. I can't imagine how it can help but I will see Mme Savigny sends you a copy in the morning. Where are you staying?'

'At the Hotel Central.'

'Of course, Mr Snow, married men do have affairs with other women and no one is more surprised than their wives.'

'There is something else. The Australian woman is called Mrs Warner. She is the director of a public relations firm in Sydney called Pacific Promotions. That company is owned by International Publicity Services of San Francisco, which in its turn belongs to the Ikolon Corporation. I understand you control Ikolon.'

'Perhaps that's how they got to know each other. A business link. I'm only guessing, of course.'

'I'd also like to see any file of correspondence Mme Savigny holds of letters from Roberts.'

'You'll have that in the morning too.'

'Mr Bernstein, you haven't asked me whether I believe Roberts committed suicide.'

Bernstein picked up his glass and drank the contents at one swallow.

'Do you believe it, Mr Snow?'

'No, I don't.'

'Why not?'

'Because I talked to Mrs Warner just before she flew out of London. I formed the opinion she was a liar.'

Bernstein said nothing for a moment. He looked as though something had upset him. He glanced down the table at Bibi, who still sat motionless. She was looking at Snow's reflection in the polished wood. Bernstein shifted in his chair and faced Snow again.

'I hardly like to think about Mrs Roberts. If there is anything I can do' – he paused – 'you must let me know.'

Snow pushed back his chair and stood up.

'I'd better be going now. My apologies for dragging you away from the reception. They'll be wondering what's happened to you.'

Bernstein stood up, his face still serious.

'Not at all . . . a real tragedy . . . any assistance I can give you. Have you a car, Mr Snow?'

'No, I shall get a taxi.'

'My car will take you back. I shan't need it for several hours.'

Leading the way, he unlocked the door and opened it. The world outside flooded in, an aroma of wine, smoke-laden heat and a babble of voices.

Outside there seemed to be as many people as ever. Faces were flushed, the laughter less inhibited now. Several people swayed slightly.

Bernstein found Mme Savigny and spoke to her rapidly in a language Snow was unable to identify.

As he left, Snow turned to say good night to Bibi. She bowed her head without saying anything, her eyes very large and thoughtful. He said good night to Mme Savigny. She stared at him without a trace of good humour.

Bernstein took Snow by the arm and led him down the wide staircase. A black Mercedes was waiting at the entrance. The chauffeur held open the rear door while

Snow climbed inside. He heard Bernstein tell him where to go.

As the car pulled away and turned into the avenue Snow looked back. Bernstein was standing under a lamp, waving his cigarette-holder.

The Mercedes sped down the avenue, past orange-coloured lanterns. On either side the park spread away into the dark, spotted with ghostly green lights, like a scene in a dream.

Leaving the avenue, the car swung on to the autobahn and hurtled through the night. Snow settled back in his seat, his eyes half closed, enjoying the unbroken momentum. There was no other traffic on the road. The Mercedes continued its uninterrupted flight through the darkness. Snow gave in to the feeling of drowsiness and fell asleep.

The car began to slow down. Snow opened his eyes as it pulled up in front of the Hotel Central. He got out, said good night to the chauffeur and started walking up the hotel steps as the Mercedes roared off down the street.

It was still incredibly warm. He took out his handkerchief and dried his hands.

He was near the top of the steps when a man appeared from behind a pillar and walked slowly down towards him. Then he stopped in Snow's path. He was a short fat man and he wore a soft broad-brimmed hat. Snow recognized the man at London Airport, the man who had left the Sapphire at Wiesbaden.

'Have you a light, please?'

Very Germanic in speech, like firing a cannon, the fat man stood holding a cigar in his left hand.

Snow took out a box of matches and handed them to him.

'You'd better light it yourself.'

He found himself remembering the revolver he had left in his suitcase.

The fat man lit the cigar very carefully, his eyes studying Snow from behind the flame. He handed back the box.

'*Danke.*'

He walked slowly down the steps. As Snow turned and watched him descend a car pulled up at the kerb and waited for the fat man. The driver peered out of the window, looking up the steps.

Framed in the window was another soft hat, the top of a fawn raincoat and eyes which seemed to see nothing. He was the man on the Henninger Tower.

The eyes stared at Snow until the fat man climbed in the back and slammed the door. The driver jerked his head inside, released the brake and left the kerb as though escaping the *Polizei*.

Walking up the rest of the steps, Snow said good night to the doorman and went inside. At the reception desk he paused to speak to the clerk, an ageless man with a moon-like face and pale eyes. Snow collected his room key and began tapping it on the counter.

'I think I know the fat man who just left, the one in the wide-brimmed hat. Can you tell me his name?'

'*Ja, mein Herr*, that will be Herr Kurt Volga. He has just registered with us.'

'Has he, now. When I arrived last night you had only one room vacant and that was because the occupant had just died. You made a joke about waiting for dead men's rooms in Frankfurt while the Book Fair was on. Had Herr Volga booked well in advance?'

The clerk took off his rimless glasses and began polishing them with a little piece of chamois leather. He looked at Snow thoughtfully.

64

'It is against the regulations to give information about the guests. I am sorry, but you will understand.'

He put his glasses on again and peered at Snow mournfully. There was no change of expression as Snow took a note from his wallet, folded it once and slipped it underneath the telephone on the counter.

'Of course I understand. As you say, the regulations. But I was hoping you might be able to do me a personal favour.'

The clerk went on speaking in a monotone voice, as though telling Snow the way to the theatre.

'It is a little odd. I am sure you will treat what I say as confidential. The two men arrived today and I believe they bought a room.'

'Bought a room? How do you mean?'

'It must have been expensive. I am only assuming that, you understand. Two men already here were sharing a double bedroom. They agreed to find other accommodation for a consideration from Herr Volga. Most unusual.'

'You said two men? There is someone with Herr Volga?'

'*Ja*, a tall thin man. Herr Heinrich Strauss. They look quite peculiar together. The long and the short, like a comedy team. Not that they ever laugh. Rather strange people, I thought.'

'Do you know anything about them?'

'I am sorry, Herr Snow. Neither of them has ever stayed with us before.'

Snow said good night and went up in the lift. When he stepped out into the corridor he looked both ways and then walked slowly up to his bedroom door. Inserting the key silently, he opened the door a fraction, reached inside and switched on the light, stood to one side and pushed the door flat against the wall.

The room looked as empty and indifferent as all hotel

65

bedrooms. Walking inside he closed the door quietly and slipped the bolt into place. The bathroom door was closed.

He unlocked his suitcase carefully, controlling the upward movement of the spring catches. The Smith and Wesson ·38 revolver lay under his shirt. The match-stick across the trigger guard was as he had left it.

Picking up the gun he crept over to the bathroom door, stood to one side and threw it open. There was nothing inside except the bath and the toilet.

He went back to the bedroom door, tilted a chair and jammed it under the handle. A communicating door to the next bedroom opened inwards into his room. It was locked. He dragged the dressing-table along the wall and moved it up against the door. By now he felt hot and sticky.

Going back to the bathroom, he perched the revolver on a stool, turned the taps full on and stripped off his clothes. He had just got settled in the bath when the phone rang. Climbing out of the bath he walked back into the bedroom and picked up the phone.

'Herr Snow. Reception speaking. I have a call for you. Fräulein Decker.'

'Put her on.'

'Mr Snow? Bibi here.'

'Don't you ever go to bed?'

'I haven't woken you up?'

'No, I was in the bath.'

'Oh! Are you . . .' A giggle.

'You've drunk too much champagne, Bibi. Get on with it.'

'I want to talk to you. Can you come and see me to-morrow, or rather today? In the morning? I've got a flat at 984 Untermainkai. That's the street by the river. Flat 88.'

'Yes, I'll come. What time?'

'About ten. I might be up then.'

'I'll be there at ten. And you'd better be up.'

'Are you comfortable at the Central? It's not much of a place.'

'Well, it's not the Frankfurter Hof, if that's what you mean. But it's all right. I've got a large double bedroom all to myself.'

'Pity.'

She put the phone down before he could reply.

6
Zenith

Snow looked at his watch. It was exactly 10 a.m. He pressed the bell.

The door of Flat 88 was opened by Bibi. She was barefooted, dressed in a man's blue silk pyjamas, the jacket hanging loosely outside the trousers. Her long black hair was well-brushed, her lipstick fresh.

'It's ten o'clock. You said you'd be up.'

'I said I might be up. It's Saturday. What do you expect? Come in.'

Snow walked inside and she closed the door. He stood in the vestibule while she tucked her jacket inside her trousers. It only served to emphasize the full mounds of her chest. She looked at him for a moment and then led the way through a glazed swing door into a huge living-room.

The far wall was occupied by a picture-window looking across the river to Sachsenhausen. The floor was covered with expensive carpet from wall to wall. Large areas of the carpet were hidden beneath Chinese rugs.

A small dining-table stood against the right-hand wall under a hatchway. Close to the table was another glazed swing door.

The rest of the furniture was mostly a collection of couches with curved ends. A monster radiogram and an open cocktail cabinet took up the middle of the left-hand wall. The only chairs in the room were those pushed under the dining-table.

Bibi walked over to the cocktail cabinet.

'Sit down. Anywhere. What would you like to drink?'

'It's a bit early, isn't it? Would coffee be a lot of trouble?'

'No. I'll join you. I've got some nearly ready in the percolator.'

She picked up a bottle, walked across the room quickly and disappeared through the swing door. There was a glimpse of kitchen as the door closed again.

Snow walked across to the window and looked down on the river. Another barge train was moving along the middle of the Main, again towards the Rhine. Sunlight blazed through the glass. He could feel its warmth on his face. Walking back across the room he sat down at one end of a couch.

The swing door opened again and Bibi returned. She was carrying a silver tray holding two straight glasses with handles. Fetching two small tables, she put one next to Snow, one at the other end of the couch and perched a glass on each table.

Sitting down at the far end she tucked her feet underneath her like a cat, her knees pressed together, her back arched against the arm. She watched Snow drink.

'What's in the coffee?'

'I've laced it with whiskey – Irish whiskey. Do you like it?'

'Laced it? You've flooded it. Anyway, this should wake us up.'

'Or make us want to sleep.'

She looked at him over the rim of her glass, eyes half-closed.

'Stop talking about bed, Bibi. You've only just got up. Now what was it you wanted to talk to me about?'

'Something rather serious. At least I think I want to

talk about it. I do and I don't, but I think I'm going to anyway.'

She frowned into her glass. Snow sat quite still, waiting patiently, anxious not to disturb her mood.

Suddenly she uncoiled her long legs and jumped off the couch.

She went over to the radiogram, humming to herself. Selecting several records, she piled them on the autochanger, pressed a switch and waited until the music began.

German dance music filled the apartment, a nostalgic tune suggesting youth and abandon.

Turning the volume down low Bibi skipped back to the couch and coiled herself up again, fidgeting with her pyjama cord. Snow drank more coffee. He could feel the warm glow spreading through him like sensual fatigue.

It was very quiet inside the apartment. The only sounds were the muted rhythm of the music and the occasional creak of a couch spring as Bibi shifted position. It occurred to Snow that she was very restless.

'Mr Snow, I've got to talk to you . . .'

'Yes.'

'You see . . . they've brought the killers in.'

It came as a quick rush of words, as though she was afraid she might never say them, then silence.

'What do you mean by that, Bibi?'

'I overheard a telephone conversation. I'm not sure what it's all about.'

'Well first of all, who are they?'

'I don't really know.'

'Which killers are you talking about?'

'I'm not sure of that either.'

'Bibi, you're not making a lot of sense.'

Snow spoke gently, watching her closely.

70

'I overheard a phone conversation on an extension. Someone called Zenith is the head of the gang.'

'Gang?'

'They're worried about something which has gone wrong, something which has been found out. I think they're frightened. They'd never have called in Zenith otherwise. Nothing like it has ever happened before.'

'What are they frightened about?'

'I think it's some information which has been discovered. By accident, I gathered. The information must never become public. That's why they've called in Zenith – to make sure the information is suppressed.'

'You mean this is a gang of professional killers you're talking about?'

'People like that do exist, don't they?'

The couch spring squeaked again.

'Oh yes. They exist all right,' said Snow grimly.

'Have you ever heard of this man Zenith?'

'You're sure Zenith is a man?'

A look of surprise crossed Bibi's face.

'Well, I just assumed it would be a man. You don't know anything about him – or her?'

'I've heard the name just twice. In connexion with two separate murders in two quite different parts of Europe, two unsolved murders. Zenith might be the code name for an organization, or it might be the head of the gang. I don't know. Where did you hear the name mentioned?'

'During the phone call. Just once. Something like "We've brought in Zenith to deal with it." Just that.'

'And who made the phone call?'

'I can't tell you. You'll have to accept that.'

'Bibi, why are you telling me all this? We only met last night.'

'Yes, I know. I suppose in a way that's the reason.

71

You're a complete outsider. I felt I'd go mad if I didn't confide in someone. And in any case, you used to be a policeman.'

'How do you know that? Because I mentioned it to Bernstein last night?'

'No, I knew before then. They all know about you.'

Snow drank some more coffee. He looked at Bibi keenly.

'You said they, whoever they are, have taken fright?'

'Yes. That's the only thing which would have driven them to get in touch with Zenith. I think it's a crazy risk to take. You hire people like that and before you know where you are they've taken over. They are giving you the orders. And there's nothing you can do about it.'

'That's a very intelligent remark. Incidentally, Bibi, are you frightened?'

'Yes, I suppose I am. Frankly I'm scared stiff. They're horrible people.'

'So you do know something about Zenith?'

She drank over half her glass at one gulp. Her face was beginning to look flushed. She flexed her hands down her legs.

'It was several years ago. Before I met Josef. I was a hostess in a club on the Reperbahn in Hamburg. One night a shipbuilder came into the place. He was a very fat man and rather drunk. I can still see him – he tried to take me upstairs. I wasn't used to things then. After he'd been there a while the manager sent him to a house just opposite. One of those places where they have girls, two to a room. About midnight there was a commotion in the street and we all ran out. It was the fat shipbuilder. He'd fallen out of a window on the third floor. His neck was broken. It was a queer business and the *Polizei* never got to the bottom of it. The following night we were all

72

talking about it and the barman mentioned the name Zenith. I asked him who Zenith was and he told me to shut up or I'd be shut up permanently. I forgot about it soon afterwards – in fact until I heard the name Zenith again during the phone call.'

Snow had listened to her with an expressionless face, sitting quite still, his glass in his hand. When she stopped speaking he finished his drink, gave her a cigarette, took one himself and lit them both.

'Is Bernstein mixed up in this?' he asked.

'No, at least not directly, I mean . . . I don't think he knows . . . I'm not sure . . . Oh, let's stop talking about it. Tomorrow I'll wish I'd never said anything.'

Snow suddenly realized the music had stopped. He got up and went over to the radiogram. One record had finished playing. The arm was withdrawn waiting for the next disc to fall. But something had gone wrong with the mechanism and the pick-up was frozen in mid-air. He tried to remember when he had heard the music stop. He thought it was just after Bibi had begun telling her story about the man in Hamburg. It could be important, if the room was equipped with listening devices. . . .

Bibi shook her head as though to clear her mind of unpleasant thoughts. It struck Snow that she was probably experiencing an emotional reaction. She stirred on the couch.

'It's very hot in here. I think I'm going to take my pyjamas off.'

Her hand moved towards a button.

At that moment the doorbell rang. Bibi got off the couch, picked up Snow's glass and stood over him.

'I'll see who it is. Quite the wrong moment, of course! Go into the bedroom – it's that door next to the kitchen. Here, take your glass with you.'

73

'Are you expecting anyone?'

'It's probably Mme Savigny. She'd better not find you here.'

'There's a chain on the door, isn't there?'

'Yes.'

'Put it on before you open it. In any case I'm staying here to make sure. If it is Mme Savigny I'll nip into the bedroom.'

'That won't work. She charges in. Now go into the bedroom and stop fussing. I'll join you after she's gone.'

She grinned impishly and skipped over to the vestibule.

Snow walked over to the bedroom door with the glass in his hand. Opening it, he walked inside and pushed the door closed, his hand remaining on the knob, holding it in the open position. He listened for a moment and then opened the door a fraction.

Bibi had gone out of sight into the vestibule. The swing door was still shuddering. Snow put his glass down on a table, placed his hand inside his pocket on his revolver and watched through the narrow gap. There was not a sound.

He was beginning to get worried when the swing door opened and Mme Savigny walked in. She disappeared beyond the gap towards the window. Snow closed the door carefully and listened again. It was impossible to hear anything.

Walking away from the door he examined the room. Standing with its back to the far wall was a huge four-poster double bed. Pink silk curtains were gathered round the posts, tied with blue cord. Against another wall stood a dressing-table backed with three long mirrors.

There was no canopy to the bed which was open to the ceiling. Immediately above the bed a large mirror was fixed to the ceiling, reflecting the entire bed area. Scattered round the room were three more mirrors, cheval glasses with adjustable hinges. All these mirrors were suggestive to Snow.

Moving around rapidly, he made a quick search, opening drawers quietly, glancing inside, not touching anything. Underneath a pillow he found a ·45 Luger automatic pistol, fully loaded. He placed the gun carefully back under the pillow and walked over to the door.

He had just reached it when the door opened in his face and Bibi peered in.

'Not in bed yet?'

'Who was it?'

'Just Mme Savigny. She's gone now.'

'What did she want?'

'Oh, this and that. She had some instructions to give me about the reception in Munich this evening.'

'Is Bernstein going to Munich, then?'

'Yes, he's catching the lunch-time train. I'm going by plane later this afternoon. Josef hates flying.'

'I agree with him. What time does the train leave?'

'It's the T.E.E. The Rhine Arrow Express. It leaves the Hauptbahnhof at 1.20 p.m. Why? Are you going too?'

'Yes. I want another chat with Mr Bernstein.'

'He'll be awfully pleased. He likes you.'

'Where can I find him in Munich?'

'He's got a permanent suite at the Bayer Hof, plus spare rooms. I'll reserve one for you. And you must come to the reception. It's at midnight. Exciting!'

She was still leaning against the side of the doorway, her eyes large and dark. Snow couldn't get past her. He took a step forward. She stayed quite still. Now he was almost touching her body.

'You're in a terrible hurry, Mr Snow.'

75

'Not much time left. I've got one or two things to do before I catch the Rhine Arrow.'

'Of course!'

'You and your mirrors.'

'There's always a couch in the lounge.'

She turned and walked slowly towards the vestibule, talking over her shoulder.

'It isn't everyone I receive in my pyjamas. I really think I must be going off!'

She glanced back at Snow, frowning in a mock huff. He slapped her through the thin material.

'You do all right, Bibi, you do all right. Where will you be in Munich?'

'At the Bayer Hof. It will be impossible to avoid me!'

The chain was dangling loose. Snow pointed to it as she opened the front door.

'When I've gone, put that thing on. And get into the habit of using it whenever you're here. *Wiedersehen.*'

When the lift arrived he looked back as he stepped inside. She was still standing there, watching him, as the lift doors closed.

7
Rhine Arrow

Inside the immense cavern of Frankfurt Hauptbahnhof the big clock registered 1 p.m. Amid the hum and stutter of impatient diesels long trains extended away down the platforms. The high metallic drone of the tannoy system, like an announcement from outer space, reported trains arriving, trains departing.

Stockholm . . . Amsterdam . . . Paris . . . Mailand . . . München . . . Wien . . . Budapest.

Passengers hurried, ran across the concourse, in all directions, colliding with each other, without apologies, exchanging brief glares. Porters were trundling giant trolleys piled high with luggage. Everything seemed heavy, solid, built to last, Teutonic. There was an absence of elegance, no sign of gaiety, only grim determination.

The Hauptbahnhof, thought Snow, was a world on its own, a world of restaurants, waiting-rooms, bookstalls, fruit shops and travel bureaux. He noticed a post office approached by an aluminium escalator, ticket offices for local journeys, long distance and T.E.E. The cavern was vast enough to deploy a tank division.

He walked through the ticket barrier to *Gleis 12*. The Rhine Arrow Express was waiting, a fantastic train, more like a rocket to the moon.

Half-way along the platform he climbed up into one of the coaches. A uniformed steward appeared immediately.

'No, I have no reservation. I understood there would be spare seats.'

'*Ja, ja.* This way, please.'

It was another superb compartment. The steward gave him a corner seat facing the engine. Snow arranged his things, put his brief-case on the seat, got out of the train and wandered up and down the platform.

He strolled backwards and forwards for ten minutes and then looked at the clock. It was time to board the train.

'Mr Snow! Mr Snow!'

A face was looking down from an open window, a figure in shirt-sleeves, brandishing a cigarette-holder. Bernstein.

'Come along in, Mr Snow, come along in. What a splendid surprise!'

Snow went back to the end of the coach, climbed up the steps and walked along the corridor. Bernstein was waiting for him outside the open door of a large compartment, almost like a hotel suite.

'Where are you off to, Snow? . . . Munich! Wonderful! We shall travel together. Now I can enjoy the journey. . . . You will take lunch with us, of course . . . just the three of us. Mme Savigny should arrive at any moment. . . . Ah, here she is. . . . Maria, Mr Snow is travelling with us to Munich. Isn't it marvellous?'

Mme Savigny looked as though she thought it was anything but marvellous. Nodding briefly, she took off her coat, placed it on a hook, sat down and then looked up at Snow.

'Why are you going to Munich? I thought you had just arrived in Frankfurt.'

'Maria,' Bernstein flourished his holder, 'Mr Snow is like me. He prefers to travel rather than stay. The world is vast and we should see it all. . . . I promised myself I would do that when I was a small boy . . . so poor I could not even buy a pair of shoes, let alone an interna-

78

tional train ticket . . . and it has all come true. . . . I enjoy every minute of it. . . . Every morning I wake up and say to myself "I have another whole day before me. Wonderful! How can I make it different from yesterday?" . . . You should never repeat yourself. . . . Change is living.'

'What part of the world was that – where you lived when you were a small boy?' asked Snow.

Bernstein laughed and waved his cigarette-holder towards the back of the Hauptbahnhof.

'The East, Mr Snow, the frozen East. . . . Six months of the year the ground was like iron, frozen under a sheet of ice, a kind of temporary death . . . the mind freezes too. Can you imagine it? . . . They say the Ice Age retreated to the Pole long ago. Nonsense! . . . There are large parts of the earth where it still returns each year to blight the human race for half its lifetime . . . indescribably dismal. . . . If they had any sense whole populations would pack their bags, leave the ice behind for ever, settle in America, South America, the Mediterranean . . . wherever the sun shines.'

The train was moving now, gliding through the hooded cavern out into the sunshine, heading away from the oceans, deep into the continent.

Bernstein sat down in an arm-chair and patted the seat beside him. Snow sat down next to him. Mme Savigny was facing Snow. She lit a Turkish cigarette, more imperial than ever, almost as though she occupied the compartment by herself.

The Rhine Arrow was picking up speed, the outskirts of Frankfurt flying away behind the window. Already it was very warm inside the train, a dry thirsty warmth.

Bernstein was pressing the bell.

'We must have something to drink; to celebrate the arrival of our guest. Champagne for me. What about you, Snow?'

'A whisky and soda for me.'

'I'll have brandy,' said Mme Savigny. 'It's going to be a hot journey.'

The steward arrived. Bernstein leaned forward, waving his holder as he gave instructions.

'Champagne . . . a crate was brought on board for me. You've got it? Good. Then some whisky and also brandy. You've got a bottle of Mme Savigny's brandy as well. . . . Bring the bottles and glasses. I'll pour myself.'

When the steward came back with a tray Bernstein had it put in front of him and shooed the steward away. He poured a huge quantity of whisky into a tall glass and splashed soda on top.

'They'll have to carry me off the train, Bernstein.'

'Nonsense! You've a head like granite, I'm sure. . . . Make the journey go quicker . . . like travelling by plane . . . the first essential is a reasonable drink . . . not that I ever do go by plane unless I'm forced to. What happens when something goes wrong in those aerial coffins? No chance at all, complete madness. . . . Boats and trains will get you anywhere. Your health, Snow.'

'Bernstein, I read those papers you sent me about Roberts.'

'Good, good. Did they help?'

'No, I'm afraid they didn't. The report he wrote about Checkers was simply a financial report. I gather that he couldn't really see it served any useful purpose. In fact he seemed to wonder whether it was worth continuing its existence.'

'Precisely. And he was right. Which is why I had it absorbed.'

'You said you would ask Mme Savigny to send me a file of any letters from Roberts.'

'There weren't any.' Mme Savigny spoke abruptly.

'Apart from the final report, any instructions or queries were dealt with on the phone.'

'Rather unusual, isn't it, Mme Savigny?'

'Not at all. Most of our business is done on the phone or by cable. Mr Bernstein thinks correspondence is a waste of time.'

'But you must have at least one or two letters from Roberts?'

'No. None at all.'

'I see.'

Snow sat silent for a moment, watching Mme Savigny, who looked straight back at him, an expression of arrogance on her face. Then he turned to Bernstein.

'Tell me, Mr Bernstein, what happened when Roberts visited you in Frankfurt a month ago?'

'I never saw him in Frankfurt.'

'Perhaps Mme Savigny . . .?' Snow looked across the table.

'Mr Roberts never came to Frankfurt.'

She spoke with decision and drank some more brandy.

Bernstein was gazing out of the window. Suddenly he turned to Snow.

'How old would you say Mrs Roberts is?'

'About twenty-five, I should imagine.'

'And the two children? One five and the other four, you said?'

'Yes.'

Bernstein turned away, inserted a new cigarette in his holder, lit it and gazed out of the window again, his expression sombre. No one spoke for some time.

The train was moving at tremendous speed, flashing through stations, never slowing down. Snow thought about the T.E.E. system. The expresses had priority over all other rail traffic. Nothing must stop them. They had been planned to link key European cities in such a way that their timetable at least equalled the speed of aircraft linking the same cities. Air passengers lost valuable time travelling to and from airports outside the cities. It was a triumph of international organization, a Bernstein on wheels.

Suddenly Bernstein roused himself.

'Lunch! I told them I'd ring when we were ready. The chef must be sweating!' He jabbed at the bell.

The steward slid aside the compartment doors.

'Lunch, steward, lunch! Have I kept it waiting?'

'*Nein, mein Herr.* It is just ready. May I serve it now?'

'Immediately! Immediately! It's *paella*. Snow, do you like *paella*? We can get something else for you, something cold?'

'It's my favourite dish.'

'Splendid! Splendid! Something to start with? Or shall we plunge straight into the main event?'

'The main event.'

'A man after my own heart! All these elaborate meals . . . course after course . . . they treat the stomach like a dustbin. It must wonder what on earth is coming next! I'm sticking to champagne but there will be wines for both of you. . . . Snow, you've half a glass of whisky left. Drink up!'

'The whisky will see me through the meal.'

Snow was already feeling light-headed. He had the equivalent of four large whiskies inside him. The heat in the compartment was torrid.

Bernstein seemed to revel in the high temperature. He was off again.

'So Mme Savigny will drink all the wine. We shall see her do it, too. She drinks anything . . . fantastic mixtures one after each other. . . . It's her disgusting French habits! White, red, rosé . . . all the colours of the rainbow. . . . I knew a Frenchman once. Only forty years old.

He had just completed a two-year treatment course in Normandy. His liver had packed up. There he was, starting all over again. Wine on every conceivable occasion . . . getting ready for his next two years, I suppose. . . . Good, here's the *paella*. No, just leave it on the table. I'll serve myself.'

Snow watched Bernstein ladling great portions of steaming *paella* out of the copper pan, piling it on plates, great mountains of it. He suddenly realized he was extraordinarily hungry.

There was Chablis for Mme Savigny, another bottle of champagne for Bernstein, a third on the table as a reserve.

Mme Savigny looked across the table at Snow, a smile on her lips, her eyes sparkling.

'You remind me of Quentin Day, Mr Snow.'

Bernstein waved a spoon in the air.

'Quentin Day? That's very good. . . . You'd better watch out, Snow . . . Maria . . . she leads a most respectable existence for months and then she spots someone she fancies and – pouf! – she pounces . . . all restraint overboard . . . unbridled passion . . . she says she's discriminating: I say she exhausts herself with some mad affair and then needs months to recover! . . . How splendid all this is. What a stroke of luck I saw you, Snow. A journey to remember!'

Snow relaxed with his whisky and his plate of *paella*. It was an extraordinary lunch, like eating with old friends who had known each other for years. Bernstein kept filling up glasses, piling more *paella* on plates, exchanging banter, the soul of enjoyment.

Mme Savigny was thawing visibly every minute, glancing across at Snow from under her long eyelashes, leaning over the table to talk to him. She seemed ten years younger. At one moment Snow could have sworn she rubbed her knee against his leg.

83

And all under the influence of Bernstein's persuasive chatter and boyish high spirits. Yet not half an hour ago he had been gazing through the window as though he saw the end of the world.

When lunch was over and coffee had arrived Bernstein produced an expensive cigar and handed it to Snow.

'And yourself?' inquired Snow as he pierced the cigar.

'Not for me. Always a cigarette with coffee. We're slowing down. It must be Würzburg.' He peered out of the window.

It was a long platform. The express stopped but the sense of motion remained. *Würzburg Hbf*. A few people got off, a handful climbed aboard. After a one-minute halt the train began to move again.

Snow looked at his watch. 2.43 p.m. It was three more hours to Munich.

Outside the window the landscape was changing into high rolling uplands drenched in sunshine, their lower slopes covered with forest. Each upland merged into the next grassy sweep; not a house in sight anywhere. There was a feeling of peace, a sense of drowsiness in the afternoon sunlight.

The Rhine Arrow was a long way east now. Snow had an impression of travelling into a vast land, extending thousands of miles until it reached the Pacific shore. People living in such a land would think differently from those who spent their lives within easy reach of the sea. His thoughts blurred and disintegrated. He fell asleep.

He woke up suddenly. The chair next to him was empty. Mme Savigny sat watching him with an expression on her face he could not quite place. Certainly it was not hostile. In front of her on the table stood a half-empty glass of brandy.

The compartment was like an oven. His shirt was damp under his armpits, his head like soggy cottonwool.

84

Snow made the effort. He stood up.

'I'd better get back to my compartment. I hope my luggage is still there.'

'You'll come back, won't you?' She spoke as though she meant it. 'Mr Bernstein will never forgive me if I lose you.' She smiled warmly.

'Where is he?'

'He's gone down the train to talk to someone. Bring your luggage along here.'

'I'll see. Give him my thanks for a wonderful lunch. It's odd to get a Spanish dish on a German train.'

'They cook it specially for him. He can't stand the sort of meal they normally serve. We'll see you soon then, Mr Snow?'

'I hope so.'

Snow pulled the doors aside, went out into the corridor, closed them behind him and walked along the train. There were very few passengers aboard. Whole compartments were empty.

He found his own compartment unoccupied, his case still on the rack, his brief-case on the seat. Tucked into the handle of his brief-case was a long white envelope, addressed to himself.

He opened the envelope and unfolded the sheet of paper inside. The message was written in German in a firm teutonic hand.

On the way call at Altdorfstrasse 4 Nürnberg. Ask for Herr Winkel.

At the bottom it was signed anonymously, *Bibi's friend.*

Snow stood looking down at the note, frowning. A ticket inspector walked along the corridor. Snow called out to him.

'Have you seen anyone enter this compartment since the train left Frankfurt?'

'*Nein, mein Herr*. There is something missing?'
'No, on the contrary, something added.'
'I do not understand.'
'It doesn't matter. How close are we to Nuremberg?'
The inspector looked at his watch.
'We arrive in three minutes' time.'
'Could you take a message to Mr Bernstein's private compartment? It's near the end of the train.'
'*Ja, ja.* I know Herr Bernstein. He often travels on the Rhine Arrow.'
Snow scribbled briefly on a page in his notebook. *I find I have to break my journey in Nuremberg. Hope to see you in Munich. John Snow.*

He tore the page out and gave it to the inspector with a note. As the inspector disappeared he picked up his bags hurriedly and took a last look round the compartment. The train was losing speed rapidly. It would probably be another one-minute stop. Stepping out into the corridor he walked quickly down the train, looking into each compartment as he passed in case he saw Bernstein.

Just before he reached the end of the coach he glanced into a compartment with only one man inside. The man had a large beaked nose and sad eyes. Dr Zimmermann.

Zimmermann looked up, stared, leaned forward and slid aside the doors. His voice expressed complete surprise.

'How extraordinary!'
'Dr Zimmermann! Are you getting off at Nuremberg?'
'No, I'm afraid not. What a pity. Had we met earlier you could have joined me for lunch.'
'A great pity. I must get along to the coach door. *Auf Wiedersehen.*'

Dr Zimmermann called out after him as he walked away.

'Perhaps we shall meet again.'

Snow reached the coach door as the express stopped. He was the only passenger to get off the train. Walking slowly along the platform he watched carefully, but no one else alighted.

The Rhine Arrow suddenly started to move again, the wheels pounding a slow thump-thump on the iron track. Glancing up Snow saw the coach containing Bernstein's private compartment.

A long window came into view. There was the man himself, looking down on Snow from a great height, leaning forward, smiling broadly, waving the cigarette-holder as he bobbed his head.

Then the rest of the coach overtook Snow. The express gathered speed and before he turned down into the sub-way the length of the train was lost behind its rear door, growing smaller and smaller. Now that Bernstein was gone Snow felt a little flat, almost lonely.

He walked down the steps and along the echoing sub-way until he reached the ticket barrier. After showing his ticket he picked up his bags and went outside the station into the blazing sunlight of a cloudless afternoon. He paused at the kerb.

A wide street ran past the station. On the opposite side, immediately facing Snow, rose the walled city of Nuremberg. It was a long high wall, broken at intervals with watch towers topped with peaked cones like witches' hats. He almost felt the towers were watching him, wait-ing for his arrival.

There was a whiff of menace in the air, a memory of evil.

The brilliant sunshine made his reaction seem all the more absurd.

8

The Toymaker of Nuremberg

Altdorfstrasse 4 was a small shop in a cobbled side-street which was little more than an alley. As the buildings on either side rose to the first floor they tilted towards each other across the street, almost making a tunnel of the road below. A narrow strip of blue sky reminded Snow of a brighter world outside.

The houses were crooked, warped with age and made of darkened wood. It was like a street out of a morbid fairy-tale. No one walked down Altdorfstrasse. There was not a soul anywhere except Snow, who stood looking at the weird shop in the strange street.

It was very small, with a bulging bay window on either side of the central door made of heavy timber covered with iron studs. The bay windows were broken up with decrepit leaded panes, the glass was thick with grime. Beyond each window he could vaguely see a jumble of German toys.

There were dolls with faces like pigs and spiky hair *en brosse*. Mixed up among the pig dolls were girl dolls, dressed in German national costumes, like characters out of Grimm. It was almost an obscene touch, mingling them with the other dolls.

Over the doorway he could faintly make out the remnants of a shop sign painted long ago. *W. Winkel*.

Snow glanced up and down the street, walked up to the shop, lifted the iron latch with his left hand and pushed the heavy door inwards. His right hand was inside his pocket, gripping the Smith and Wesson.

The door lurched as it dropped over the lintel, the hinges creaked. As he stood inside the doorway a clapper bell above his head tinkled furiously.

It took him a moment to adjust his eyes to the darkness. A counter ran the full width of the shop. The walls were lined with shelves full of more wooden toys. Snow noticed a steep-roofed doll's house, more hideous dolls and an ancient cannon. The place was more like a nightmare than a child's Saturday afternoon.

He closed the door with difficulty, heaving it back over the lintel, and walked to the counter.

Someone was sitting behind it, perched on a high stool, holding a stick of white wood in one hand and a carving tool in the other. He was a tiny man with a hump on his back. On his head he wore a crumpled cap with a pointed top, like a jester's hat. He was a grotesque figure. What child would come to buy toys from him?

The dwarf kept glancing at Snow and then looking away. He had started to whittle madly at the wood with his knife.

'I've come to see Herr Winkel.'

'*Ja, ja*. I am Winkel.'

'My name is Snow. I understand you have something to tell me.'

'I can see you are Herr Snow. Look.'

He reached under the counter and dropped something on top in front of Snow. It was a piece of white wood similar to the one he was holding. But this stick had been crudely carved into the head and shoulders of a man, the head and shoulders of Snow. It was primitive sculpture but the likeness was unmistakable. Snow picked it up.

'How did you do this?'

'There are many mysteries inside the walls of Nuremberg.'

The dwarf chuckled, a harsh racking sound.

'Someone gave you a photograph of me? So you could recognize me?'

'*Ja, ja*. It was a very good photograph of you sitting in a train. You are like your photograph. Some people aren't. Then they complain about the carving.'

There was an odd wheezing sound, the dwarf breathing.

'Well, what have you to tell me?'

'A message, Herr Snow, a message. You are to go to my workshop this evening. Someone will meet you. You must be there at seven o'clock.'

'Where is your workshop?'

'Here. I will show you on the map.'

Winkel produced a printed street plan of the town and marked a cross with his knife on the city wall.

'That is the tower. The door will be left open. You go straight in.'

'Is that your workshop? In such a place?'

'*Ja, ja*. I have just told you.'

'Who asked you to give me this message?'

'A woman.'

'You were told to say that when I asked you the question?'

'*Nein, nein*. I have given you the message. That is all.'

'Describe the woman, then.'

'I must say nothing more, otherwise I do not get the money.'

The dwarf was whittling furiously at his stick, hissing away to himself as small pieces of wood flew all over the counter. Snow picked up the map and put it in his pocket.

'You haven't been paid yet? Then it must be a large sum they are giving you.'

'I do not understand you.'

'Anyone would want to be paid in advance for passing a message. Unless the sum was very substantial and to be paid only if the instructions were carried out faithfully.'

'It is difficult to understand your German. The English cannot speak German.'

As he worked away with his knife, Winkel's eyes bulged, almost like the eyes of the pig dolls in the window.

Snow took out a cigarette and lit it while he watched the dwarf's hands trembling with furious activity. The stick was taking shape now, like the first stage of a sculpture. It was another head-and-shoulders carving.

Placing his hand on the counter, Snow drummed with his fingers on the wood to emphasize what he said.

'I want to know who I am supposed to meet at the tower. If you don't tell me I am not prepared to go there.'

'What does it matter to me? It is to your benefit, not mine.'

'Except that if I don't go you can never prove you gave me the message. Then they won't pay you any money.'

The dwarf continued whittling, but it seemed to Snow he was carving more slowly, as though he was thinking about Snow's remark.

Snow leaned forward, drumming with his fingers.

'Then again, Herr Winkel, it might be a matter for the *Polizei.*'

The dwarf suddenly stopped whittling and jumped down off his stool. He was incredibly small, his face just coming above the counter, like an evil child peering from behind a hiding-place. The hand with the knife came over the edge and its point pricked the back of Snow's hand.

'Get out of my shop. Do you hear me?'

His voice was in insane shriek, his face white with fury. His teeth chattered without saying anything.

'Don't point that knife at me. It's rude.'

Snow spoke very mildly.

The dwarf jabbed the knife forward again. Snow's right hand swept over the counter, grabbed the dwarf's wrist and twisted sharply. Snow was half-way over the counter now, staring down at Winkel, who was screaming blasphemies, his arm doubled behind his back. The knife clattered to the stone floor and Snow released his grip.

'You would like to buy this?'

The dwarf shoved forward the whittled stick he still held in his left hand. It was the head and shoulders of a girl, of Bibi Decker.

'Who gave you her photograph?'

Snow's voice was cold with anger. He took a step towards the counter flap. The dwarf looked uncertain for a moment.

'You don't want to buy it?'

There was a savage grin on Winkel's face.

'No.'

Winkel suddenly stooped down. He came up again with the knife in his hand, dropped the stick on the counter and slashed the head off. His knife flashed towards the stick carved with Snow's image. Too late!

Snow's clenched fist smashed down on the dwarf's hand with crushing force. Winkel screamed with pain. He staggered backwards, moaning.

Picking up his own stick, Snow walked to the door,

heaved it open and walked into the street. Behind him he could hear the rattle of the clapper bell.

At the end of Altdorfstrasse he dropped the stick down a drain and walked rapidly back to his hotel. When he arrived he went straight into the panelled dining-room. It was nearly six o'clock. He ordered dinner and said he was in a hurry.

It was 6.45 p.m. when he left the hotel. The sky was dark purple, slashed with streaks of red in the west. It was almost dusk and the streets were full of stale warm air. It was going to be another oppressive night.

As he walked along a hot dry wind began to filter into the town, the first wind for weeks. It brought no welcome coolness, simply a movement of the fetid air.

In the distance the ramparts of the wall were black against the setting sun. Snow sensed a medieval atmosphere, like going back a thousand years to a time of cruelty and terror.

All around him people strolled through the half-light as though it was any normal town.

9
The Witch's Tower

Snow paused and looked straight up the inside of the vast conical tower. The only light came from an ancient lantern hanging from a beam near the roof. The lantern was swaying slightly, so that enormous shadows trembled as though the tower was about to collapse.

Running up the centre of the tower, like a giant wooden spring suspended in space, was a spiral staircase, with open steps of wooden planks. A low banister rail spiralled up above the steps.

The staircase appeared to end at a platform almost at the top, about the level of the witch's hat. There was no one in sight anywhere. The wind outside had a strange drawn sound, like a man being strangled slowly.

The circular floor was covered with straw, giving the impression of a horse barn. Round the walls stood curved benches, duplicating the curved surface of the tower.

The benches were littered with wood shavings, power tools, vices, presses and an assortment of knives. Here and there amid the sea of shavings rose a half-finished wooden toy, a Ferris wheel dangling small cabins, a high-gabled house, strange mad-looking dolls.

Snow walked round the wall, his feet scuffing through the straw, until he reached the point he had started from. There was no one there, nothing but toys. He found the silence uncanny. Even his feet made no sound treading through the straw. The tower had an air of unreality, rather like a dream. Outside the wind was quietly choking itself to death again.

Then he heard a noise, high up above him, half-way to heaven, the clump of a foot, just once.

Moving into the cover of one of the huge shadows on the wall he looked up. The staircase was deserted. At the summit of the tower the platform was masked in deep shadow.

He stood for five minutes without moving, listening, watching. There was nothing to see, not even the hint of a sound. Someone else had the same capacity of waiting, someone inside the witch's hat.

Suddenly Snow made up his mind. Taking off his shoes he hid them in the straw. He transferred his revolver from his holster to his coat pocket and walked silently to the foot of the twisting staircase.

With great deliberation he began to move up, step by step, testing each plank gently for creaks. The banister rail was very low. His hand hardly reached it unless he bent down slightly. It was a banister for a dwarf.

As he climbed he looked up, his eyes never leaving the edge of the platform, his left hand on the rail, his right hand on the revolver. He was aware that he was mortally exposed, like a man on a tight-rope.

When he was half-way up he glanced down. The drop was frightening. The fact that he was looking down into an expanding cone made the risk of dizziness all the greater. The moving shadows were alarming. He almost had the impression the tower was revolving round the staircase, which snaked away below him in hypnotic S-shapes. He looked up again quickly. The platform was deserted, as far as he could see, which was not far enough.

He started his climb again. The lantern, suspended from a long chain attached to a hook, came steadily

95

nearer. He could feel the breeze now. There must be an aperture somewhere. The fear had gone now and was replaced by a coldness, a physical coldness. His nerves were as alert as an animal's. He guessed the attack would come when he was almost up to the platform, perhaps six steps from the top. Then the unseen man in the shadows would see his head rising above the edge of the platform ...

Snow felt sure he had made no sound during his long ascent, but he felt equally sure the man waiting knew he was coming, like two invisible beasts in the jungle, sensing each other's smell.

The low rail bothered him. If he went over the side that would be the end. No one could survive such a drop. He looked down again. The floor seemed a mile away. The insidious circular wall began to spin. He looked up again and counted the remaining steps. Ten more.

Nine ... eight ... seven ... six ...

His head was above the platform level. Something moved in the pool of shadows. A man emerged, a short fat man wearing a broad-brimmed hat. Kurt Volga.

He was holding in front of him something which looked like a long broom-handle. At the end of it was a large round drum of rubber, vaguely resembling a stomper. At that moment Snow heard a noise far below.

He snatched a glance downwards and then immediately switched his gaze back to Volga. At the foot of the staircase he had seen a man staring up, holding something in his hand. It was probably Strauss.

Volga was advancing now to the edge of the platform, the stomper thrust forward. Suddenly he lunged down viciously at Snow. By the time the rubber disc reached him Snow had grabbed the rail with his left hand, his right hand free from his pocket. The disc crashed into his chest and unbalanced him. He felt himself going over sideways, the rail acting as a pivot behind his knees to carry him right over the edge. His left hand was sticky, slipping off the rail. . . .

He made a supreme effort and forced himself downwards, his knees slamming square on to the step above, his left hand clenched round the rail, his body pressed against his arm, twisting backwards, to preserve some sort of balance. Volga was forcing the disc against his chest. In another moment he would go over backwards.

His right hand grasped the handle beyond the disc. Jerking it savagely sideways, he suddenly pulled it downwards past him with all his remaining strength. The movement was so unexpected Volga nearly came over with it but he let go just in time. The stomper hurtled over the edge into the pit.

Volga staggered on the brink of the platform, recovered and slipped his hand under his armpit. In seconds he completed three swift actions but as he performed them Snow had also moved.

Jumping up off his knees, he ran up four steps, his left hand sliding up the rail, his right hand outstretched. The gun was half-way out of Volga's holster when Snow's hand gripped his left ankle and pulled with a quick jerk. Volga lost balance and toppled forward. He lay across Snow's shoulder for a moment and then the shoulder lifted and twisted in the same motion. Volga slipped forward and shot out over the rail, his shoe kicking Snow behind the ear. Then he was gone with one long last shriek which ended in a distant thud.

Snow climbed the last two steps to the platform and looked down. Volga's body lay to one side of the staircase, a vague crumpled heap. The shadows cast by the swaying lantern shifted eerily round the walls of the funnel.

Strauss was now a quarter of the way up the staircase, standing quite still, his arm lifted, pointed at Snow. An explosion echoed weirdly inside the tower. Snow felt the bullet go past him. Stepping away from the edge into the darkness he looked quickly around him.

A few feet away was a doorway, the door open at right-angles to the frame. The glow of the lights of Nuremberg outlined the shape clearly. He peered outside.

Beyond the door there was a walk along the top of the wall. In the distance he could see the silhouette of the next witch's hat. Midway between the two towers a staircase led down the inner side of the wall. He could detect no sign of life.

As he watched the wind blew in his face and brought with it the sound of dance music. He thought he heard distant laughter and a clink of glasses. Saturday-night revels.

Stepping back inside the tower he made sure the door was not self-locking and then closed it with a tremendous slam. The sound spiralled down through the tower. Making no noise in his stockinged feet, Snow crept back towards the platform edge. He stopped near the top of the staircase, still hidden in shadow, his revolver in his hand.

Silence returned to the tower for a short time. Suddenly Snow heard a clatter of footsteps coming up the staircase rapidly. Strauss must have wondered whether it was a trap, but Snow was counting on the assumption that these men had received orders that on no account must he escape.

As he heard Strauss coming closer, making no attempt to conceal his ascent, Snow realized that the gunman was convinced Snow had fled. But Strauss was a professional. When he came over the top his gun would be ready, just in case. It was going to be a matter of timing.

Snow almost left it too late. The shape of the tower played tricks with the echoes. As he began to move forward Strauss ran up the last few steps, his gun in his hand but pointed downwards.

Strauss suddenly saw Snow waiting for him. A look of amazement flashed across his face. In that moment of astonishment Snow released the pressure on his trigger and gave Strauss a tremendous kick, in the stomach.

The thin gunman doubled up in agony, wobbled, half-recovered himself, reeled, lost his footing and fell back over the edge of the platform. He dropped soundlessly, spinning as he fell.

Snow gazed down inside the tower for a minute and then went back to the door. Opening it slowly he looked outside. There was nothing but the wind and the wall. He closed the door again and walked back to the staircase.

As he descended he was careful to look at the next step all the way down. At the bottom he paused and listened. Then he searched under the straw, found his shoes and put them on quickly.

Standing up, he brushed straw off his trousers and walked across to examine the two bodies. Both men were dead. He searched Volga's pockets. They were completely empty except for a wallet containing about five hundred Deutschmarks. He found nothing else, no means of identification if anything went wrong. Strauss's pockets yielded the same result. They were anonymous men, their only ability a talent for killing.

Snow had just finished searching the two bodies when he heard a car approaching in the distance. It would probably drive straight past but it struck him he hadn't heard any other traffic since entering the tower.

Running across to the staircase he began climbing rapidly. He was three-quarters of the way up when he heard the car engine stop just outside the tower. As he ran up the few remaining steps he was almost out of breath. He heard the door open far below when he reached the platform. Keeping back in the shadows he peered over the edge.

Several men came rushing into the tower. Voices drifted up through the cone, speaking in German.

'God in heaven! It's Strauss. . . . Look, Volga's over here. . . .'

Snow stepped back quickly and walked over to the door. Opening it, he slipped out into the night and closed it carefully behind him. He started to run along the walk between the parapet walls.

The hot wind was blowing strongly now. It was rather like being on top of a mountain. To the right lay the roofs of Nuremberg, a long way down, resembling the waves of a tile sea. In the distance the Burg was floodlit, a gaunt castle out of a legend, the one-time home of Nazi war criminals awaiting trial. He could faintly hear the dance music again.

When he reached the top of the wall staircase he looked back. There was no sign of pursuit yet. He began to hurry down the steps. Again they were made of wooden planks, but this time each straight flight led down to a landing and then turned down another flight. At the bottom he found himself at the entrance to a narrow lonely street. He started walking back towards the centre of the town.

Snow walked painfully. His back ached where he had lifted Volga over the edge. His left arm felt almost dislocated. Every step reminded him of his bruised knees. He thought about the episode in the tower.

It had been planned to look like an accident, another fall from a great height. Zenith seemed to specialize in accidents. The *Polizei* might have their suspicions but murder required proof. Probably Herr Winkel would have 'discovered' his body in the morning at the foot of the staircase. The note he had found in his compartment on the Rhine Arrow would have been destroyed. It would have seemed odd, difficult to explain, but still an accident.

When he reached his hotel Snow went straight upstairs, collected his bags and came down again to the reception desk. The severe woman behind the counter looked at him with surprise.

'I have to leave unexpectedly,' said Snow. 'Make out my bill for the night, please. I'm in a hurry. And can you tell me the time of the next train to Frankfurt?'

She made out his bill first and then fetched the timetable.

'You could catch the 10.35 p.m. train,' she informed him. 'There's plenty of time.'

'Let me have a look.'

He took the timetable across to a chair while she made out his receipt. Turning to the trains to Munich, he found there was one leaving Nuremberg at 8.51 p.m. He could catch it easily.

He went back to the desk, returned the timetable, stuffed the receipted bill in his pocket, picked up his bags and walked out into the night. With luck any inquiries about the whereabouts of Herr Snow should be misdirected to Frankfurt.

The wind had dropped now. It had almost been a freak wind. The atmosphere in the streets was like the inside of a boiler house.

He walked into the Hauptbahnhof at 8.30 p.m. After

buying a single ticket to Frankfurt he fumbled at the barrier and dropped his passport on the concrete. The ticket collector picked it up for him slowly, looking at the name.

'*Danke.*'

The subway was deserted. He met no one as he walked up the steps leading to the platform for Munich. Glancing around, he slipped inside a waiting-room. It was empty. He sat down, mopped his head with a handkerchief, lit a cigarette and kept an eye on his watch.

Promptly at 8.45 p.m. the Munich express arrived. As soon as it stopped Snow climbed aboard and walked along the corridor until he found an empty compartment.

He settled in his seat and looked out at the deserted platform until the train began to move again, heading east.

10

The Demonstration

Snow climbed down the metal coach steps and started walking along the platform, a bag in each hand. A station sign read *München Hbf*. A straggle of passengers trailed in front of him. Most of the platform bays were empty. The clock hands pointed to 10.45 p.m.

Above Snow's head curved the glass vault of the most modern station in Europe. Greenish lights coloured people's faces, like characters in a bizarre film.

There was an atmosphere of fatigue, a washed-out feeling, the end of the day. It would take one last effort to reach hotel or home. The heat inside the vault was intolerable. Travellers put down their bags to wipe their foreheads, gazing around hopelessly. Then came the final trudge to the exit, a sound of feet flopping on hard concrete.

Snow passed through the ticket barrier and walked across the concourse into the hall beyond. He stopped to look at the glass display cases indicating hotel vacancies. He saw dozens of hotel names. Beneath each name was a green window and a red window, green for vacancies, red for full up. There was a blaze of red lights inside every case, not a green in sight.

He noticed some posters on a wall advertising three beer festivals, all being held at once in Munich. The city would be packed, no accommodation anywhere, just like Frankfurt. He would have to go to the Bayer Hof.

Picking up his bags he walked out of the station. On the opposite side of the road a wall of hotels faced him, alive with lights. Voices were shouting in the distance, an alcoholic sound. The festive week was in full swing.

'Herr Snow?'

At the kerb stood a chauffeur wearing a peaked cap. He was holding open the rear door of a red Rolls-Royce.

'Yes?'

'Mr Bernstein . . .'

Snow kept his bags as he stepped inside the car. There was a soft click when the door closed. Slipping into his own seat the chauffeur sat very erect, on duty. The car glided away from the kerb.

With a sense of resignation Snow sank back in comfort and watched the road ahead, thinking. They were obviously scared of letting him out of their sight. Well, this saved him all the bother of searching for them. It just depended on the way you looked at things.

The Rolls turned out of the traffic and pulled up. They had arrived at the Bayer Hof, one of the famous hotels in Germany. Snow noticed a reek of luxury in the reception hall. Men and women strolled about in evening dress. He caught only the vaguest impression of his surroundings. Suddenly he realized he was almost swimming with fatigue.

He heard a sound of dance music nearby, something familiar about the tune. Then he remembered. It was one of the records which had been playing in Bibi's flat while he listened to her story of Zenith. Where was Zenith now?

'Herr Snow? Your room number is 47. The porter will take care of your luggage. May I have your coat? This way please. Mr Bernstein . . .'

They were all waiting for him in the hotel lounge. He

104

saw Bernstein in evening dress, Mme Savigny wearing a peacock-blue evening gown, Bibi in a full-length dress of golden duchesse satin, belted at the waist. Again it was just like Frankfurt.

The thought crossed Snow's mind that they were like a group of travelling players. 'Opening Tonight in Munich . . .' But this time a new performer had been added to the cast, a fat man, vast inside his dinner-jacket, polishing his glasses with the intensity of a lens-grinder.

Bernstein rose to greet Snow, waving his cigarette-holder like a baton. Did the fellow never stop smoking?

'My dear Snow, we had a car meet each train. We were beginning to get worried. Everything all right, I hope?'

'Well, I'm alive. That's always something to be thankful for. Wake up every morning and there's a whole new day before you. . . . You know the rest, Bernstein.'

'Was there some trouble in Nuremberg? You look a little strained.'

'Trouble? In Nuremberg? What an idea! A quaint old town. Such interesting people.'

'You think so? Curious. I thought it a horrible place. I went there once to spend the day. I left it after two hours. Couldn't stand the atmosphere.'

Bernstein stood watching Snow thoughtfully, a certain reserve in his manner. Then his mood changed. Animation returned.

'Snow, you must meet a very good friend of mine . . . Peter Sternberg . . . President of the Süddeutsche Bank . . . Mr Snow from London. . . . He will be joining us at the reception . . . Mr Snow speaks your awful language!'

The fat man stood up heavily, very tall, his huge shoulders crouched forward like a bear, a massive hand extended.

'I am very pleased, Herr Snow, to welcome you to our beautiful city.'

'You live in Munich, Herr Sternberg?'

'*Nein*, my home is in Frankfurt. This is my southern G.H.Q., if you will excuse the military term. My wife says I should become a Muslim. Then I could have a wife in each port – is that not how you say it? – and she could stay in Frankfurt instead of living in airport lounges. But I tell her if I had two other wives like her I should have no strength left to run my businesses.'

He laughed harshly, his huge face creased with his own merriment, his eyes watching Snow between puffed lids, as though the laughing man was a different person.

'You look strong enough for anything – ten wives in fact.'

'Ten wives!' Sternberg exploded in a gale of laughter. 'You do not know German women. Take this little pearl of German womanhood.'

He turned and placed a hairy hand on Bibi's bare arm.

'I'm not German,' said Bibi sharply.

Bernstein broke in:

'It's a midnight reception, Snow . . . stimulating! Munich is alive tonight . . . a galaxy of people from all over Europe . . . the States too. We shall be leaving in a minute. You will want a bath. The car which brought you from the Hauptbahnhof will be waiting at the door. Come when you are ready. Heaven knows when the party will finish! . . . Please excuse us, we must make sure everything is organized. Peter always fumbles it! . . . Bibi will take care of you. Have you had anything to eat? . . . An early dinner? Bibi, look after Mr Snow. . . . Until the reception, then.'

Bernstein inclined his head, gave a little salute and

walked rapidly across to the doorway, Mme Savigny by his side, Sternberg lumbering in his wake.

Snow turned to Bibi and made a face at her. She laughed.

'Josef is exhausting, isn't he?' She came and stood close to him. He caught a faint aroma of perfume.

'Does he always go on like this?'

'Always. He's never still for a moment. He never stops talking. And he hates to stay in one place for more than three days. Now, Mr Snow, upstairs to your room and your bath. I'll organize something to eat and drink. I'm going to be your secretary tonight.'

'I'd like a ham omelette and . . .'

' . . . coffee.' They spoke at the same moment and laughed.

He went upstairs while she disappeared in search of room service. His room was on the first floor. In fact it was a complete suite, a living-room, a large double bedroom and a bathroom. He made a quick search and found nothing which disturbed him.

After turning on the taps he stripped in the bedroom, grabbed his dressing-gown out of his case, went into the bathroom full of steam clouds, went back into the bedroom, collected his gun from his coat pocket, returned to the bathroom, perched the gun on a stool, locked the door and stepped into the bath. It was too hot. Switching off the taps he eased himself down into the steaming pool.

He lay there for some time, soaking up the heat. Then he heard the bedroom door open. Sitting up quickly he dried his right hand and reached out for the revolver.

The door handle turned and was released. There was a tap on the door, then Bibi's voice.

'You've locked me out. Do you think I'm dangerous?'

'Yes, very.'

'Scared of a girl! You ought to be ashamed of yourself. Let me in.'

'Nothing doing. A man taking a bath is a private affair.'

'Hurry up then. I've got your food. The omelette will spoil.'

'Coming.'

He climbed out, hauled up the plug, went under the shower, switched it from warm to cool, to cold, stepped out, dried himself, put on the dressing-gown, slipped the gun inside his pocket and opened the door.

Bibi was sitting in the bedroom at one end of a long couch. Near the other end was a low table supporting a tray which contained a covered dish, a plate of bread, butter, a dish of fruit, two cups and a coffee-pot.

She got up as he walked over and sat down by the table.

'It's probably ruined now.'

She whisked off the silver cover, revealing an enormous flaky omelette.

Pouring two cups of coffee she left one on the table and took her own to the other end of the couch. Bending down she scooped up her dress almost to the waist. Snow was eating huge quantities of omelette. She sat down on the couch, tucked her legs underneath her and carefully arranged the dress well above her knees. In the electric light her legs looked bare.

Snow was ravenous. He piled butter on bread, helped himself to forkfuls of omelette, drank half a cup of steaming coffee, then drank the other half.

Bibi sighed, got up again and came over to fill his cup.

'Black, please, this time.'

'My, we're feeling stronger.'

'We're still capable of improvement.'

Refilling the cup, she walked back, lifted her dress again and went through the pantomime of settling herself. Looking up, she caught Snow glancing at her exposed upper legs.

'You're always half-undressed,' he remarked, balancing the last of the omelette on his fork.

'It will give you an appetite.'

'I'm satisfied now. Too late.'

Bibi leant back against the couch, her arms behind her head, fingers trailing through her soft black hair. Her belt was tight round her slim waist. Her breasts filled the cloth above it, thrusting forward against the satin. She was gazing at the ceiling, dreamily.

'The reception goes on all night. Let's go later. We could stay here and . . . talk.'

Her voice was soft, almost sleepy.

'I'm getting dressed now, so you're going to be chased out. You can read a magazine in the living-room.'

He stood up and walked over to her.

'Come on, Bibi. Make the effort.'

'Have you got anything on under that dressing-gown?'

'No. Satisfied?'

She grinned wickedly and shook her head.

'I don't want to get dressed in the bathroom, but I'm quite prepared to.'

She got up and shook her head again.

'Englishmen! Quite impossible!'

'Off you go.'

She skipped over to the door and looked back.

'Is your dinner suit still in decent condition? I could get you one.'

'It'll do. I can usually pack my stuff twice so it comes out all right.'

She opened the door, went out and then popped her head back.

'Mr Snow, I've just had a thought.'

'What is it now, Bibi?'

'One of us is always ready for bed while the other's still dressed. We'll really have to get together some-time.'

She slammed the door as he picked up a cushion.

Ten minutes later he was ready. He took a last look in the bathroom mirror. Reasonable, all things consid-ered. In fact he felt completely recovered, ready for any-thing!

He finished the black coffee, put his coat on and opened the door into the living-room.

Bibi was sitting at the end of a couch, this time with her feet on the floor. She was wearing a short black coat over her gold dress. A gold handbag lay on the couch be-side her. Putting down a copy of *Der Spiegel* she stood up and gave him a mock frown.

'Ready at last? You've been ages.'

'I imagine it takes you an hour to get ready.'

'No, it doesn't. I'm very quick. I can't stand women who fiddle.'

The red Rolls was waiting at the hotel entrance. The same chauffeur opened the rear door. Snow followed Bibi inside and waited for the soft click. The chauffeur settled in his seat, stiff-backed, and the car moved off.

'Bernstein seems to drink a lot of champagne,' Snow remarked.

'He has it for breakfast, for lunch and for dinner. And between meals too.'

'Does he ever drink anything else?'

'Never. He even has a supply in this car. Look at that metal thing by the front seat.'

Snow had noticed the odd cradle mechanism in front of the passenger seat on his way from the Hauptbahnhof.

'What is it?'

'A special stabilizer, like those things they have on transatlantic liners. It's a miniature version to hold the champagne bucket. It stops any movement of the car disturbing it.'

'Let alone the bottle inside it?'

'Exactly. He always takes a crate of his special brand with him everywhere, even aboard trains. He says it helps him to think.'

'And does it?'

'I think he'd be lost without it.' She laughed. 'I've often said you could trace Josef's movements all over the world if you had a chart of his strategically placed champagne deposits!'

'But doesn't it have any ill effect on him at all?'

'Absolutely none. He's so used to it. I suppose he gets through over a thousand bottles a year, but only in small quantities. A glass at a time, spread throughout the day.'

Snow lowered his voice to a whisper. Unnecessarily she leaned over until her ear almost touched his lips.

'Bibi, have you heard anything more about Zenith?'

'No, not a word.'

'Does Bernstein have a bodyguard, or perhaps two?'

'Good heavens, no! I once suggested the idea to him. He just laughed and said it would be ridiculous. I remember he said who would want to kill him. He was much too valuable to people alive.'

'I'm thinking of two men. One short and fat. He always wears a broad-brimmed hat. The other's tall and thin, with eyes like a dead fish.'

'They sound a lovely pair. I'm glad to say I've never met them.'

They sat in silence for a few minutes, watching the street lights of Munich flash by. It was a warm night. The moon floated in a clear black sky.

Snow took out his cigarette-case, gave one to Bibi, took one himself, lit them both and settled back, his arm on the seat divider. Bibi lifted her arm and dropped her hand on top of his. There was no pressure, it just rested there.

'Where is the reception being held?'

'At the Mozart. It's on the outskirts of Munich. Josef likes the place. It has the biggest room in Bavaria. The number of people who are coming tonight, we shall need it.'

'Who is coming, then?'

'Everyone, so Josef says. There'll be some people from England. You'll see. Here we are.'

It was an imperial room, almost as vast as a parade ground. Hundreds of people in evening dress rubbed shoulders. There was a flavour of wealth, a sense of power.

Snow and Bibi stood side by side near the entrance, watching it all. From the massed crowd came a hum of voices like a flight of bees, a clink of glasses. Above the glittering gathering towered an immensely high ceiling, moulded with intricate decoration, supported by stone pillars. Elegant chandeliers sparkled above the heads of the crowd. It was like a remembrance of centuries of Habsburg rule, a scene of monarchy.

Bibi gripped Snow's arm.

'Isn't it magnificent? I wish I'd been born a hundred years ago.'

'The plumbing was a bit primitive.'

'Englishmen!'

'Is this Bernstein's own reception?'

'Yes. He holds one here each year. It costs him a fortune.'

'Why does he do it?'

'He says wealth breeds wealth.'

A figure appeared out of the crowd, all smiles, waving a cigarette-holder.

'There you are. . . . Come along, Snow. I insist you enjoy yourself . . . a night of nights. Everyone is here: Paris, New York, London, Zürich, Milan . . . almost all the great financial interests of the West under one roof . . . and in the heart of provincial Bavaria! A party to end all parties. A glass of champagne? Now, come and meet my friends.'

Bernstein was more full of life than ever, completely in his element. He took Snow's arm and guided him into the multitude.

As he approached, groups of chattering people fell silent and opened into a semi-circle, as though before the arrival of a rajah. There was a hush in the conversation as Bernstein made the introductions.

'Lord Eastcastle, Chairman of . . . The Comte de Puy, President of . . . Mr Hughes, Governor of. . . . My friend, Mr Snow of London.'

Lord Eastcastle was a steeple of a man, silver-haired, with a great beak of a nose and a sardonic expression, smoking a cigar and looking down from a great height.

'What's your line of business, Mr Snow?'

'You might say I'm an assessor.'

'Ah, insurance?'

'No, an assessor of people.'

'People, eh?' Lord Eastcastle smiled vaguely. 'Detecting the genuine from the fake? That sort of thing?'

'Something like that.'

'See any fakes here tonight?' He lifted an eyebrow and glanced at his cigar ash.

'It's a little early to say yet. I've only just arrived.'

'Hear that, Josef? Snow says it's a bit early to say yet. Only just arrived. Rather good that!' Eastcastle spoke automatically, as though his thoughts were miles away.

Bernstein was smiling broadly but for once he said nothing, his eyes watching Snow intently.

The Comte de Puy was a small man, thin as a rake, with a tight mouth and a bored expression. He spoke English rapidly with great precision.

'You are an assessor, M. Snow? What is the present feeling in the City? Excellent, I suppose?'

'I have no idea.'

'Because we are thinking of raising money in London soon. The terms would have to be favourable, of course, but we would like to establish closer links in view of your people's connexions with the Far East.'

So it went on, with Bernstein escorting Snow from group to group, a few words here, a few words there, all in the same terse conversation.

Snow had an impression of millions . . . marks . . . dollars . . . pounds . . . lire . . . francs . . .

There was talk of arrangements between bankers, deals between governments . . . 'considering a loan to . . . get in before the Americans. . . . No, not to Brazil, not yet . . . financing the Africans . . . Japan is interested . . .'

And always there was the same reaction as Bernstein arrived. Conversation ceased, the group made a semi-circle, heads bowed attentively. Bernstein talked while others listened . . . an emperor among kings.

In spite of the size of the room the heat was building up again, a torrid alcoholic heat. Men stirred uneasily inside their dinner jackets. Women dabbed their hands surreptitiously with tiny lace handkerchiefs.

Snow's neck felt too large for his collar. A layer of blue cigar-smoke floated round the chandeliers. Voices were raised a little louder. People began to bump into each other with muttered apologies, looking slightly dazed.

Bibi had been left behind long ago as Bernstein plodded insatiably among the crowd. There were more introductions, more talk, more bankers, more money.

Suddenly Bernstein let go of Snow's arm.

'Time to liven things up, Snow. People are beginning to wilt. We'll have a little entertainment . . . all a matter of timing.'

He said it just like a stage director producing a show.

Walking away rapidly towards the end of the room, he left Snow standing next to the buffet bar, looking at the tables laden with food and an army of bottles. He saw something dark and spotty in bowls, probably caviare. The waiters behind the tables were beginning to look limp, running up and down with harassed expressions, their white jackets creased and rumpled.

Snow helped himself to a glass of whisky, squirted in soda and drank slowly. That was better. Second wind.

'Herr Snow!' The voice boomed, deep and guttural.

Snow glanced up. Peter Sternberg was rumbling through the crowd like a tank, a glass of beer in his fist. He stood beside Snow and surveyed the room.

'Look at them, Herr Snow. All these people. Imagine a bomb dropping now! In a moment they are all gone. Think of it. Who would rule the West, then?'

'There must be a few of them elsewhere tonight – the rulers of the West.'

'Anyone who is not a friend of Mr Bernstein . . .'

Sternberg dismissed them with a wave of his hand. He looked towards the end of the room and slammed his glass down on the table.

'Come, Herr Snow. Josef is just going to set it in motion.'

'Set what in motion?'

'Come.'

Sternberg began his armoured progress down the room. He trod on a woman's foot and pressed on past her without a word. Snow stayed where he was for a moment, changed his mind and followed Sternberg.

At the end of the room stood a wide raised dais, almost completely concealed by crimson curtains draped round the platform like a bell tent. At the foot of the dais stood Bernstein, clapping his hands for attention.

A wave of silence spread gradually to the far end of the room. Bernstein began a little speech.

'It is good to see you all here this evening . . . but the party is just beginning. . . . It is a hot night. . . . We will cool it down a bit.'

Reaching up his hand he gripped a tasselled cord hanging from the curtain and pulled. Two things happened at once. A sound of falling water filled the room and the curtains divided and slid aside.

Near the back of the dais an immense cascade of water began to pour down. At the foot of the waterfall lay a huge pool. There was an island in the centre of the pool, covered with strange green plants and exotic flowers. Bernstein had brought a fragment of the tropics to the outskirts of Munich.

Cool air flooded into the room amid gasps of surprise and excited chatter. The crowd surged forward. Women pushed their way to the front and stood gazing at the cascade. A team of fresh waiters appeared carrying trays loaded with glasses of champagne. A grab of hands reached for them and a buzz of conversation started up again.

Snow turned and made his way towards the entrance. He pushed past a slim Swede and found himself face to face with Mme Savigny, looking more imperial than ever.

'Are you enjoying yourself, Mr Snow?'

'It's an experience.'

'Mr Bernstein always times things so perfectly. The waterfall came just at the right moment. People will stay another hour or two and go home happy and exhausted.'

'They will certainly be exhausted.'

'You're not going, surely?'

'It's been a long day, what with one thing and another. Give my regards to Mr Bernstein. He should have been an impresario.'

Snow moved past her and continued edging his way between people towards the doorway. He noticed the limp waiters behind the buffet had been replaced by the fresh team.

'Herr Snow!'

A raucous shout. It was Sternberg again.

'What is it, Sternberg?'

'You like the waterfall?'

'Fantastic.'

'I supervised its construction myself. Most ingenious. German engineering.'

'I thought you were a banker.'

'*Ja, ja.* But I help Herr Bernstein with everything.'

Snow moved on. He had nearly reached the doorway.

'Mr Snow, you've deserted me.' Bibi grinned at him. She was wearing a different evening gown.

'You've changed your dress, Bibi. I suppose somebody poured champagne over you.'

'Of course not! A change freshens me up.'

'You must be tired. Why not go back to the Bayer Hof? They'll all be tight soon.'

'I can't. I've got another two hours yet. Josef may need me.'

'Well, I'm off. I'll see you tomorrow?'

'Of course. I'm taking you somewhere special tomorrow night. Up in the mountains.'

'What happens in the mountains?'

'It's a surprise.'

'Not another one? And everyone will be there? They always are.'

'Don't be such a bear.'

Bernstein appeared at the edge of the crowd. He walked rapidly towards Snow, his step as springy as ever.

'There you are, Snow. Mme Savigny told me you were leaving. What do you think of it all?'

He waved his hand round the room, like a school-master indicating his prize pupils.

'Well, you've asked me, so I'll tell you. I'm not all that impressed. Some of them look a bit simple-minded. The financial aristocracy of the West, you said. I doubt if they'd recognize a fake if he was held under their noses.'

'I don't quite follow you, Snow.'

The cigarette-holder was motionless by Bernstein's side. He had an attentive expression on his face.

'I think you brought me here this evening to give me a demonstration, to overwhelm me with all this. But I told you in Frankfurt I used to be a policeman. At one time I was with the Fraud Squad. It wasn't so much the men who manipulated money outside the law who interested me, as the people they took in. I found men responsible for vast sums of money could be taken in like little children. I rather fancy I've seen some of the little children here tonight. You'll excuse my frankness, but you did ask for my opinion.'

Bernstein was standing quite still, an odd expression on his face, as though he could hardly believe his ears.

'These are some of the leading men in the Western world you are talking about.'

'Yes, I know. I'm going now.'

Snow turned to leave. As he did so Bernstein put a hand on his arm, in the friendliest way.

'Take care, Snow. There could be danger in the most unexpected quarters.'

The strange thing was Snow felt Bernstein meant what he said. There was no trace of a threat. It was rather a warning which had slipped out reluctantly. The two men stared at each other for a moment. Snow was surprised to see a look of admiration in Bernstein's expression, a sense of respect between two opponents. It was almost like a brief armistice, Christmas Day between the trenches. Snow nodded and turned away.

At the main entrance he found the Rolls waiting for him. During the swift drive through the night he sighed with relief at the thought of a few hours of sleep. For a brief time he catnapped. Then the car stopped outside the Bayer Hof.

Inside the reception hall he went up to the desk for his room key. The clerk handed him an envelope. Snow took out a sheet and read the brief message which was typed.

There is something urgent for discussion. I shall wait for you at the Süddeutsche Bank, Karlsplatz. Peter Sternberg

'Who left this message?'

119

'A man brought it about two hours ago.'

'Did you recognize him?'

'*Nein, mein Herr*. I have never seen him before.'

Snow looked at his watch. It was 2.30 a.m. He stood thinking for a moment.

'Have you a street map of Munich?'

'*Ja*. Can I find somewhere for you?'

'No, that's all right.'

Snow put the map in his pocket and went up to his room. Unlocking his case, he took out his revolver, checked its action and dropped it inside his pocket. After studying the street plan he had a wash, locked up the suite, went downstairs and walked out of the main entrance.

The Rolls was still standing at the kerb. At Snow's approach the chauffeur got out and opened the rear door.

'Why are you waiting for me?'

'I was told you would be going on to the Süddeutsche Bank shortly after you returned.'

'Who told you that?'

'Herr Sternberg.'

Snow said nothing, climbed into the back seat again and relaxed. He knew if he thought about it he would feel very tired.

It was a short ride. A high moon flooded the empty streets with pale light. Enormous shadows hid the dark buildings. Snow thought it was more like a stage setting than a real city. They came round a corner into a huge square. Looming behind the buildings were the twin onion domes of the Cathedral, suggesting a tinge of the East.

As the car pulled into the kerb Snow quickly opened the door himself and got out. The Süddeutsche Bank was in front of him. Walking across to the huge double doors he pressed a bell. There was no sound from inside and no trace of lights. But after a moment the door on the right opened a crack, as though he had been expected.

'Is Herr Sternberg here?'

'Who are you, please?'

'Snow. He's expecting me. Is he here?'

'Come in.'

The door opened wider and was closed as soon as he stepped inside. An old uniformed attendant led Snow across a large hall to the foot of a wide staircase. One lamp was lit at the back. Snow could vaguely make out counters running down each side of the hall.

He followed the attendant up the staircase and along a corridor, again lit by a single lamp. There were panelled wooden doors on either side. The attendant paused before a door near the end.

'I shall be waiting downstairs to let you out when you are ready.'

'Thank you.'

Snow walked into the room and the attendant closed the door silently behind him. It was very large and had a polished wood-block floor. Facing Snow was a huge desk in front of an uncurtained window.

Sternberg sat behind the desk, like a heavy wooden statue, with his back to the window. He acknowledged the arrival of Snow by ignoring him. Then he simply waved an outsize hand at a chair in front of the desk. Snow sat down, took out a cigarette and lit it.

'We will speak in English, Mr Snow. It is important we understand each other.'

'As you wish.'

'This business must stop at once, Mr Snow. Immediately.'

He spoke in a guttural bullying tone.

'What are you talking about?'

'If it doesn't stop, we may have to take steps.'

'Stop talking in riddles and get to the point. You're lucky I came to see you at this hour.'

'This business of pestering Mr Bernstein wherever he goes. Anyone would think he associated with criminals.'

'Doesn't he?'

'Is that an accusation?'

Sternberg was roaring now. He leaned across the desk, his corn stubble hair almost seeming to stand on end. Snow smiled.

'It's a question. You raised the point. In any case you're not making much sense. Mr Bernstein always seems glad to see me. He sends cars to meet me off trains, books rooms for me at hotels, plies me with champagne. Sternberg, are you sure you're feeling all right? Perhaps you had a little too much tonight?'

Snow spoke politely, mildly, rather like humouring a tiresome child. His manner increased Sternberg's rage.

'I repeat, this persecution must stop.' A clenched fist pounded the desk-top. Sternberg was almost beside himself with fury.

'Or there will be consequences?'

'*Ja.*'

'I take it you are threatening me. Does Mr Bernstein know about this?'

'This matter is between the two of us.'

Sternberg had quietened down now. Producing a long cigar he picked up a lighter, carefully lit the cigar and sat back in his chair. Beyond the window Snow could see the buildings on the other side of the street at the rear of the bank. The buildings were very close. He guessed the street was little more than an alley.

'Mr Snow. My associate Mr Bernstein is one of the wealthiest men in Europe. He is probably our foremost international financier.'

'What's that got to do with what we are talking about?'

'A man in Mr Bernstein's position, followed about by a detective.' Sternberg spread his hands graphically. 'No, Mr Snow, we will not tolerate it.'

'What are you frightened I shall discover? For a banker you are showing a certain lack of finesse.'

Sternberg got up from his chair and slowly ambled round his desk. He stopped by Snow's chair, looking down at him, his smoking cigar held like a knife poised to strike. His voice sank to a deep whisper.

'Naturally you will require some consideration for your nuisance value. I put it no higher.'

'I suppose you are going to offer me money now?'

Snow had lifted his voice. He could just hear the faint hum of a hidden tape recorder as it sucked in the conversation.

'Money, Mr Snow?'

'Yes, money, Sternberg. I presume you have some?'

'Mr Snow, are you asking me for money?'

Sternberg was booming again, as though addressing a public meeting. He put his cigar back in his mouth.

'Because if you were thinking of offering me some you can save your breath – and your money.'

Snow was looking directly up at his opponent now, rather unpleasantly. In the distance he thought he could hear the sound of a car engine ticking over.

Sternberg went back to his chair and sat down. Pulling a face at his cigar he dropped it into a crystal glass ashtray. Then he leaned forward and hunched his shoulders. His hands were spread in an open gesture.

'Mr Snow, let us try again, on friendly terms. In my

123

capacity as President of the Süddeutsche Bank I felt it might be mutually profitable if we discussed this matter and came to a sensible arrangement.'

'What sort of arrangement?'

'We do not like the way you are pestering Mr Bernstein with trivial questions about a minor incident, almost as though you wished to manufacture a scandal, perhaps for your own personal gain.'

Snow had stood up, his face expressionless, rather white.

'This minor incident . . . you are referring to the death of David Roberts?'

'Whatever his name was . . .'

'Sternberg, you have practically accused me of blackmail, in your capacity as President of the Süddeutsche Bank, of course.'

'I was talking about the possibility of an arrangement . . .'

'You seem extraordinarily worried about the so-called minor incident. You must be tired, Sternberg. Your reflexes aren't quick enough in the early hours.'

'As President of . . .'

'Do you own the whole bank, then?' interrupted Snow.

'I am responsible to the shareholders. What has this to do with what we are talking about?'

Sternberg was standing up now, his head thrust forward as though about to charge.

'I see, just an employee.' Snow's manner was insulting.

'Mr Snow, this interview is terminused.'

'Terminated, Sternberg, terminated. Terminus is the end of the line, which it may be for some of you.'

Snow turned round and walked towards the door. Behind him Sternberg thundered away.

'Kindly use the back door to get out. On your right down the corridor. The attendant has gone home.'

Snow opened the door, walked out and closed it quietly. He turned left and went back the way he had come in. At the bottom of the stairs the ancient attendant emerged from the shadows, unlocked the front door and stood aside to let him out.

The square was deserted. There was no sign of the Rolls. The Cathedral's onion domes looked like balloons in the moonlight. Snow paused on the pavement. It was a strange time of night for an interview.

Turning left he walked along slowly until he reached an alley running down the side of the bank. The back entrance probably led into the street below Sternberg's window. He moved quietly down the alley. At the end he peered round the corner.

It was a very narrow street, hardly wider than a passage-way. There was no pavement and the buildings on either side were a sheer wall. A little way along the street a car was parked facing the other way. The vehicle took up nearly the full width of the street and its engine was ticking over gently. In the driver's seat Snow saw the outline of a man.

It seemed fairly clear to Snow. The back door from the bank must be some distance beyond the waiting car. If he had followed Sternberg's suggestion he would have come out of the back door and started walking along the narrow street. Whichever way he had walked would have made no difference. The car would have run him down.

He turned round and walked back into the square. After checking his street map by moonlight he made his way to the Bayer Hof.

He was walking over to the lift when the reception clerk called him back.

'Herr Snow, a phone call for you.'

He went back to the desk and took the receiver.

'Snow speaking.'

'You will not know me, but I should like to meet you this morning. I have information for you.'

'Who is this speaking?'

'My name is Schmidt. Please listen to me. I have very little time.'

'Where are you calling from?'

'Munich. But that does not matter. I will see you at the Café Rheinhardt at 11 a.m. It is in the Oststrasse. Please sit at the table by the window just inside the door. I will come and join you.'

'I shall want to know more than that before I agree to meet you. What are you talking about?'

'Herr Snow, I must go now. I know what happened to Roberts.'

11
Scardale

There was a peaceful atmosphere on Sunday morning in Munich. People strolled through the streets, men arm in arm with their girls; families all dressed up for an outing. Among the crowd foreign visitors to the beer festivals walked along slowly, a glazed look in their eyes.

Sunshine radiated down out of a blue sky between fleecy clouds, giving a feeling of relaxation, of sauntering through layers of warmth. The city was full of smiling faces and the weather forecast had given no sign of a break in the Indian summer.

Snow stood on the edge of the pavement, the sun on the back of his neck, looking across at the Café Rheinhardt on the other side of the street. He had been standing there for some time, watching people enter and leave.

The windows were wide open. Inside he caught a glimpse of polished wooden tables and panelled walls. A handful of customers sat chatting, drinking coffee and eating pastries. The window table by the door was empty.

Stepping down into the street he walked across, his hand on the revolver in his pocket.

The change from blazing sunshine to the semi-darkness of the café made him blink. He stood just inside the doorway for several minutes, surveying the room. Something in his manner must have been intimidating. Certainly he felt in no mood for compromise. People gradually began to notice him standing there. As they looked up, one by one, conversation faded and died.

Snow stood perfectly still, his eyes moving from face to face, searching for a tell-tale sign. The entire room was gazing back at him now, as though in the presence of a hostile force.

Ultimately a waiter could stand it no longer. He moved tentatively towards Snow, a nervous smile on his face.

'May I show you to a table, *mein Herr*?'

'I'll take the one by the window.'

Snow did not look at the waiter as he replied. His eyes continued to rove round the room.

'This way, please.'

Snow sat down at the table sideways, facing the door.

'Actually, *mein Herr*, this table was reserved.' The waiter twisted a serviette between his hands restlessly.

'Who reserved it?'

'A Herr Schmidt.'

'That's all right. He reserved it for me. You know him?'

'*Nein*, he made the reservation by phone.'

'When was this?'

'Early this morning. The phone was ringing when I arrived. Will you wait for your friend?'

'No. Bring me some coffee. Quickly please.'

The babble of conversation had started again. The water came back with a huge pot of coffee and hurried away. With a yawn Snow poured himself a cup, drank it quickly and then refilled the cup. He lit a cigarette and settled back to wait.

Customers paid their bills and left, glancing at Snow on their way out. New people strolled in. Snow poured more coffee, glanced at his watch and looked out of the window.

There was nothing unusual in sight. It seemed a normal Sunday morning.

It was half an hour later when he noticed a tall lean man with hard eyes walk in from the street. He was dressed casually in an English sports jacket, slacks and an open-neck shirt. In his hand he carried a walking-stick of polished wood.

After a quick look round the café the lean man strode across the floor and sat down at a table behind Snow next to the wall. The waiter came over. Snow heard the man behind him order beer in poor German.

Snow looked at his watch again. It was 11.45 a.m. An aroma of smoke drifted across his face. The man behind him had lit a cheap German cigar. The minutes dragged past like wounded soldiers.

He had just lit another cigarette when he was aware of a slight movement behind him. The man with the cigar had leaned closer. When he spoke the message came over as a clear whisper in English.

'If I were you, Super, I'd move over to this table out of range. There's a man across the street watching you. The open window on the first floor, the one with the lace curtains behind the balcony. He's got a telescopic rifle.'

Snow put his cup down and glanced across the street.

He could see the balcony. Behind it were two French windows, one of them open. Lace curtains fluttered faintly in the breeze. He could see nothing else.

Snow sat very still, watching the window, a slight frown on his face. A cloud had hidden the sun. The lace curtains might have been opaque and it was impossible to see beyond them.

Suddenly the sun came out again, shining direct on the building opposite, making the curtains almost transparent. Silhouetted behind them was the outline of a seated man, gazing straight across the street at the Café Rheinhardt. Then the breeze blew more strongly and for a moment the curtains parted, making a triangular opening like the entrance to a tent.

Snow had a split-second exposure of a rifle barrel. He caught a flash of light on something glassy . . .

Then the curtains closed again. The sun went behind another cloud and the window recovered its innocence.

Snow stood up, moved away from the window and sat down at the table of the man with the cigar, his back to the wall.

'That's better,' the stranger remarked. He drank some beer.

'When did you spot him?' asked Snow.

'A couple of minutes ago. You'll have to watch it, Super.'

'How do you know who I am?'

'I should do by now. I've followed you all the way from Dover.'

'Have you. Do you mind telling me who you are?'

'Detective-Inspector Scardale, C.I.D.'

Snow looked across the table. Scardale was about thirty years old. He had a long thin moustache and thick black hair. Cold blue eyes like bullets stared at Snow above high cheek-bones. There was a suggestion of arrogance in his manner.

As Snow kept looking at him without speaking Scardale hitched his hands inside the tops of his trousers and returned the gaze steadily, almost as though posing for a photograph.

'Satisfied, Mr Snow?'

'No.'

'I should have let him blow your head off.' Scardale laughed.

'I'm going across to look at that room. I'll be back.'

'I'll come with you.'

'No. Wait here.'

'I'm supposed to protect you. All right, be a lone wolf.'

Snow got up, dropped some coins on his table and walked out into the street. Immediately below the balcony was an open doorway leading to a narrow staircase.

Crossing the street Snow walked inside and went up the staircase two steps at a time. At the top a landing led back towards the street. He walked quietly towards a closed door at the foot of the second flight.

There was no sound from inside the room. He waited a moment and then took out his revolver. Turning the handle noiselessly he suddenly threw the door open and jumped to one side.

Beyond the open doorway he saw a window overlooking the street. Lace curtains stirred in the breeze. In front of the window stood a hard-backed wooden chair facing the Café Rheinhardt. Behind it was another chair, facing the same way. The first was to support the rifle, the second for the assassin to sit in. The room was empty and the weapon had gone.

He searched the room quickly and found nothing, not even a trace that the room had been recently occupied. Going back on to the landing he closed the door and returned to the café.

Scardale was still sitting at the table, a fresh glass of beer in front of him.

'Find anyone?'

'No. Just an empty room.'

'He must have pushed off when he saw you coming.'

'There wasn't time.'

'Well, when you changed tables, then.'

Snow sat down again and ordered more coffee. Inside

the café the temperature was rising. The sun was out once more, filling the street with brightness.

'Have you any means of identification, Scardale?'

'Don't take much for granted, do we? Here you are.'

Scardale tossed a leather folder across the table. He drank some more beer while Snow examined it.

'Scardale, you said you followed me all the way from Dover. Do you mean that literally?'

'No, I lost you on the Rhine Arrow. Where did you slip off the train? At Nuremberg?'

'Never mind that. How did you pick me up again?'

'Easy. You were following Bernstein around, so when you gave me the slip I kept tabs on Bernstein and hung around the Bayer Hof. I saw you roll up in his car. He must have known which train you were arriving on.'

'If you followed me from Dover you should be able to give me the details of my trip. I'd like to hear them.'

Scardale looked annoyed. He glared at Snow and drank the rest of his beer.

'They said you were a careful Charlie. All right, here goes. Thursday you caught the boat from Dover. At Ostend you caught the Sapphire Express, arriving in Frankfurt at 10 p.m. You toured the town looking for a room and ended up at the Central. Friday morning you went to Bernstein's suite at the Frankfurter Hof. Then I lost you. In the evening you went to Wiesbaden for the big reception. On Saturday morning you visited Bibi Decker at her flat by the river. Afterwards you went back to your hotel, packed up and caught the Rhine Arrow about lunch-time. Fair enough?'

Scardale grinned and put his hands inside his trousers.

'All right, Scardale. Now what's this all about?'

'It's about Roberts.'

Wiping beer froth off his mouth with the back of his

hand, he picked up his cigar and re-lit it. Snow sat well back in his chair and shook his head.

'I don't follow you.'

'Yes, you do.' Scardale blew out the match. 'That's why you're here.'

'Stop fencing and get to the point.'

'You don't really think we swallowed the suicide yarn, do you?'

'That was the coroner's verdict.'

'Window-dressing. You should know. The whole business looked queer. Not that we're sure, but it looked queer enough to investigate.'

'You think it was murder, then?'

'I don't know. That's what I'm trying to find out.'

'Where do I come into this?'

'I hoped you'd tell me.'

'What do you mean by that?'

'Who's fencing now? Look, Snow. We know that you went to see Mrs Roberts. What's your next move? You visit Mrs Warner just before she makes a moonlight flit to Sydney. The following morning you pop along to a travel agent and buy a ticket for Frankfurt. We decided you were on to something and I was detailed to tag on behind and see what you were up to. So here I am, drinking lousy German beer half-way to the Iron Curtain.'

'On the way, did you notice anyone else following me?'

'No, should I have?'

'It was just a thought.'

'What have you found out about Roberts?'

'Nothing, so far. What about yourself?'

'I'm as far ahead as you are, Snow. Where does Bernstein fit into all this?'

'He may not fit at all. But he controlled the Checkers

Group and Roberts had just finished working on their books when he died.'

'That's a pretty flimsy connexion.'

Scardale put his hands on the edge of the table, his eyes a blue glare.

'It's the only link so far. It's a question of waiting for something to happen. Most people can't help talking. Some of them can't stop talking. Sooner or later they say too much if you listen long enough. If people didn't have this compulsion to talk I'd never have solved a single case. The closed mouth is the policeman's dead end.'

'Here endeth the lesson.' Scardale grinned aggressively. 'What made you leave the Force, Snow? A superintendent at thirty. You must have been mad to resign.'

'I had my reasons. For one thing, I prefer to work alone.'

'I heard that too. Well, this time you've got company.'

'What do you mean by that?'

'I'm tagging along on this one, Snow. Wherever you go, I go, from now on.'

'We'll discuss that later. It's time for lunch. We'd better find somewhere before the festival crowds think about eating. By the way, did you have any trouble getting accommodation here last night?'

'Funny question. I'll say I had trouble. Two hours it took me to find somewhere.'

'Where are you now, then?'

'At a lovely little place called Gasthof Weber off the Donaustrasse. It's worse than a doss-house. The lavatory is quite something. I think they disconnected the outlet pipe a couple of years ago. I'll describe it over lunch.'

They paid their bills and wandered out into the midday sun. It was incredibly warm. The bright light hurt Snow's eyes for a moment.

As they left the Café Rheinhardt he glanced at the window across the street. The breeze had dropped and the lace curtains hung close together, quite motionless, like a woman's veil hiding her secrets.

They came out of the restaurant into a hot cloudless afternoon. Snow looked at his watch. It was 2.30 p.m. Standing by the kerb, Scardale flexed his large hands across his stomach.

'That's better, Snow. I like this German meat.'

'Where's this Gasthof Weber you're staying at?'

'Over there. Let's get inside out of this heat.'

They crossed the road and walked underneath a stone archway into a side-street. It was narrow and cobbled and very quiet, like a village street in the heart of the Bavarian countryside. When they had almost reached the end Scardale turned into a tiny courtyard.

'Here it is, the lap of luxury.'

Snow followed him through an open doorway flanked by windows thick with dirt. Ahead stretched a long lobby with small tables and chairs on either side. Scardale pointed to the tables, his mouth wide with derision.

'The dining-room!'

At the end of the lobby was a bare wooden counter. Behind it sat an old man with dusty grey hair and pebble glasses. Scardale collected his room key and turned up a flight of stairs.

The carpet was worn through in the middle of each stair tread. There was a musty atmosphere, like a neglected greenhouse. As they reached the landing Snow winced. A rank odour of faulty drains polluted the stale air. Scardale grinned.

'That's the lavatory. You should see it.'

'Some other time.'

Scardale unlocked a door and walked inside. Snow followed him, closed the door and looked round the room. There was a single bed covered with grey blankets, a cracked wash-basin and an alcove for clothes curtained off by a piece of aged green cloth suspended from a metal rail.

'At least there's a view of the Karlsplatz,' Scardale remarked, looking out of the window.

'As you said, a doss-house.'

'I've slept in worse places. Not from choice though. Why do you think Roberts was murdered?'

Scardale asked the question off-handedly, still gazing out of the window.

'For one thing Mrs Warner didn't react the way she should have done when I saw her. For another thing, I noticed the curtain rail.'

Scardale was still looking across the square. He asked the question over his shoulder.

'Curtain rail? Which one?'

'The one in Mrs Warner's living-room over the fire escape door. It's next to the window Roberts fell from. It was a new rail and had very recent scratches on it. The curtain had been taken away. Mrs Warner said there wasn't one there while she occupied the flat. I think she was lying.'

'I still don't see the point.'

'A man could have hidden behind that curtain. Then if Roberts was persuaded to go and look out of the open window the person behind the curtain could have slipped out behind him and toppled him over the edge before he knew what was happening. So the curtain had to be taken away, otherwise it might have given people ideas.'

'That's really rather bright.' Scardale spoke slowly, almost reluctantly.

'It's only a theory.'

'Only a theory! Snow, you ought to sign on again.'

'You noticed the scratch-marks on the rail?'

'Go on, rub it in. I missed them – by a mile.'

'Well, we're in Munich now. What's your next move?'

'My next move, Snow, is to find out who the character in that grey Citroën parked across the square is.'

Snow moved over to the window. There was no traffic in the square. In the distance he saw the grey car, with a man sitting behind the wheel. He was too far away for recognition.

'He's watching us,' remarked Scardale. 'I saw the sun shining on his field glasses.'

'You've got good eyesight.'

'You can say that again. I'm off. Wait for me.'

'He'll see you coming.'

'He may not spot me in shirt-sleeves.' Scardale dropped his jacket on the bed and went out of the room.

Snow stayed watching at the window. Two or three minutes slipped away. The Citroën was still parked at the kerb as Scardale appeared round a corner. Stepping off the pavement he started his long walk across the square with a swinging stride, the walk of a hunter.

He had reached a point half-way across the square when Snow saw a black Mercedes approaching at speed, heading straight for Scardale.

He cupped his hands and bellowed at the top of his voice.

'Scardale! Look out! The Mercedes!'

Scardale paused and looked back at the black monster roaring towards him. Then he began to run, heading for the Citroën, his long legs whipping backwards and forwards.

The Mercedes curved sideways in a furious arc at the same moment as the Citroën left the kerb, also heading for the running figure. The two cars were executing a pincer movement, like two bulls in a ring charging the same matador. Snow knew he would never make it.

Then an extraordinary thing happened. Scardale changed direction, running midway between the on-coming cars, compelling them to drive straight at each other. Snow waited for the collision.

The driver of the Mercedes lost his nerve first. He suddenly swerved away from the Citroën, and away from Scardale. At almost the same time the Citroën changed course. Both cars sped along the square and out of sight.

Scardale was standing alone in the sunshine, his white shirt showing up clearly against the grey square. He waved his hand, walked across to the pavement and began striding back round the deserted Karlsplatz.

Snow turned quickly away from the window and went over to a suitcase lying at the foot of the bed. Bending down he tried the catches. It was unlocked. He searched the case quickly and found Scardale's passport among the folded clothes. Near the bottom he came across a file. Inside was a typed report of the inquest on David Roberts, a photograph of Roberts and a slim notebook. He flipped over the pages. They were all blank except for one page which contained a list of names.

> Mme Savigny?
> Peter Sternberg?
> Bibi Decker?
> Dr Zimmermann?

Slipping everything back into place, he closed the case. Then he searched the jacket on the bed and a coat behind the green curtain. He found nothing interesting. When Scardale opened the door Snow was standing in the middle of the room, lighting a cigarette.

'That was a close thing, Scardale. Did you recognize either of the drivers?'

'No, I was a bit too preoccupied.'

His forehead was damp with sweat. He went over to the basin, turned a tap and sloshed water over his face. As he dried himself he looked at Snow, his mouth tight.

'I think this business is going to need the two of us. When do you meet Bernstein next?'

'I'm not sure. In any case I've got to go somewhere this evening, alone.'

'You must be crazy. Well, it's your funeral.' He put his jacket on and lit a cigar.

'Possibly, but that's the way it's going to be. Are you all right now?'

'Fit as a fiddle. I needed the exercise. When shall I see you again?'

'I know where you are now. I'll be in touch.'

Snow went out, closed the door and made his way back to the main street. Underneath the archway he paused to check his street plan and then walked away towards the centre of the town.

The main post office was open on Sunday for telephone calls. Inside he gave a London number to the phone clerk and then sat down on a bench to wait for the call. After ten minutes the clerk beckoned to him.

'Booth No. 2. Over there.'

He went inside the kiosk, pulled the door shut and lifted the receiver.

'Snow speaking. Is that you, Slope?'

'Hello, Snow. All the way from Munich, eh? You do get around. It's still almost a heatwave here. What's it like down in Bavaria?'

'Boiling. What have you found out?'

'In a nutshell, Bernstein controlled Checkers.'

'Yes, I know. I found that out myself. Anything else?'

'Well, yes there is. I've got really absorbed in this thing.

139

I'm now hard at work finding out what controls Ikolon. It's like a Chinese puzzle, almost as though it's been made as difficult as possible for anyone to find out what goes on.'

'But Bernstein controls Ikolon, doesn't he?'

'Yes, but it appears to be only one unit in a really staggering financial system. I've got people all over Europe making inquiries. Ikolon is a giant in itself but it seems to be one of a family of giants. So far I've got back to a Swedish holding company called Stromfors. It controls Ikolon and God knows how much else.'

'But who owns Stromfors?'

'Bernstein. He apparently controls a most colossal combine.'

'Combine?'

'Yes, combine. A monopoly composed of monopolies.'

'How does he do it?'

'By offering ten per cent.'

'Go on. There must be more to it than that.'

'He offers ten per cent interest, much higher than you can get anywhere else safely, on any sum. And he always pays – and promptly too. The man in the street doesn't realize it but there are enormous sums floating about looking for the most profitable place to be invested. Bernstein is the most profitable place.'

'I still don't see how he pays such a high rate.'

'He's an amazing money organizer, an organizer of trusts, if you like. He gradually buys up a whole industry in one country and then buys up the same industry in another country and so on.'

'That must take a lot of time.'

'Not with Bernstein. He always offers a tempting price when he wants to buy and this enables him to buy quickly.'

'The thing to do is to find out what controls Stromfors, then?'

'I'm working on it now. I may know the source of the whole combine in a day or two.'

'I'll phone you when I can.'

'Where are you moving on to next?'

'I'd like to know that myself. Good-bye.'

Snow went back to the counter, paid for his call and started walking to the Bayer Hof.

When he reached the hotel he found a message waiting for him. *Please call me at the number below. Bibi.*

He went up to his suite, sat down and asked the hotel operator to get the number. The phone rang almost at once.

'Snow here.'

'And about time too. You've deserted me again.'

'It's Sunday, Bibi. Busy day.'

'I thought it was a day of rest.'

'You'd be surprised how busy Sunday can be. What's the trouble?'

'No trouble at all. It's about tonight. You've got to be ready at eight o'clock this evening. I'll pick you up at the Bayer Hof.'

'What are we going to do?'

'Take a trip into the mountains. You'll be away all night. Bring your pyjamas and toothbrush. And wear your dinner jacket.'

'Bibi, what are you up to?'

She giggled. 'Don't worry. There'll be other people there. I must go now.'

Snow put the phone down. He suddenly realized he felt very tired. He had a bath, put on his dressing-gown, lay down on the bed and fell fast asleep.

12

The Illuminated Mountain

The car skimmed through the night like a speedboat crossing a calm sea. Ahead the lamp beams spotlighted the road's way through the forest. On either side an overhang of black firs pressed down as though to swallow up the curving strip of concrete, climbing ever higher, bend by bend. The air was mountain fresh, almost heady.

Snow revelled in the coolness. He glanced sideways at Bibi. Her hands rested on the semi-circle of wheel, her eyes following the beams, her lips slightly parted with contented excitement. She had not spoken a word for some time.

Reaching into his pocket Snow took out his case and extracted a cigarette.

'Me too, please,' said Bibi.

He lit one and handed it to her. As he lit his own he watched her profile in the match flare. Her lipstick was deep red.

'What part of the world do you come from?' asked Snow.

'Let's just say the East. My mother anyway. My father was half German, only half. The whole Bernstein family comes from the East. I don't think Josef trusts anyone from west of Leipzig.'

She laughed as she said it, sweeping the car round a great curve without slackening speed, so much so that

Snow lurched against her shoulder. She looked at him and grinned.

'The Bernstein family?'

'Well, Josef, Mme Savigny and myself. It's just a phrase of mine. We're not related, of course.'

'Where does Bernstein come from, then?'

'I really don't know. You'd better ask him. I mean that. It's not a thing I'd ever ask him myself and so far he's never told me.'

'And Mme Savigny?'

'She comes from Bucharest. She escaped from Rumania to France just after the war. I gather she had an awful time. She managed to smuggle herself aboard a Russian ship on the Black Sea and slipped ashore at Istanbul. Then she made her way to Paris. The upper-class crowd in Rumania used to speak French and that helped her. Really, you shouldn't ask where people come from over here. They can be sensitive about their backgrounds.'

She grinned impishly, glancing at him out of the corner of her eyes.

They drove on in silence for a few minutes. The air had an edge to it now. The speed of the car gave a feeling of great exhilaration.

'Are you married, Mr Snow?'

She looked at him quickly as she asked the question, then switched her gaze back to the road.

'Yes, I am.' Snow spoke slowly, wondering how to put it. 'My wife went away with someone two years ago.'

'Can't you find her? You're a detective.'

'She didn't want me to.'

'I'm sorry. Josef is always scolding me for asking the wrong questions.' Her tone changed and became matter of fact. 'I haven't told you where we're going. We're spending the night at the Schloss Ludwig. We should be there now.'

She had no sooner spoken when the car turned a corner and suddenly emerged from the forest. The Schloss Ludwig rose above them, a short distance away.

'I know this road so well and yet it always takes me by surprise, even in daylight,' said Bibi, changing gear and slowing down.

The Schloss stood on a small hill, a mock castle built in recent times. On the roof was a series of turreted towers placed at different levels. The windows were filled with single sheets of plate glass.

Below the castle lay a vast car-port, open on all sides and filled with cars arranged in neat rows like a parade in a tank park. Dance music drifted down from the Schloss, a strangely nostalgic sound in the night, like the ghost of a ball held long ago.

'Your room's in the Tower,' said Bibi, nodding her head towards the left of the castle.

The Tower was quite separate from the Schloss. A round slim column ten storeys high, it appeared to be built of glass, like a transparent tube. Curtains were drawn across some of the windows but others were filled with light. Snow could see straight through them.

'That's an odd building. Are the rooms circular?'

'Yes. It was Josef's idea. He thought it would be an interesting architectural experiment. People rave over it, but it's not for me.'

She pulled up in front of the car-port and started backing and manœuvring it into an empty slot between a Ferrari and a Rolls-Royce.

'Why don't you like it?'

'All that glass! Just imagine getting undressed.' She glanced at him ironically, her left eyebrow arched.

144

'You can always draw the curtains.'

'People do, of course. But you still feel naked even when you're dressed. Can you imagine making love up there?' She was concentrating on the final drive-in.

'You're in the Schloss, then?' Snow had his hand on the door, ready to get out.

'Yes, I am. My room faces east. I can see the dawn break over the mountains. A sight to last you all your life. When I'm old and grey, Mr Snow, I'll always feel young again when I remember the dawn at Schloss Ludwig.'

They got out of the car. Snow walked beside her, carrying his case. A narrow flight of stone steps led up to the main entrance. At the top they walked past heavy double doors covered with iron studs into the reception hall. It was rather like entering a hotel. There was no one about except the receptionist, a fat smiling man who relieved Snow of his bag.

'Good evening, Fräulein Decker. Herr Bernstein is with the guests on the terrace.'

'Thank you, Joachim. So it's lit up already?'

'What is?' asked Snow.

'You'll see. Joachim, get the porter to take Mr Snow's bag over to the Tower. He can inspect his room later. I have something to show him first.'

They started walking down the long narrow hall towards the back. Bibi suddenly darted into a side room.

'The bar! I'm dying for a brandy. I don't really like Josef's champagne.'

The bar was like a cave. There were huge stone flags on the floor and the walls were constructed of limestone blocks. The counter was a low stone wall supporting a beam of pinewood. Lighting came from old lanterns perched inside rock alcoves. The room had a subterranean character, the lanterns glowing redly as though the cave was on fire. It was deserted except for the barman.

Snow ordered brandy for Bibi and a whisky and soda for himself. The brandy came in a large balloon glass, holding a generous quantity. Snow took out his wallet to pay.

'That's not allowed, Mr Snow. You're a guest.'

They drank in silence. Bibi held her glass in both hands, gazing into space, while Snow examined the range of bottles behind the bar.

Swallowing the last of her brandy, Bibi put the glass back on the counter. As they left the room she linked her arm inside his, pressing her thigh against him. Snow wondered if she were a little high with the mountain air and the brandy. In the bar she had drunk three quarters of the contents of her glass at once, with a certain abandon, as though to hurry things up. He glanced down at her and at the same moment she returned his look, her eyes sparkling with mischief.

At the end of the hall they walked through another double door out of the rear wall of the castle. A path led up a hillside into a wood. Green lanterns hung from the trees, swaying slightly in the breeze, lighting the way. It was like a walk through a haunted wood.

After a few minutes they emerged into the open again, looking down on a broad terrace behind a stone balustrade.

The terrace was full of tables covered with glasses and bottles, mostly champagne. People in evening dress sat round the tables. They sat very quietly, hardly speaking. There was almost a hush, broken by the occasional clink of a glass. They were awestruck.

It was a fantastic sight. Snow had never experienced anything like it. Immediately beyond the balustrade the hill plunged sheer down a tremendous depth into a valley, somewhere far below. Swirls of white mist drifted up out of the abyss.

But it was not this which trapped and held the gaze. It was what lay beyond.

In the distance rose a mountain, an illuminated mountain. Triangular in shape, it rose dramatically from a narrow base, its sheer walls climbing to a white-capped peak high in the sky.

From the base, at intervals up the slopes, searchlights shone over every yard of the shark-toothed giant. It had a monstrous beauty which almost overwhelmed the spectator. Snow stood quite still, gazing at the summit.

Bibi squeezed his arm and chuckled happily.

'The Stagenwand. It almost makes me light-headed.'

'You are light-headed.'

A man got up from a table and walked briskly towards them, cigarette-holder in one hand, champagne glass in the other.

'Welcome to the Schloss Ludwig, Mr Snow. What do you think of it?'

He waved his holder across the valley.

'Mount Bernstein,' suggested Snow.

'Did you hear that, Elise?' Bernstein turned to a plump woman at the nearest table. 'Mount Bernstein!' He was delighted.

'How did you manage it?' asked Snow.

'Like everything else, a question of organization. We photographed the Stagenwand from all angles by helicopter. Then we reduced it to a scale model and planned where to site the searchlights. The greatest difficulty was getting them up to the higher slopes. But we managed, we managed.'

It seemed to Snow that this was the nearest he had come

147

to seeing Bernstein affected by his champagne. His walk was steady but his face appeared flushed. Everyone seemed a little high tonight, except himself. He began to dislike his own self-restraint.

'I'll get you some more whisky,' said Bibi. She was reading his thoughts now.

When she came back she handed him a long conical glass. He tasted it, almost pure whisky. He didn't really mind. He was prepared to enter into the spirit of things. A night to end all nights.

Bernstein had finished chatting to Elise. He took Snow by the arm and led him over to an empty table on the edge of the terrace. A waiter hurried across with a silver bucket containing a bottle of champagne. Globules of water speckled the glassy surface. Snow sat down facing Bernstein.

'Come, Snow, a toast: to this wonderful summer which never ends: to the mountain: to life itself. . . . How considerate of Bibi to bring you here tonight. She knows I enjoy your company. A wonderful child! I am very fond of her . . . always so gay, enjoying herself . . . full of life and laughter, the way people should be. I find her enormously stimulating. So many people are serious, spending all the days of their brief lives with long faces. You would think they expected to live three hundred years! . . . Now we will drink to Bibi, one of the family. You are almost a member yourself now, Snow.'

Bernstein was bubbling over with enjoyment, a fountain of vitality, his gestures animated, a sparkle in his eye, never still for a moment. He waved across the terrace to new arrivals, flourishing his cigarette-holder, smiling ceaselessly, the soul of life.

'Tell me, Snow, are you married?'

'Yes.' Here we go again, he thought, but Bernstein immediately resumed his conversational barrage.

148

'Unlike myself. I never married. Too poor when I was young, too determined to make my way in the world. Later, success came and I was absorbed in my work. Later still, I found myself surrounded with beautiful women . . . it seemed too late . . .'

'No regrets, then, Bernstein?'

A pause, while Bernstein lit another cigarette.

'Well, Snow, I would have liked to have had children. Bachelors are impermanent people. They come and they go. . . . Who cares? It would give a feeling of endurance to perpetuate all this . . .'

He waved the holder like a magic wand towards the mountain, and continued, 'but perhaps as things are, it is for the best the way things are. In any case I have a family of a sort. I have the pleasure of women's company to enjoy. In fact I found women were the only ones I could really rely on. They have a strange form of loyalty you never find in other men . . . Bibi and Mme Savigny . . . they would do anything for me. I met them, by the way, when I was penniless. All the rest . . . loot-pickers!'

Just then a group of people entered the terrace. Bernstein jumped up, gave his apologies and a promise to be back, and went over to the new-comers.

Snow sat watching the mountain for a while. Finishing his whisky, he got up from the table and wandered towards the woodland path. He felt in a holiday mood, completely relaxed. A bare arm entwined itself round his arm. It was perfect timing.

'Mr Snow, you will not elude me tonight.' Bibi hugged his arm, looking up into his face.

They walked back down the path between the trees. High above them the firs rustled gently. The air was incredibly pure and heady. In the distance Snow could hear dance music again.

'Bibi, where is that music coming from?'

'I'll show you. They'll be dancing now. At least the younger element.'

'I doubt if I fit that category.'

'You need a little encouragement.' She giggled. 'In fact for some things you need a lot of encouragement.'

'Whereabouts in the mountains are we?'

'On the Austrian border, due south of Munich.'

'Which is the nearest city, then?'

'Probably Innsbruck, but it's a long way off. Here we are.'

They had arrived in front of a large arched doorway at the back of the Schloss. Beyond was a huge room with a wood-block floor polished like glass. They walked inside.

At one end of the room a German dance band in dinner jackets was playing a fast quickstep. Couples glided across the crowded floor. Several on the fringes were twisting and jiving in mad gyrations. Snow sensed an air of abandoned gaiety, a party to last the whole night long.

'I haven't danced in ages,' remarked Snow, as they moved on to the floor.

'Just relax and enjoy yourself.'

Gradually they moved into the centre of the floor, their feet flowing, Bibi anticipating Snow's every change of direction. He began to enjoy himself, moving faster, improvising steps. They were in the very middle of the crowd when Snow bent down and whispered into Bibi's ear.

'There's a photograph in my breast pocket. Take it out and tell me if you've ever seen the man in it.'

She extracted the photograph and examined it as they danced. Then she slipped it back inside his jacket.

'No, I've never seen him before. Who is it? Roberts?'

'Yes.'

They took another turn round the floor. The band never stopped. It had inexhaustible energy, eight men blowing through brass, tapping drums, pressing piano keys. Their faces gleamed with sweat but they seemed tireless, playing their instruments with ferocity, each number faster, louder than the previous one. The heat was equatorial.

'Mr Snow, are you investigating Mr Roberts' death just because his wife asked you to?'

'Yes, she needed some help.'

'If I had a husband who died like that I should ask you to do the same thing.'

'Why? You hardly know me.'

'Because I know you'd never give up till you found out what really happened.' Her mood changed. 'Look, drinks!'

They were passing a buffet bar. Walking off the floor they ordered drinks, brandy for Bibi, whisky for Snow. Bibi asked for a large double and swallowed it in three gulps. Then she took Snow's arm again and piloted him back on to the floor.

'Bibi, you're insatiable.'

'I love dancing. Look at that couple over there.'

A red-headed girl in a green dress was dancing with a blond young German, slowly and deliberately. She had both her arms round his neck, her body pressed against him as they swayed to the rhythm.

'That looks nice.' said Bibi.

She placed her arms over Snow's shoulders and moved up close against him, her lips just below his, the faint scent of her perfume drifting up to his nostrils, a dreamy expression on her face, her breasts compressed against his body. They stayed in the centre of the room for several minutes, swaying with the music.

'Bibi, we're not in bed.'

'Not yet.'

Over her bare shoulders Snow could see Bernstein on the edge of the floor, talking to several people, looking across at Bibi, smiling broadly. He brandished his holder when he caught Snow's eye.

'Bernstein's over there, looking very pleased with himself.'

Bibi opened her eyes. 'What time is it?'

'Just after midnight.'

'Blast! I'll have to leave you for a while. I have some phone calls to make for Josef. I'll be back. Don't go wandering after strange women.'

She led him firmly off the dance floor, her hand inside his. Then, pulling a face, she slipped away through the crowd.

Snow lit a cigarette and watched the animated scene. The dancing was getting a little wild now. A blonde girl had tucked her long pink dress inside the top of her pants and was jiving madly with a young American in rimless glasses. He seemed a little out of his depth.

Looking round the room Snow saw Mme Savigny by the bar, a glass in her hand. He made his way round the floor. Stopping beside her he ordered another whisky.

'Good evening, Mr Snow. Still worrying about Mr Roberts?'

'Not worrying. Wondering.'

'Why not forget the whole thing and enjoy yourself? He committed suicide. You know that.'

'That was the official verdict. There may have been a mistake. I'm beginning to think there was.'

'Have you any reason for saying that?' She held her glass ready to take a drink.

'For one thing the most extraordinary precautions were

taken to conceal the fact that Roberts stayed at the Frankfurter Hof on the night of September 1. That's why the hotel registration records were stolen.'

'You are simply theorizing.' She looked very white, almost nervous.

'I always start with theories, Mme Savigny. They can lead to the truth in the end. Have you ever heard of someone called Zenith?'

There was a crash of breaking glass as the tumbler slid through her fingers and splintered on the floor. A waiter rushed round the bar counter and started mopping up with a cloth.

'I'm sorry I startled you, Mme Savigny. You have heard of Zenith, then?'

'It's the name of some American corporation, isn't it? Mr Snow, you must excuse me. There are things I have to do for Mr Bernstein.'

She refused the fresh drink the waiter brought her and walked away, very erect.

Snow finished his drink and walked out of the ballroom into the reception hall of the Schloss. The receptionist put away a magazine and stood up. Snow shook his head and went over to look at a large relief map of Germany and northern Austria which hung on the wall. He studied it for a few minutes and then walked into the cave bar and sat down in a corner. Again it was empty except for the barman. Leaning his head back on the top of the armchair he closed his eyes and fell asleep.

He was woken up by someone coming into the bar. There was no sign of the barman and the man who had just come in was Sternberg. Snow got up and strolled towards him.

'Good evening, Sternberg. Have you got any more cars outside? You know, with the engine running and a chap at the wheel, just waiting for me to step out of the back entrance?'

His tone was jocular, almost friendly.

'You are talking in riddles, Snow. I find your manner impertinent.'

'Don't worry about it, Sternberg. What are you having? Beer, I suppose. Let's see what we've got.'

Snow walked round the end of the counter to the other side of the bar and started looking at bottles.

'Ah, here we are. Some lager. That should do you. Now where are the glasses? Here they are. Won't keep you a minute.'

'I can go to the ballroom . . .' Sternberg stood uncertainly, taken off guard.

'Not a bit of it. There you are. Make a new man of you. Help your reflexes in the early hours.'

Snow pushed the glass across the counter, beaming all over his face. Pouring himself a whisky he clinked Sternberg's glass, gave a solemn wink and drank half the contents. Leaning on the counter he smiled genially at Sternberg, who was standing quite still, glass in hand, more like a wooden statue than ever.

'You know, Sternberg, I've always wondered what it was like to be a barman: seeing life from the other side of the counter, rather like going behind a mirror. Drink up, man. You look as though you need it. By the way, so far we've checked the combine back to Stromfors in Sweden. It shouldn't be long now.'

'I find you difficult to understand, Herr Snow. What is this about Stromfors?'

'You mean you don't know that Bernstein controls Stromfors? A confidential matter, perhaps?'

'I am not prepared to discuss Herr Bernstein's affairs. You would have been wise to accept my offer.'

Sternberg drank half his beer and thumped the glass back on the counter. He seemed disturbed at the sight of Snow behind the bar. It was an unorthodox situation, a social distortion, almost an outrage. He looked at the doorway as though afraid someone might come in.

'Let's try again, shall we, in a friendly manner?' Snow was enjoying himself enormously. 'Ikolon, the giant Ikolon, is just one unit in a vast international system. But where does it all start from? That is the question. I'm beginning to think you don't know yourself. I'm sure there's something wrong somewhere. Probably they haven't told you.'

Sternberg gave a roar, his fist crashing on the counter.

'You will regret it, Snow. Coming over here and meddling in matters which do not concern you. You will regret it.'

As he stormed out of the bar Sternberg's face was purple with fury.

Snow sat down on a stool behind the bar and lit a cigarette. In the distance he could hear dance music faintly. It looked as though the party would last all night. He glanced at his watch. It was 2.45 a.m., time for bed. He felt wide awake. When he had finished his cigarette he got up and walked out of the cave.

For several minutes he searched the whole ground floor. There was no sign of Bibi. He stood at the entrance to the ballroom for a while. They had a fresh band now. The dance floor was packed, the music wilder than ever. He could still see no sign of Bibi. She had probably gone to bed. He went back to the reception desk.

'I haven't been to my room yet. Have you a key?'

'Here you are, *mein Herr*. You are in the Tower. Floor 7.'

'Isn't there a room number?'

155

'You have the whole floor. The lift will take you up. It is automatic.'

Snow said good night and walked out of the front entrance. There was not a soul in sight anywhere. Pale moonlight cast horror shadows in front of the Schloss, shadows of a crooked castle. In the distance the low-roofed car-port looked like an insect museum housing dead beetles.

As he went across the forecourt towards the glass tower he noticed a band of light round the top floor. The other floors were in darkness.

At the base of the tower he entered an open doorway leading to a small lobby. The glass walls were curved from floor to ceiling, like the inside of a goldfish bowl.

The lift door was in the left wall. Snow pressed button 7 and waited. The doors opened with a gentle hiss. When the lift reached floor 7 the doors slid back with another hiss and revealed a closed door. Inserting his key, he opened the inner door and walked into a small vestibule illuminated by a blue night-light. He pressed down a master-switch and pushed open a swing door.

The living-room beyond was unlike any other room he had seen before. The right-hand wall dividing the circular floor in two was straight, but the outer wall was a continuous curve masked with heavy curtains. Furnished like a stateroom aboard ship, it contained couches, armchairs, a cocktail cabinet and a TV set let into the wall.

Snow walked over to a door in the straight wall and opened it. He looked out into a narrow corridor with three doors leading off the opposite wall. Walking down the passage he glanced inside each room. The end wall was always a portion of a curve.

He found a bathroom, the walls lined with mirrors, and a kitchen full of electric equipment. The third room was the bedroom, containing a double bed, twin hand-basins and a built-in wardrobe. His case was at the foot of the bed.

Sitting down on the bed, he lit a cigarette, stripped off his dinner jacket, tie, shirt and vest, and bent down to unlace his shoes. It was very hot inside the tower. He suspected hot air was being piped into the room.

Then the phone rang. Snow sprawled over the bed and lifted the receiver.

'Mr Snow?'

'Yes, Bibi. I looked for you but you'd disappeared.'

'Never mind that. I want to come over and see you.'

'Now? It's after 3 a.m.'

'Josef has gone.'

'How do you mean?'

'Can I come over? The telephone . . .'

'All right.'

He put the phone down, tied up his shoes again, slipped on his shirt and went back to the lobby. He remembered he hadn't locked the door. He had left the key in the living-room. Perhaps he was tired.

He stood smoking until he heard the lift hiss. When he opened the door Bibi was standing inside the cage. She stepped out into the lobby and waited while he closed the door.

She was dressed in a black sweater and black ballet tights. Snow almost had the impression her body was naked, covered with a film of black paint. She grinned as she watched his inspection, twirling a small handbag slowly.

'What have you changed for?'

'I don't really like formal clothes. When I had work to do for Josef I changed into this. They're my working clothes.'

'What's all this about Bernstein leaving?'

'Are you going to keep me standing in the lobby all night?'

'Sorry, I think I must be tired.'

They went through to the living-room. Bibi pointed to a couch.

'Sit down. I'll make some coffee. Unless you want something stronger?'

'Coffee will do nicely. But is there any?'

'I brought it up myself earlier this evening. Now sit down and relax.'

She disappeared through the door towards the kitchen. Snow went over to the curved wall and pulled aside a handful of curtain. He looked down on a view straight across the Schloss between the turrets. The mountain was still illuminated, but by moonlight now. There was no sign of life. He might have been a visitor to Mars.

He let the curtain fall back into place, went over to a couch and sat down, his back against the end. After a few minutes Bibi came into the room, carrying a tray containing two steaming glasses. It was just like the morning in Frankfurt, except this time she was dressed.

She put the tray down, brought over two small tables, put one at each end of the couch, placed Snow's glass on his table, went back to her end of the couch and curled up in her cat position. In her tights and sweater she looked rather like a black cat in a pantomime.

'Anybody would think we were married,' said Snow, 'always doing the same old thing together.' He regretted the remark as soon as he had made it.

'Do you like the coffee?'

'You've laced it again. There's more whisky than coffee here.'

'Aren't you lucky?'

She leant sideways to pick up her glass. As she did so her sweater slipped up away from the top of her tights, exposing a band of white flesh.

'Bibi, have you got anything on under that outfit?' Another remark he immediately regretted.

'You're not exactly overdressed yourself. Incidentally, have you had anyone up here with you? I noticed the bed was all rumpled.'

'You're the most suspicious woman I've ever met. Now, to get back to Bernstein. What's happened to him?'

'He left for Vienna hours ago. He's driven to Salzburg to catch the night train. He left in a frightful rush. I didn't even know he was going.'

'Doesn't the man ever stay in one place for more than five minutes? He seems to have a mania for moving about.'

'Oh, he's always been like that. He says he gets bored if he stays in one place too long.'

'Have you ever known him to dash off in the middle of the night before?'

'No, not without telling me, if I'm around. That's the odd thing.'

'How did you find out?'

'The reception clerk told me. I think he went off with Sternberg.'

'He couldn't have done that. I saw Sternberg recently. Are you sure he's gone?'

'Quite sure. He's taken all his bags. The reception clerk saw Sternberg go out to his car and assumed he'd gone too. Perhaps he was just seeing Josef off.'

'Where will he stay in Vienna?'

'At the Sacher. He always stays there. He pays for a suite and other rooms to be kept all the year round.'

Snow drank the last of his coffee. The glow was spreading through him again, any easy relaxed warmth, a mellow feeling. Bibi uncoiled herself, got off the couch and came over to stand beside him. Folding her arms she hoisted her breasts up, her expression serious for once.

'That photograph you showed me in the ballroom . . .' She paused.

'Yes?'

'I told you a fib. I have seen Roberts. Just once, at the Frankfurter Hof.'

'When was this?'

'About a month ago. In the evening, quite late. About 11 o'clock, I think it was.'

'Where exactly did you see him?'

'He had just come out of Josef's suite. We bumped into each other.'

'You're sure it was Roberts?'

'Quite sure. We were face to face for a moment. Then he walked off down the corridor. I never saw him again.'

'Then Bernstein did see him in Frankfurt?'

'Not necessarily. He's only there part of the time. I don't even know if he was in then.'

'Who else has access to that suite at night?'

'Mme Savigny has a key. She can go there any time.'

'What about Sternberg?'

'I shouldn't have thought so, but it's not impossible.'

'Why didn't you tell me you recognized Roberts when I asked you earlier this evening?'

Bibi dropped down on her knees and folded her arms in Snow's lap. She looked up at him.

'Because I was frightened someone might overhear us, Mr Snow. Everyone's been so on edge this evening, or rather last night.'

'Who's everyone?'

'Mme Savigny, Sternberg – even Josef hasn't been quite himself. Not that an outsider would have noticed. It's just little things.'

'Have you heard any more references to Zenith?'

She pulled a face. 'No. Let's not talk about him. I'm going to get some more coffee.'

Jumping to her feet she collected the empty glasses and tray, looked down at Snow for a moment and vanished into the kitchen. He lit another cigarette and leaned back against the couch. It seemed to be getting even warmer inside the room. He would have liked to take off his shirt but instead he loosened it above his trousers. As he sat smoking it struck him he was beginning to wake up again. He noticed the outer door key on a table and was just going to get up to lock the door when he heard Bibi coming back.

He couldn't see her until she came round the end of the couch, carrying the tray again, which she put down on her table.

Snow's face showed no reaction. He just sat looking at her.

She had taken off her tights. Her black sweater was rolled up to just below her breasts and below that she was completely naked. Her superb legs looked even longer. Round her bare waist he could see the red line of the elastic at the top of the tights she had taken off.

She picked up a glass of coffee, walked to his table and put the glass down on top of it. Then she placed one hand on the back of the couch, the other on the arm, leaned herself over him and kissed him slowly full on the lips. Her blue eyes looked enormous behind her half-closed lashes. Snow put a hand behind her neck and pulled her closer to him.

Easing herself upright again she went back to the other

end of the couch. She sat down sideways and rested her back firmly against the end of the couch. Lifting her right leg she extended it along the couch and planted her bare foot hard into Snow's stomach. He felt his muscles tense.

'Bibi, you'd better get dressed.'

'I'll get dressed . . . afterwards,' she said and pressed her foot into him again.

Everything might have happened but at that moment the doorbell rang harshly, impatiently.

Bibi looked across towards the lobby and smiled with doleful resignation.

'She would have to call now.'

'Who?'

'Mme Savigny. I had to phone New York. She'll want to put the information in code and cable it to Vienna. Josef will expect it when he arrives. I'd forgotten all about it.'

'Send a cable? At this hour of the night?'

'Oh, she keeps the same hours as Josef. Then she's always available when he wants her. He stays up half the night and then sleeps till mid-morning. She does the same thing.'

'You mean Bernstein and Mme Savigny. . . ?'

'Don't be silly. Of course not. The only thing Josef thinks about is making money. No, that's not quite fair. He's very kind. Look, I've got to get something on.'

She ran out of the room and came back carrying her tights and shoes. Then she stood in front of Snow, grinning at him as she hitched her tights up and rolled them over her upper legs.

Snow felt he was seeing the same film round twice, even including the arrival of Mme Savigny. It was just like Frankfurt. He watched her legs disappear behind the telescoping cloth.

162

'She hasn't rung again,' he remarked.

'No, she thinks we're in bed. She's giving me what they call a decent interval. There.'

'Perhaps you'd better go back to the Schloss with her.' He wasn't speaking in a very firm tone of voice.

'I'm sleeping here tonight, or rather this morning.' She spoke as though it were a command, an impish smile on her face. Waving him a kiss she disappeared through the swing door into the lobby.

Snow drank some more coffee. He wasn't sure now whether it was putting him to sleep or waking him up. It seemed to do both things at the same time. His cigarette had gone out, so he lit another one. There was half a glass of coffee left. He drank some of it. When she came back he must make the effort and get her out of the tower. He'd better escort her back to the Schloss. It was very late. No, it was very early in the morning, as she kept pointing out. When she came back . . . he'd be standing up. He stood up. It was a step in the right direction. He looked down at the second table. She hadn't touched her coffee. He'd have to wait while she drank it. . . . He liked the girl enormously. Not a trace of malice or meanness. Why not. . . . ? A thought crept into his mind. She'd been out there a long time.

Suddenly he walked across the room and pushed open the door into the lobby. He stood there for a moment in the open doorway, his teeth clamped hard, his senses acutely alert.

Bibi was lying in front of the lift door, which was closed, one naked leg bent under the other. She was lying face down on her stomach, the black handle of a knife protruding from underneath her left shoulder-blade. They had taken her tights off. She was dressed almost as she had been on the couch a few minutes before.

He walked forward and bent over her, feeling her pulse and the artery at the side of her neck. She was dead.

Somewhere outside the tower he heard a noise. Running back into the living-room he switched off the lights, felt his way to the window and pulled back the curtain. The landscape was still flooded with pale moonlight. Beyond the car-port he saw a car moving down the hill. It disappeared into the forest. At that distance it was impossible even to see the make of car. He dropped the curtain, went back to the door and switched on the lights again.

He walked back into the lobby and stood looking down at Bibi for a long minute. He felt as cold as ice. He knew he had lost all his colour.

Then he began his search. Underneath her body he found a handkerchief, tinged with blood in one corner. It was a handkerchief taken from his own case. Folding it up carefully in his own pocket handkerchief, he tucked them both away inside his trouser pocket. Then he examined every inch of the lobby swiftly and thoroughly.

Underneath an aluminium umbrella stand he found a coat button with the torn threads still attached. The button look familiar. He had completed his examination when it occurred to him that Bibi's tights had been taken away.

Walking through to the bedroom, he lifted his case on to a luggage stand and unlocked it. One of the buttons was missing from a suit jacket, torn away roughly from the cloth, a button like the one he held in his hand. He tucked it inside the breast pocket and repacked the case. Then he walked over to the phone to call the *Polizei*.

His hand was poised over the receiver while he stood still, thinking. They had counted on this, of course. An ex-policeman must call the *Polizei*. He took his hand away

164

from the phone and went back to his case. In five minutes he had changed into a day suit and packed his evening clothes.

Going back into the living-room he collected his own coffee glass and the ashtray. He took them into the kitchen, lost the contents down the waste disposal unit, dried the glass and the ashtray, put the glass back into a cupboard and took the ashtray back into the living-room. On his way back to the bedroom he deposited the tray from the living-room in the kitchen.

He took a last look round the entire suite and carried his bags into the living-room. Putting them down, he started to look for Bibi's handbag. He found it down behind a cushion in an arm-chair. The contents included two lipsticks, a powder compact, a comb, two tiny handkerchiefs and a set of car keys. He dropped the car keys inside his jacket pocket and replaced them with the suite-key he had never used after entering. If he had . . . He brushed the thought out of his mind. Then he took the room key out of the bag again, wiped it with his handkerchief and dropped it back inside the bag.

Picking up his case he walked out into the lobby and put the handbag on the floor near Bibi's body. Before pressing the lift button he paused for a moment, looking down.

When the lift doors opened his hand was resting on his gun inside his pocket. He stepped inside and turned round. As the doors closed he caught a last glimpse of the crumpled figure.

In the ground floor lobby he paused cautiously and then walked towards the entrance. His foot felt something hard on the carpet. He went back a few steps, stooped down and picked up a small leather button, moulded with a triangular design. Loose threads were hanging from it. This time it was not one of his own buttons. It could have come from the coat of a man or a woman, impossible to say which. He put it carefully inside his waistcoat pocket and walked back to the entrance.

It was a long walk across the moonlit forecourt and down the hill to the car-port. He tightened his grip on his bag, watching the darkened windows of the Schloss. In the late moonlight it had a derelict look, as though abandoned long ago.

The car-port was still half-full, but the cars on either side of Bibi's had gone. He opened the door with her keys, put his bag inside and looked at the gently sloping bank just beyond the edge of the car-port. It led down to the road which fell gradually away to the forest.

He put the car in gear and released the brake. Then he started to push. Fatigue clogged his muscles. He gave another heave. Suddenly the car began to move forward. He scrambled to get inside, slipped, recovered, flopped into the seat and grabbed the wheel.

Under its own momentum the car ran down the slope and on to the road, picking up speed. It was inside the forest before it began to slow down. Snow stopped the car and listened for a moment. Then he started the engine. It sounded incredibly loud. Switching on the headlights he eased his foot down. The car shot forward into the night.

The road to Munich was well signposted. He met no other traffic during his swift drive through the night. He had covered half the distance to the city when he pulled up inside a wood. Getting out of the car he walked several yards into the trees. After listening for a moment he bent down and scooped a hole out of the earth using the flame of his lighter for illumination. Then he burnt the two handkerchiefs and buried the remnants in the hole.

He listened again, went back to his car and drove on towards Munich.

13
Eight Hours to Vienna

The streets were filled with early morning gloom as Snow pulled up outside the Bayer Hof. It was still quite dark, the stale end of night, with a chill in the air. As he climbed out on to the pavement he shivered.

Behind the entrance doors the reception hall was palely illuminated with sick light. Snow closed the car door, went inside and collected his room key from the sleepy-eyed desk clerk.

'No messages for me?'

'*Nein, mein Herr.*'

'That's a change. I've left one of Mr Bernstein's cars outside. Have it put in the garage. And have you a railway timetable? I want trains to Ostend. Thank you, I'll take it up to my room.'

As soon as he was inside his suite he locked the door. He stood for a moment looking at the couch where Bibi had sat waiting for him. It seemed a long time ago. For a second he thought he caught a whiff of her perfume. It was pure imagination, of course. He glanced round the room wearily. A strange hotel suite at five o'clock in the morning was like a forgotten tomb.

He nearly sat down on the couch and then moved over to a chair instead. Opening the timetable he ran his finger down the columns. A train was leaving for Vienna at 6.08 a.m. He got up, went through the bedroom into the bathroom and had a wash. He was drying himself in the bedroom when he heard a soft tapping on the outer door.

He stood quite still and waited. There was another tattoo, more urgent this time. He walked quietly back into the living-room, his revolver in his hand, and stood to one side of the door. When the tattoo was repeated he turned the key silently and called out.

'Come in!'

The handle turned and the door moved inwards. A man carrying a bag took a step into the room.

'What are you doing here, Scardale?'

'Nervous, aren't we?' He gave a wide-mouthed grin.

'I don't expect friends at this hour of the morning.'

'You're right, of course.'

Scardale shut the door and put his bag on the floor. Hitching his hands inside his trouser tops he gazed round the room.

'Better than the Gasthof Weber. Much better!'

'What made you come over so early?'

'I called here last night and heard you'd gone off on a trip. I had an idea you might be moving on this morning so I got up bright and early, packed my things and here I am. Anything happening?'

'Bernstein's given me the slip. He's gone to Vienna.'

Scardale sat down in a chair, took out a cigar, lit it and blew smoke at the ceiling.

'So what do we do next, Snow?'

'I'm going after him. There's a train to Vienna from the Hauptbahnhof just after six.'

'We'll have to hurry, then. You won't get a taxi at this hour.'

'We?'

'I'm coming with you.'

Snow stood looking at Scardale for a moment. Suddenly his manner changed, became more brisk and business-like.

'Yes, Scardale, I think you'd better. Well, hurry up!'

They went out of the suite together and walked down the stairs to the reception desk. Snow handed back his key.

'I'm leaving. Have you my bill?'

'You are Herr Bernstein's guest. He has made all the arrangements.'

'I'd prefer to pay myself.'

'I'm sorry, *mein Herr*. The bill is already dealt with.'

'Mr Bernstein didn't know how long I was staying.'

'We have instructions to debit his account, no matter how long you stay.'

'Good night, or rather, good morning.'

Another reminder of Bibi.

Snow and Scardale walked silently out of the hotel and into the pre-dawn streets. Cold light was beginning to filter into the eastern sky. Their feet echoed along the stone pavements like ghost sentries patrolling a dead city.

Here and there was an occasional square of light behind a lonely window. Was it an early riser or someone who never slept? Snow's hands, holding his cases, were quite chilled now. He thumped his feet on the pavement to warm them up.

Nearer the Hauptbahnhof they were joined by other solitary figures trudging in the same direction, pale listless shadows of people. Bavaria was dragging itself into another day.

It was almost empty inside the huge concourse of the Hauptbahnhof. A handful of people sat waiting on seats. One man was sprawled out fast asleep, a pile of luggage near his head.

There was snail-like activity at *Gleis 6*. Porters with faces like robots trundled trolleys through the ticket barrier. A long train stood by the platform. The Vienna Express.

'There's a coffee stall,' said Snow. 'We've got time.'

'What about tickets?' asked Scardale.

'The counter's over there. Here's some money. As you insist on coming along you might as well make yourself useful. First class for me.'

'I usually travel second.'

'That's all right. We'll travel in separate compartments!'

Snow watched the porters loading up the express as he drank coffee. Two *Polizei* in uniform strolled along the concourse, glancing at people mechanically.

A group of last-minute travellers came hurrying into the station and formed a queue at the ticket office. As Snow finished his coffee Scardale came striding back, two first-class tickets in his hand.

'I have to justify my expenses you know, Snow. First class!'

'You'll find it expensive travelling with me. Nothing but the best! Remember, it was your idea. Come on. Five minutes to go.'

They found an empty compartment and settled themselves in corner seats, facing each other. Snow was checking his timetable when the train gave a lurch and started to move out of the station.

It was getting quite light outside. Another dawn, another day. Snow eased himself back in his seat. He suddenly felt exhausted, all reserves dissipated. The moving picture beyond the train window seemed like a dream.

'I'm going to take a nap, Scardale. Wake me at eight o'clock for breakfast.'

'I'll be peckish before then.'

'Well go and get it by yourself.'

Snow closed his eyes and immediately fell asleep.

The sound of someone calling out woke him. The dining-car attendant was going down the corridor announcing breakfast was being served. Scardale was still sitting opposite, his long legs sprawled half way along the compartment, staring out of the window.

Snow sat up straight and yawned. Beyond the window a rolling plain stretched away for miles, bright and peaceful in the morning sunlight. In the distance rose a pale mountain range. It was the Bavarian Alps, almost unreal, like a mirage.

The train was moving at speed now. The coaches swayed from side to side as they followed the curving track.

'I'll join you for breakfast,' said Snow.

'Good man. I'm famished.'

They started to walk along towards the dining-car. As he followed Scardale down the corridor Snow glanced into each compartment. There were not many passengers. Most of them were asleep or sitting up gazing vacantly into space. As they crossed from one coach to the next Snow called out to Scardale.

'I'm going to have a wash. See you in the dining-car.'

He waited until Scardale had disappeared and then went back into the previous coach. Stopping outside a compartment he opened the door and looked down at the solitary occupant.

'Good morning, Dr Zimmermann. And where are you going to this time?'

'Mr Snow! What a pleasant surprise! You will join me for breakfast, of course?'

'I'm afraid not, I'm with someone. Otherwise it would have been a pleasure. Where did you say you were going?'

'Vienna. How strange the way we keep bumping into each other.'

'Yes, isn't it. You are a much-travelled man, Dr Zimmermann.'

'Like yourself, Mr Snow, like yourself. Are you also going to Vienna?'

'It depends. Perhaps I shall like the look of somewhere *en route*. It's pleasant to break a journey on impulse.'

'*Ja, ja*. That is so. You have come from Munich?'

'Like yourself, Dr Zimmermann, like yourself.'

'If you do go on to Vienna, perhaps you would join me for dinner one evening? I shall be at the Hotel France.'

'Most kind of you. Shall we see what happens? I must get along to breakfast now. *Auf Wiedersehen.*'

Snow closed the compartment door and went along to the dining car. He found Scardale sitting at a table for two, explaining carefully in bad German exactly what he wanted. The waiter nodded his head repeatedly as though he understood it all and handed the menu to Snow.

'Scardale, where did you learn your German?'

'Berlitz. A short course, a very short course.' He grinned contemptuously. 'Enough to get by on. In any case these people should all speak English. It's an international train, isn't it?'

When the waiter had gone away Scardale leant across the table, his eyes glaring.

'Snow, I've been thinking. These people who tried to knock me down in Munich may have followed us on this train.'

'You're very wide awake this morning.' Snow had started to butter a roll.

'How do you mean?'

'I happened to be thinking the same thing myself.'

'If they are on the train they may try something else before we reach Vienna.'

'I should think that's more than likely.'

'I've got an idea. I think we can put them off the scent.'

'How?' Snow was plastering thin marmalade out of a small pot on to his buttered roll.

'There's another way to get to Vienna. By paddle steamer on the Danube from Linz. We reach Linz at 10.25 a.m.'

'Surely it would take ages. By paddle boat!'

'Only eight hours to Vienna. I think there's a paddle steamer, a fast one, which leaves Linz about eleven o'clock. If I'm right we can catch it easily. It's worth a try.'

'How do you know all this, Scardale?'

'The wife and I were coming here on holiday. We thought it would be a novelty to arrive in Vienna by boat, so I looked up the times. I remember it took eight hours and the boat reached Vienna about seven o'clock at night. We thought it would be just in time for dinner. I could check the times with the attendant.'

'No, don't do that. Someone might ask him what had happened to us. Mind you, eight hours on a boat is a long time.'

'You can get a private cabin. I remember it was quite cheap.' Scardale coloured as he saw Snow's expression.

'I'd like to think about it while we eat.'

The waiter arrived with breakfast. The coffee was hot, steaming and tasteless. The boiled eggs were as hard as pebbles. Snow ate and drank as he looked out of the window.

It was a lonely countryside, brilliant in the blazing sunshine. The express curved round the edge of a large lake, just below the railway. It was like a Chinese painting, azure water decorated with a single flat-bottomed boat, occupied by a motionless man holding a fishing-rod.

Snow drank some more coffee and made up his mind.

173

'All right. We'll get off as soon as the train reaches Linz and make straight for the boat. We'll have to take a chance on the sailing time. I'm going to get a shave now. I'll see you back in the compartment.'

He left some money on the table, got up and walked back down the train. Dr Zimmermann's compartment was empty. Snow collected his shaving kit and made his way to the toilet.

At Salzburg they had a glimpse of the castle perched on a hilltop. Passport Control and Customs men came aboard and wandered through the train.

Snow sat in the compartment reading a book. He could feel the warmth of the sun shining through the glass on his face. Scardale was fast asleep, his arms folded.

When the express steamed into Linz Hauptbahnhof they were both standing by the coach door. They made a quick dash down the steps as soon as the train stopped. *Ausgang* was to the right. They were the first passengers to pass through the ticket barrier.

Inside the taxi they sat in silence as it sped through the city. Snow was half-asleep, the sound of the train wheels still echoing in his ears. Afterwards he could not even remember what Linz looked like.

Then they reached the Danube. Moored to the quay-side lay a paddle steamer out of a story book. The hull was painted cream and green. One slim funnel rose above the decks. Snow particularly noticed the enormous covered paddle, half-way along the steamer, painted bright red.

Scardale bought the tickets and they crossed the gang-plank.

'They hadn't got any double cabins so I got two singles. You can be on your own. I'm sure that will suit you.'

'Yes, Scardale, it will. I should be able to finish my report before we reach Vienna.'

They were walking along inside the boat now as the steward conducted them to their cabins.

'Report?'

'Yes. I'm writing this whole business down and posting it to the Commissioner as soon as we reach Vienna. Then if anything happens to me someone else can carry on.'

'Well, I'm here to carry on.'

'They may get you as well.'

The steward showed Snow inside his cabin and then went away with Scardale. As soon as he was alone Snow settled down at a table and began writing. He continued writing when the engines started to vibrate.

Outside he could hear orders being shouted in German, the scrape of the gangplank being hauled aboard, then a noise like a waterfall. The steamer slowly sheered away from the quayside.

It was getting hot inside the cabin. He stopped writing, went over to the door, locked it, took off his jacket, sat down and resumed his writing. Beyond the cabin wall he heard the giant paddle turning, like a huge multiple scythe threshing the Danube water as the boat picked up speed and throbbed downstream.

He was half-way through his report when Scardale arrived, complaining that he was peckish. They had lunch together in the dining-saloon. Scardale hardly spoke during the whole meal. He seemed tired and lacking his normal exuberant self-confidence. Snow watched the view through the windows.

The shore line of the Danube was farther away than he would have expected. It was more like steaming across a lake. In the distance flat fields baked in the sunshine.

Snow was aware of a sluggish atmosphere in the dining-saloon, as though the passengers were drugged by the vibrations of the boat. There was a timeless feeling, no urgent destinations, just a gentle drifting along.

After lunch they parted company again and Snow went back to his cabin to continue his report.

He finished writing as the steamer left Melk. Folding his report once he tucked it inside his breast pocket, next to his wallet. After a quick wash he left the cabin and started to walk round the boat. His gun was in his pocket.

As he passed a lounge he thought he saw someone familiar, sitting in a corner with his back to the door. Snow peered inside. The seated figure was quite unmistakable, even without seeing his face. Dr Zimmermann. Snow quietly withdrew and continued his walk.

He found the front of the boat deserted. The scenery had completely changed now. The steamer was inside the Wachau Gorge. On both sides huge cliffs towered up from the river shore. The Danube was narrower, faster flowing, compressed inside the rock walls. Brown choppy water raced and tumbled round the steamer. Ahead the river disappeared behind an abrupt bend. It almost seemed to stop at the foot of a vertical cliff.

Standing by the railing Snow looked back at the covered wheel. The paddle was chopping and mincing the river into a mad gyration, hurling countless gallons of water backwards as it propelled the boat towards Vienna. The sound of the paddle chop and the hiss of foaming water had an almost hypnotic effect. Snow reminded himself he must be very tired. He felt almost light-headed.

He sensed rather than saw the sudden movement behind him. Instinctively he jerked his head sideways. He was too late, but the blow struck him on the side of his head instead of full force on top. It was still sufficient to stun him.

He was vaguely aware of a curious sensation of being

176

lifted upwards by his ankles, his body pivoting half over the rail. Then he was plunging head first forward at alarming speed. The splash of cold water as he went under brought him to his senses and suddenly he was terribly afraid.

It flashed through his mind that he was straight in the path of the oncoming paddle. The monstrous spoiler of water, its great blades driving downwards like some diabolical battering machine, would reach him any second. He had a brief muddled vision of being smashed to pieces, his broken body spewing out of the paddle wake . . . the drowning suction round the wheel area . . .

He lunged out desperately in a direction he hoped was away from the boat. Then he heard it . . . an incredible roaring sound . . . like Niagara . . . too late . . . the paddle blades . . . over him . . . no, past him . . . a feeling of being sucked under . . . frothy water . . . the cream hull sliding past . . . gone.

He began to swim. The current was very strong. Not far to go, surely. If he could only cross the current. He was being carried along. The bank seemed a mile away. Swim. Swim. Swim. For ever.

He could hear voices somewhere, and then an engine sound. Silence again. Something was grabbing at his jacket. He felt hands under his arms, hauling him upwards. He looked up. Several men were leaning over the side of a motor-launch.

Then he was flat on his back at the bottom of the boat, gazing up at the blue sky and a circle of anxious faces. He lay there for hours it seemed. Then he made the effort. He sat up.

He felt in his side pocket. He still had his gun. His wallet and passport were safe but the report was gone, sucked away into the Danube. The launch was close to the bank now. He felt he could talk.

'I'm very grateful . . .'

'What happened?'

'I fell overboard. From the steamer. No, I'm all right now.'

A fat Austrian with a face like a clown stood looking down at him.

'You must see a doctor.'

'No, thank you. I'm feeling much better already. How can I get to the railway?'

'Railway?'

'Yes, the main line to Vienna.'

'The nearest station is St Polten. But you must see the doctor.'

'It's not necessary. I'm perfectly all right. How do I get to St Polten?'

'My brother runs a taxi service. He could take you. But the doctor . . .'

'When we get ashore, take me to your brother. I can pay – in wet marks.'

As he climbed out of the launch Snow looked down the river. The steamer had vanished round the bend. There was no other vessel to be seen anywhere.

14
'Bibi won't be there . . .'

Snow climbed down the coach steps on to the platform of the Westbahnhof in Vienna. He started to walk. It was dark and the evening was oppressive. The clock pointed to 8.20 p.m. Snow felt irritable, like the hour before the storm. His forehead was moist, his hands were sticky.

He walked through the ticket barrier out on to a concrete landing facing an immense glass wall. In the middle of the landing were showcases indicating hotel accommodation. A dazzle of green lights met his eyes.

He went down a wide flight of steps and through an exit in the glass wall. At the kerb stood a blue Rolls-Royce. A uniformed chauffeur was scanning the weary faces of the passengers.

'Herr Snow?'

It was the reception committee again. The chauffeur already had the rear door open.

'I'm Snow. How did you recognize me? You have a photograph, I suppose?'

'*Ja, mein Herr.*' The chauffeur produced a photo.

'I'll take that. You can go home now. No, I shan't be needing you.'

He walked across to a file of taxis and spoke to the first driver.

'Find me an hotel as close to the Sacher as possible.'

The taxi drove round the square in front of the station and turned on to a long straight road leading to the heart of Vienna.

Snow leaned back in his seat, only vaguely aware of his surroundings. He had an impression of an endless line of solid drab buildings and the occasional clang of a tram bell. The dark night seemed to press down on the glow over the city.

They were almost there now. He noticed the Opera House Square, trams everywhere, a bustle of traffic and crowds of people. They were going to the Opera, perhaps. Then he caught a glimpse of the Kärntnerstrasse, modern shops blazing with lights.

The taxi drove round the Opera House and stopped in a quiet side-street.

'The Astoria, *mein Herr.*'

'*Danke.*' Snow got out, paid the driver and walked inside the Astoria Hotel.

At the reception desk he booked a room, paid in advance when they asked for his luggage, and walked straight out again. Street girls were strolling along the pavement, stopping to chat to each other as they kept an eye open for solitary men. A blonde girl said something to Snow as he passed her.

He went down the Kärntnerstrasse and turned into another side-street. Already he sensed a feeling of gaiety in the air, a lack of German tension, an absence of German rush. It was even possible to cross a main street while the traffic was moving.

Then he arrived at the Hotel Sacher. He walked through the main entrance into a reception hall.

Immediately he had the effect of going back a hundred years to the time of the Habsburgs. The reception hall had an ancient elegance; the decorations were richly ornate.

Guests in evening dress strolled about. There was plenty of time, no need to hurry. This was Vienna.

Snow stood for a moment just inside the entrance, getting his bearings. His manner was grim, almost hostile. Then he looked grimmer as a figure came through a doorway into the hall, a cigarette-holder clamped between his teeth.

'Ah, Snow! There you are. We were wondering what had happened to you. . . . I see you've bought yourself an Austrian suit – just right for the Vienna Woods! . . . Come along, you're just in time – but then you always are . . . there's a room waiting for you.'

'I'm staying elsewhere . . .' A face like stone.

'. . . and I sent the car to meet . . .'

'I dismissed the chauffeur. I preferred to come by taxi.'

'I positively insist . . .'

'Bernstein, where can we talk? *Now*.'

'Upstairs in my suite.' The smile had faded away.

They rode up in the lift without speaking, Snow looking straight ahead, Bernstein glancing at him sideways.

When the doors opened Bernstein led the way down a long corridor and into an elaborately furnished room. It was lit by glass chandeliers. He closed the door behind them and went over to an open cocktail cabinet.

'You look tired, Snow . . . a long day . . . a drink is the answer.'

'Suit yourself. Not for me.'

Snow sat down in an arm-chair and watched Bernstein pour a single glass of champagne. He said nothing as Bernstein walked across and sat down facing Snow.

Bernstein drank half the glass, put it down, inserted a cigarette in his holder, lit it, then remembered to push the cigarette-box across the table to Snow, and drank the rest of the champagne. Finally he made the effort and began talking.

'I was saying, Snow, you've arrived at just the right moment: we're holding a reception tonight, a magnificent affair at the Schönbrunn. Everyone will be there: the President of Austria. . . . You are invited, of course. Mme Savigny will take you in her car. . . . Like an imperial reception given by Franz Josef. People have been flying in all day . . . extra planes put on from Zürich . . .'

'Bibi won't be there.'

Bernstein looked grey. Only his eyes retained their brilliance. He sat quite still for a moment, like a beaten man. Then he picked up his empty glass, went over to the cabinet, refilled it and came back to his chair.

'I know, Snow. I heard the news.'

'Of course, you can easily replace her. Perhaps you've done so already?'

Bernstein was lifting his glass of champagne as Snow spoke. He suddenly threw the contents in Snow's face.

Champagne streamed down Snow's chin and dripped on to his shirt. For a moment he didn't move, his face white and taut. Then he took out a handkerchief and mopped himself.

'I prefer to drink it in the normal way, Bernstein. In fact, I think I said I wouldn't have any.'

'I am sorry, Snow, very sorry. It was quite inexcusable. I lost control. But you shouldn't have said that. The news was a terrible shock. I don't know how I'll get through this reception. I'll find you a new shirt.' He started to rise.

'Don't bother. It's a hot night. It will dry in no time. Now just exactly what news did you receive?'

'Bibi was found stabbed early this morning. A workman found her in a car by the roadside, half-way to Munich.'

'In a car?'

'Yes, on the road from the Schloss. Nobody can understand what she was doing there.'

Snow lit a cigarette. Bernstein looked badly shaken. There was an expression of sadness in his eyes, something listless in his manner, as though he felt an illness coming on.

'Bernstein, you left the Schloss Ludwig very suddenly last night. Why?'

'Not at all. I was just looking in for the evening. I was on my way here. I move about quite rapidly.'

'Yes, I know you do, but you're not telling me the truth. Bibi told me you left quite unexpectedly, in a great rush in fact. In such a rush you didn't even tell her you were going.'

Bernstein got up and started walking round the room, smoking furiously, glancing at Snow each time he completed a circuit. Then he sat down again. He seemed calmer.

'You're quite right, of course, Snow. I did leave in a hurry. Sternberg pressed me to leave immediately. He said something was going to happen and I shouldn't be there. I gathered it was something to do with you . . . that he was going to persuade you to return to London. Halfway to Salzburg I nearly turned back . . . I . . .'

He stopped suddenly, got up again and started pacing round the room.

'When did Sternberg leave the Schloss?' asked Snow.

'I've really no idea. I think he caught a later train from Salzburg. I've really no idea at all. He's here at the Sacher tonight. . . . Everything seems to be going wrong all at once. What a terrible business.'

'Murder is terrible, Bernstein. And incidentally it knows no frontiers. The police will pursue their investigations to the bitter end, no matter who is involved.'

'Will they? I wonder. You're English, Snow. I've heard that some of the continental police forces can be very discreet if important people are involved.'

Snow leaned forward, his expression grim.

'I can promise you, Bernstein, I shall exercise no discretion at all. Absolutely none.'

'I know. That is why I was relieved to see you arrive this evening.'

'I don't understand you, Bernstein. I don't understand you at all.'

Bernstein sat down again, throwing away a half-smoked cigarette. He inserted a fresh one and lit it.

'You must understand, Mr Snow, I cannot possibly be held responsible for Bibi's death . . . a man in my position . . . I have to be very careful. . . . This is a crime we are talking about.'

'Precisely.' One word, like the click of a safety-catch. It seemed to spur Bernstein on to greater efforts.

'You must realize . . . some of the people who depend on my financial influence are not so scrupulous. They are capable of being frightened: the stakes are tremendous. Your own conscience cannot be completely clear . . . prowling round the continent after me like a tiger . . . dropping hints . . . upsetting people.'

'Tell me, Mr Bernstein, what exactly did Bibi do for you?'

Snow sat back in his chair to wait for the answer. Bernstein paused for a minute, frowning.

'Well, she was a kind of aide, an assistant . . .'

'Bernstein, she showed me her apartment in Frankfurt. I saw the bedroom.'

There was another pause. Bernstein stubbed out his cigarette, again half-smoked.

'Bibi was a remarkable girl. When I first met her she was washing dishes in a cheap restaurant . . .'

'I see.'

'No, Snow, I don't think you do. When I first met her I was a telephonist. The same with Mme Savigny. The three of us joined forces when we could hardly afford a hot meal on a Saturday night.'

'I'm sorry. Go on.'

'Bibi had a gift for capturing the confidence of intelligent men, men highly placed in the financial world. She entertained them, in her flat. Prominent bankers, big industrialists, those sort of people. There was even a German Cabinet Minister. . . . I needed to know certain things these gentlemen would never have told me . . . but they told Bibi.'

'I understand.'

Bernstein lit another cigarette. He looked steadily at Snow.

'I wonder if you do? High finance isn't a game for children, Snow. You have to use every method. It's like living in the jungle. If you're going to win you must have information. Bibi got it for me.'

Snow grunted. 'These people she entertained. I take it they paid her money?'

He wondered why he had asked the question. He really must be very tired.

'Of course they did. But you don't think she lived on that, do you? You saw her apartment. Just think of the monthly rent. The money she got from her guests wouldn't have kept her in petrol! You have no idea, Snow, how mean these respectable bankers are with their girl friends.'

Snow stood up. His legs ached. His left arm still felt bruised. He really must get some sleep.

'You'll have to get off to your reception, Bernstein, but I want to talk to you in the morning. Somewhere quiet.'

'All right, Snow. Where do you suggest?'

'We'll drive round in your car, otherwise we'll find someone like Sternberg bursting in on us.'

'I'll be ready at eleven o'clock. Call for me here.'

The door opened and Sternberg lumbered in. He stopped abruptly when he saw Snow and glared. Nodding to Bernstein, Snow walked straight past Sternberg without even a glance.

The reception hall was full of people in evening dress. There was an air of excitement, as though they were looking forward to an experience. They were probably off to the reception.

As he walked out into the street someone tapped Snow on the shoulder. It was Scardale. He had an annoyed look on his face. He fell in beside Snow, who kept walking up the street.

'I thought I'd find you here, Snow. Why the devil did you leave the boat. You might have known I'd catch up with you.'

'I got fed up. I jumped overboard.'

'Not very funny. I suppose you slipped off at Melk?'

'Near there, anyway.'

'Then why leave your bags on board?'

'You saw them in my cabin?'

'No, they weren't there. That's what made me think you'd got off at Melk. One of the crew found them just before we docked at this end. They were under a pile of other people's luggage. What on earth is going on?'

'I'm staying at the Astoria. It's in the next street. Where are you?'

'At the Europa. I've got your bags there.'

'Europa? Expensive!'

186

'It'll make up for that dive in Munich. Every room has a bath.'

'Can you get the porter at your place to put my bags in a taxi and send them over tonight?'

'I'll bring them over myself. There's a lot to discuss.'

'Not tonight.'

'All right, I'll come over just after breakfast.'

'Don't do that. I'm in conference with Bernstein in the morning. I may see you later in the afternoon. This is my place. Good night.'

Snow turned in to the Astoria and left Scardale standing on the pavement, a look of bewilderment on his face.

15
The Road to the East

Snow walked towards the entrance to the Sacher. It was another golden morning. Sunshine streamed down out of a clear blue sky. Housewives in short-sleeved dresses strolled along the pavements, out shopping. A driver pulled up to let a woman carrying a cake box cross the road. Beyond the Opera House Snow could hear the cheerful clang of tram bells.

Bernstein stood waiting outside the hotel, dressed in a light tropical suit.

'Good morning, Snow. Here is the car. . . . What a splendid day for a drive! The woods will look marvellous: the leaves should just be turning. The last time I walked through them I found a whole field of autumn crocus. We'll start at once . . . after you.'

'Not with the chauffeur.' It was almost an order. Snow's manner was distant, almost icy.

'I don't drive . . .'

'I do.'

'Splendid, splendid. . . . Heinrich, you are in luck. Take the morning off.'

Snow climbed into the driver's seat of the Rolls. Bernstein sat beside him. As the car moved away from the kerb, Mme Savigny appeared in the hotel entrance, a look of astonishment on her face. Bernstein waved cheerily back at her.

Guiding the car round the Opera House Square, Snow

turned into the traffic and moved along the Ring. It was like driving through a Parisian boulevard, he thought. Bernstein sat quietly smoking, occasionally glancing down side-streets. Snow concentrated on driving.

The car glided across another square. On the far side rose the twin spires of a large church. Snow pointed to a building at a corner.

'Bernstein, look. There's the Creditanstalt Bank. I once read about it. The great Wall Street crash of 1929 was triggered off by the collapse of that bank.'

There was no reply.

Snow drove on, past the Ring Tower, across the Augarten Bridge over the Danube Canal. They were passing through a shabby decrepit district now, second-class Vienna. Bernstein seemed lost in thought.

The car picked up speed. It crossed the Floridsdorfer Bridge above the River Danube, broad and brown. The sun was quite hot now, the air fresh. It was more like a spring day.

Snow accelerated, speeding through the outskirts, past old residential areas, into the open countryside. Away to the left Snow could see a spur of forested hillside. At the summit was the long wall of the Kahlenberg terrace, which overlooked the whole of Vienna.

Beside him Bernstein still sat smoking quietly, a faint frown on his face, saying nothing. In front of him the neck of a champagne bottle protruded from a silver bucket cradled in the stabilizer. His right hand rested on the door handle, almost absent-mindedly, as though to check his balance as the car swept round corners.

'Where are we going, Snow?'

'Just somewhere out of the way. So we can have a talk without fear of interruptions. It's time we came to some arrangement.'

'I see.'

Bernstein took his hand away from the door to insert a new cigarette in the holder. When he had lit it his hand stayed in his lap. He began looking out of the window, his manner relaxed.

Snow smiled grimly to himself as he increased speed. The road was getting quieter all the time. Already Vienna seemed very remote.

The Rolls was moving so fast now it seemed to hover above the road. For half an hour Bernstein sat preoccupied with his thoughts while Snow kept up the tremendous speed.

It was a day to remember. The sun blazed down on the lonely countryside. In all directions the flat plain ran away into the distance, like a world going on for ever.

As they went over a crossroads Bernstein reached out for the champagne bottle. Holding the wheel with one hand, Snow leaned sideways, snatched up the bottle and threw it out of the window. He heard it hit the road with a dull crash.

'You can wait for your next drink until we've had our talk.'

Bernstein's face was expressionless, an exercise in self-control. He took out a cigarette and slowly inserted it into the holder. Lighting it with care he looked away from Snow, watching the countryside stream away behind the car.

They rarely met a car coming in the opposite direction. There was hardly anyone else on the road except an occasional farm wagon, drawn by oxen treading wearily down the hot road leading into space.

At one point in the middle of nowhere they came to a road junction. Snow reduced speed, looked at the sign-post, took the left turning and accelerated again. As they passed the signpost Bernstein looked at it sharply. The sign pointing left read *Horn 10 km. Prag 200 km.* He sat up suddenly, taking the holder out of his mouth.

'Haven't we gone far enough, Snow? This is the road to Prague.'

'Interesting part of Austria this, Bernstein. Do you know it?'

'No. Now look . . .'

'It's the province of Niederosterreich, the one least known to tourists. In the north it has a common frontier with Czechoslovakia, a very long one. This is Iron Curtain country. The population is very primitive. . . . You've seen the oxen-carts. . . . Over to the right of us there's a tiny village called Eggenberg . . . it's near there they found a petrified crocodile from millions of years ago. . . . That's a strange thing, Bernstein. Until they dug this one up . . .'

'Yes, but . . .'

'. . . they didn't know crocodiles existed so long ago . . .'

'Fascinating, Snow, but . . .'

'. . . . It's in a museum . . .'

'Yes, Snow, but . . .'

'. . . in the village. Pity we couldn't go and see it but there really isn't the time.'

Snow was enjoying himself. I sound just like a Cook's guide, he thought. Bernstein was frowning again. They travelled in silence for several miles.

As they approached the outskirts of a town Bernstein sat up and took notice again. It was a small place with a tiny square surrounded with steep-roofed houses. They never saw a single person. It was like a town abandoned in the path of a hostile army. The last buildings slipped away behind them. They were out in the open again.

'That was Horn,' remarked Snow. 'The last town

before the Czech border. You come from the East, don't you?'

'Snow, I'd like you to stop this car at once. We can have our talk here. God knows we couldn't be more alone.'

The car increased speed through more endless country-side. They passed another oxen-cart, the driver hunched up in his seat like a figure made of clay.

'The next town, Bernstein, is Gmünd. You've probably never even heard of the place. It's actually right on the border. In fact the frontier almost runs through the town itself. You do come from the East, don't you, Bernstein? It will be almost like going home again.'

Snow was in a genial mood, an amiable expression on his face, as though starting out on holiday.

Bernstein looked at the empty champagne bucket several times. Once he glanced at the speedometer. Then he stared at Snow.

'When you brought me out here, Snow, I understood you wanted a talk. You spoke about an arrangement between us. Why the devil do we have to come all this way just to come to an arrangement?'

'You haven't understood it at all. I think I did mention an arrangement. But that was when I was worried you might jump out of the car before I could pick up speed. It was a question of tactics, Bernstein.'

'Kidnapping is a serious offence, Snow. I may have to report this to the police.'

'Talking about police, I understand the police in eastern countries have an excellent fingerprint system. A man may go away for years but if he ever goes back they can always identify him. They never throw any records away.'

Bernstein sat up straight. He spoke very firmly.

'Stop the car. I'll agree to any reasonable suggestion.'

'But supposing the suggestion is unreasonable?'

'I'm willing to agree to quite a lot if you'll stop this car. The way you're driving we'll be at the border soon.'

'In about five minutes, I should say.'

Bernstein stubbed out his cigarette and fiddled with the holder.

'Snow, the wife of that accountant could probably do with some money, a lot of money.'

'She could do with a husband, the one that was murdered.'

'I'd like to help her. People can always use money.'

'Not Mrs Roberts. I've told you before, it isn't money she wants.'

'Are you sure?'

Snow made no reply. His expression was grim. He gazed straight ahead.

The road was beginning to wind up into hill country. The horizon had disappeared. They drove through a small forest where the trees came up to the roadside. The car swept round a bend and emerged from the wood. In the distance rose the outline of a hill range.

Bernstein's hand reached towards the ignition key. Snow increased speed.

'If you do that, Bernstein, you'll kill us both. Make up your mind.'

Bernstein sighed and withdrew his hand. Instead he jammed a new cigarette into the holder, but this time he didn't light it. He sat quite still, the holder clenched between his teeth. The strain was beginning to show. Drops of moisture gathered on his forehead. He wiped his hand on his trouser leg.

'What is it you want, Snow?'

'Information. Otherwise we cross the border.'

Close ahead Snow saw the beginnings of a town, a building on the left, a chimney like a stone finger on the right, a line of trees in the distance. He pointed through the windscreen.

'Those trees are in Czechoslovakia.'

'For God's sake, Snow, what are you going to do?'

'I've been here before. The frontier post is just ahead. It's not heavily guarded – just a couple of sentries and a pole across the road. I'm going to drive straight through without stopping. By the time the Austrian guards have recovered their wits we shall be in Czechoslovakia.'

'They will arrest you as well.'

'Of course, but only temporarily. They don't hold my fingerprints in their Central Records. I believe the British Embassy in Prague is very efficient. I'll be released in a matter of days.'

They had reached the edge of the town. The car was still travelling at speed. Snow started talking again, watching the silent street.

'It's a straight run through the middle of the town to the border post. Don't try and jump out at this speed. You'll be dead as soon as you hit the road.'

'Snow, what do you want to know?'

'Who killed Roberts?'

'What a question. I don't know. Don't you think I'd tell you if I knew? At a time like this I'd tell you anything.'

Snow was bothered. He glanced at Bernstein. It sounded as if he might be telling the truth. In fact it was just possible that Bernstein didn't know.

They were inside the town now, driving down the narrow main street at a slower pace. Strange old buildings lined the edge of the deserted street, buildings not seen elsewhere in Western Europe. The roofs were steep, the frontages narrow, all joined together. At intervals archways led to inner courtyards, high archways built long ago to let inside huge wagons drawn by oxen.

When the car turned a corner the frontier post lay ahead. It was just a pole across the road with a sentry box on either side. An Austrian guard was sitting down with his back to them, facing the border. As he heard the approach of the Rolls he began to get up and turn round.

Just beyond the sentry boxes, on the edge of the tree line, rose a peculiar tower with a cabin at the top, like a look-out post for forest fires. Snow nodded towards it.

'That's one of the watch towers where the Czechs site their machine guns.'

'I don't know. I just don't know.' Bernstein sounded worn out, resigned to his fate.

'A London stockbroker I know is checking the chain of corporations you control. So far he's got back to Strom-fors in Sweden. Where does the chain start? Quick.'

'Vaduz.'

Bernstein spat the name out, his gaze fixed on the pole dividing East from West.

Snow eased his foot off the accelerator and jammed on the brake. The car stopped as though it had run into a wall. Both of them nearly went through the windscreen.

They sat side by side in silence. Somewhere nearby Snow heard a bird chattering furiously. A column of blue smoke rose from behind the trees and climbed vertically into the afternoon sky.

Opening the door Snow stepped out and went round to the front of the car. The bonnet was barely a foot from the pole. Bernstein was still inside the car, staring ahead. The guard came running up.

'What's this damn barrier here for?' demanded Snow. 'We might have gone right through it.'

'You are on the border. The border. You nearly went through into Czechoslovakia.'

'Border? You must be mad. We are going to Vienna.'

'There it is.' The guard pointed indignantly. 'Over there is Czechoslovakia. You have just come from Vienna.'

Snow turned to Bernstein. 'What a lucky escape! We must have taken the wrong turning at Horn.'

The guard was still indignant. 'Please show me your passports.'

Snow produced his and handed it to the guard.

'While you're looking at it, I'll point the car the other way. I'll feel happier.'

He got inside, reversed carefully and turned the Rolls round until it faced the way they had come. The guard came to the window and handed Snow his passport. He looked across at Bernstein.

'Who is your companion?'

'Josef Bernstein, the international financier. If you ever read the papers out here you'll know him.'

The guard peered in again at Bernstein, this time with a certain respect. He opened his mouth to say something.

'We must get on,' said Snow. 'We're very late already and Mr Bernstein has an appointment in Vienna. Thank you.'

He drove off down the street before the guard could reply. The town was still quite deserted, a sleepy little town on the edge of two worlds.

Snow glanced at Bernstein, speaking in a matter of fact tone.

'When we get to Horn I'll leave you and try and find a car to take me back. I don't imagine you'll want my company all the way back to Vienna.'

'Why not? You brought me here. I can't drive this thing. The least you can do is to take me back to the Sacher.'

'Just as you like.'

As it turned out, they stopped in Horn for lunch. They had an indifferent meal in an ancient tavern. The locals kept glancing at them surreptitiously as they ate.

They reached the Sacher in the late afternoon. Bernstein got out of the car and walked straight into the hotel. After he had locked up the Rolls and handed the keys to the doorman Snow went round the corner to the Astoria.

He took the lift to his floor, locked the bedroom door and asked the operator to get him a number in London. Five minutes later the phone rang. Slope's voice came over the line as clearly as if he were sitting opposite Snow.

'Hello, Snow. Vienna now? You do get around. What's the weather like out there. We're all in shirt-sleeves.'

'It's still an Indian summer. Slope, what have you found out?'

'A lot. Most of it I don't understand.'

'Well, get on with it. These long-distance calls can get chopped off.'

'Always in a rush. Well, here it is. Bernstein controls, or has major shareholdings in, a fantastic number of international corporations.'

'Yes, but where does it all start from?'

'Vaduz, in Liechtenstein. It's a toy state on the Swiss border. Most people know it only for stamps, but it's useful for registering companies. It can save a fortune in taxes.'

'I could have told you all this. In fact I found it out this morning. I practically risked my neck to discover what you've got through making a few phone calls.'

'A few phone calls?' Slope snorted. 'I've had an army of searchers on this thing. People all over the States, friends of mine in Stockholm, Frankfurt, Paris, Zürich and God knows where else have been working like beavers. Half my staff is recording the information as it comes in. It's costing me a small fortune . . .'

'I said I'd pay . . .'

'Good job your uncle left you some money just before you retired from the police!'

'I mean it . . .'

'Not on, old chap. This is useful grist for my own mill. It could be a bit shaking. I just don't understand it.'

'Don't understand what?'

'There's been some strange manipulation of cross-holdings between certain continental units, so it's not easy to get to the bottom of it. But it's a combine, all right. And to back it up there are immense hidden assets some-where – in Vaduz, in fact. I reckon at least £500 million.'

'How much?'

'Five hundred million. Are you going to Vaduz?'

'Yes, I'm starting out tonight.'

'Well, take down this list of companies. They're all registered in Vaduz. They belong to Bernstein. You go to the registrar of companies place in Vaduz. Ready?'

Snow took down the names and checked them back over the phone.

'That's the lot, Snow. All I want to know is what their assets add up to. Could you phone me from Vaduz? In fact I'm holding off investing money till I hear from you. There are one or two funny things happening.'

'What sort of funny things?'

'Certain American banks are in difficulties. A big Dutch company has just gone down the drain. This boom has gone on for so long . . . one major crash could trigger off. . . . Oh, never mind. Any idea when you'll phone?'

'Probably tomorrow morning. You realize Vaduz is at the other end of Austria?'

'I'll wait for your call. Don't get shot.'

Snow put the phone down and went over to open the french windows. He stood gazing down into the street for several minutes and then had a wash. He was lighting a cigarette when he heard the tattoo on his door.

Opening the inner door, he unlocked the outer door three feet beyond it and pulled it inwards cautiously.

'There you are, Snow. I thought you'd run off again.'

Scardale walked into the room carrying his jacket over his arm. His tie was pulled loose.

'Still chasing me around, Scardale? What is it now?'

'Time for a talk. What's the idea of the double door?'

'Insulation. The winters here are like Siberia. All the windows are double too.'

Scardale dropped his jacket in a chair and sat on the bed, pulling at his tie.

'What's been happening, Snow?'

'I think Bernstein's on the run. I took him out for a drive this morning. Nearly ran him across the Czech border. He cracked. Literally on the border.'

'What's the border got to do with it?'

Snow sat down in an arm-chair and leaned forward.

'Look, Scardale, this man Bernstein has iron self-control. He must have, otherwise he would never have got where he has. You could hold him up with a gun and get nowhere. But people have dropped hints that he originally came from the East. I gambled on the fact that he daren't go back there. It's the one thing he fears.'

'Well, did he tell you who killed Roberts, if anyone?'

'No, I don't think he knows. But I got something else out of him.'

'What was that?'

'I'm not sure. I'll know tomorrow. We're going to Vaduz.'

'We?' Scardale looked astounded.

'Yes, you're coming with me. If I leave you hanging round here you'll only get lost.'

'Thanks a lot.'

Scardale glared bleakly, his hands tight over his knees.

'So you might as well make yourself useful. We'll catch the night train to Zürich. Go along to the Cosmos Bureau. It's on the Ring near the end of the Kärntnerstrasse, facing the tram stop. Book two separate sleeping compartments. First class, of course! The train leaves the Westbahnhof at 8.35 p.m.'

When Scardale had gone Snow took out his revolver and checked the action thoroughly. The Danube water had not affected its efficiency.

16
Night Train

'More coffee, please.'

Snow watched the dining-car steward refilling his cup for the third time.

He sat stirring the coffee, looking out at the darkness beyond the windows. The express rumbled on through the night, like an armoured monster heading for battle.

Snow had a slight feeling of relief that every mile carried him farther west, away from the Iron Curtain which hung poised over eastern Austria. It was an absurd emotion, but one impossible to dismiss completely.

The dining-car was nearly empty. The other passengers had finished their dinner and returned to their compartments, leaving behind crumpled table-cloths strewn with bread-crumbs.

Scardale sat opposite Snow, his legs sprawled sideways, so that waiters had to walk round them. His hand held a glass of brandy. The two men had not spoken for some time.

Finishing his brandy, Scardale wiped his hand over his mouth and looked at Snow.

'This chap Bernstein, I suppose he's a Jew. Strikes me the whole thing could be an international conspiracy.'

'For heaven's sake, Scardale, what a ludicrous idea! I very much doubt whether Bernstein is Jewish at all. Mind you, I think it may suit his book for people to think he is. The Jewish race has a reputation for throwing up money wizards. It creates the right impression. I'm sure his real name isn't Bernstein, anyway.'

'Where do you think he comes from, then?'

'It could be anywhere north of the Danube or east of Vienna, possibly Czechoslovakia or Poland. Maybe even Rumania. We shall probably never know.'

'What do you think he's going to do next?'

'I haven't the slightest idea.'

'It strikes me we aren't getting very far, and we're on our way home. What do you expect to pick up at Vaduz?'

'With a bit of luck, the key to the whole business.'

'I'm beginning to think we're chasing a wild hare.' Scardale took out a cigar and lit it, throwing the spent match on the floor.

'We should know in the morning,' said Snow.

'What time do we get there?'

'We get to Buchs at 6.25 a.m. It's the nearest stop to Vaduz. No breakfast, by the way. They don't put the buffet-car on till Sargans, the stop beyond Buchs.'

'What an ungodly hour to be up. And no breakfast. I'll be peckish. What happens at Buchs?'

'You wait there for me while I get a coach or taxi to Vaduz. It's just across the Rhine from Buchs.'

'I'll come with you.'

'No, you won't. I have an idea this may be the most dangerous part of the trip and one of us has got to survive.'

'You think they'll try something again?'

'We'll know when it happens. I'm off to bed.'

They paid their bills and walked back down the corridor of the swaying train. When he reached his sleeping compartment Snow said good night, closed and locked the door, and sat down on the made-up bed.

He lit a cigarette and smoked while he thought, listening to the iron hammer of the wheels on the track. It was hot and airless inside the little room. He got up and lifted the blind. The window was closed. With an effort he turned the handle until the window was lowered several inches. The noise was appalling now, a crescendo of sound.

Before taking off his shoes he went along to the lavatory. On the way he noticed the conductor's seat facing down the corridor was empty. He had smelt brandy on the man's breath earlier. He was probably in his own compartment having a drink. No, the compartment door was open and it was empty inside. Very unusual.

In a few minutes he came back along the corridor. The train was racing along now, the coach wobbling from side to side, almost as though the express might leave the track. In the corridor the conductor's seat was still empty.

Snow went back into his compartment, shut the door and slipped the chain on. He took off his shoes, jacket and tie, and wriggled under the sheets in his trousers. Switching on the blue night light, he turned off the main overhead light. He was just going to lie down when he heard a fly buzzing. He paused, propped on his elbow, watching the insect darting in and out of the blue light. Then the fly landed on the middle of his pillow. Picking up a newspaper he folded it carefully, lifted it and swatted at the pillow. The dead fly came away from the pillow stuck to the paper. Snow sat quite still, his teeth clenched together.

Where he had struck the pillow something was protruding through the linen, something thin and needlelike. The newspaper had a tear in its underside.

He got out of bed and switched on the main light again. Kneeling down on the floor he opened the end of the pillow and peered inside. Then he inserted his hand carefully. He brought out of the pillow a strange object, rather like a metal hedgehog.

The oval base of the hedgehog was made of rubber, and hollowed at the base, so that it had a suction effect. Once pressed against any surface it would keep its upright position.

The top consisted of several steel needles, projecting at right-angles from the rubber base. Each needle was about an inch long, the ends smeared with a glutinous substance.

Snow shivered slightly as he looked at the hedgehog. He had no doubt he was holding in his hand a fiendish murder weapon. The needle points would be tipped with quick-acting lethal poison. But for the accident of the buzzing fly he would have flopped his head on the pillow and the poison needles would have penetrated his scalp.

He put his shoes on again and went down the corridor to Scardale's compartment. After listening for a moment he knocked gently.

'Snow here. Open up.'

He heard the rattle of the chain, the click of the lock turning and then the door opened.

'What the hell is it?'

Scardale was sitting up in bed in his pyjamas. His hair was tousled and he looked sleepy.

'Ever seen one of these? I found it inside my pillow.'

'What is it?'

'The needles are poisonous. I was supposed to lie on it.'

'God!' Scardale was wide awake now. He glanced at his own pillow.

'There won't be one there. If there had been, you'd be dead by now.'

Scardale started to get out of bed, his face grim.

'Snow, we'll search the whole train. Get the chief guard first. He can come with us.'

'It's no use. Whoever put this thing in my compartment won't be carrying another one. And it will be someone we've never seen before. No, we'll stay in our compartments until the train is close to Buchs. It will be safer. You'd better check everything in here. Watch the bedding, the floor and the racks particularly. And keep the window closed. The train stops during the night. They might try and drop something through an open window from a platform.'

'I still think we ought to search the train.'

'Please yourself. I'm going back to tear my place to pieces. See you in the morning. Pleasant dreams!'

As Snow walked back to his compartment the sleeping-car conductor appeared, his walk not quite steady, an aroma of brandy preceding him.

'Just a minute. Have you seen anyone enter my compartment during the last hour?'

'*Nein, mein Herr.* No one has entered your compartment. The train is quiet tonight. I am on duty. I would have seen them.'

'No, you wouldn't. You weren't here a quarter of an hour ago. Your seat was empty.'

'Then I would be in my compartment. But only for a moment. I am on duty.'

'Your compartment was empty too.'

'Is something missing, then?' His manner was becoming aggressive.

'Nothing missing. Someone called and left me something.'

'What is that?' The conductor was staring stupidly at the hedgehog in Snow's hand.

'Never mind that. Who gave you the brandy?'

'Brandy? Brandy? Are you accusing me of something?' The conductor's expression was one of tipsy indignation.

'You'll tell me who gave you the brandy and asked you to keep out of the way or I'll report you as soon as we reach Innsbruck. This is a police matter.'

The conductor felt inside his pocket and pulled out a flat bottle. His manner was servile now. He had a cringing smile on his face.

'I always carry some with me . . . it's a long night . . . you get your sleep, but as for me . . .'

It was quite hopeless. Snow went back to his compartment, locked and chained the door, and set about turning the room inside out. He found nothing. When he had finished, he packed the hedgehog with wads of newspaper, surrounded it with dirty clothing and put it inside his brief-case. Then he rolled up a spare blanket, propped it at the end of the bed and leant back against it, facing the door, his revolver in his lap.

The clatter of the train wheels reminded him of the open window. He got up again, lifted the blind, closed the window tight, pulled down the blind and stretched out on the bed. It was going to be a long night the conductor had said.

The express stopped four times during the night. At each stop Snow got up and stood in the corridor until the train moved off again. He had reached the stage of imagining a sticky bomb being plastered to the outside of his compartment window while the train was stationary.

To keep himself awake he stood up every hour and had a wash at the corner basin. He was beginning to run out of cigarettes. The atmosphere inside the compartment was like a furnace. His eyes were heavy with lack of sleep, his limbs stiff with fatigue.

Occasionally he interrupted the monotony by opening the door and looking down the corridor. Always at the end of the coach he saw the conductor, sitting on his seat, gazing back sullenly, as motionless as a waxwork. He could have been dead. He was certainly drunk.

Just after dawn Snow pushed up the blind. A white mist floated outside the window. It was impossible to see anything. The compartment was dense with stale smoke. He opened the window and cold air rushed in.

Lighting another cigarette he sat down again, trying to think coherently. What day of the week was it? He was losing all sense of time. He worked it out from the Sunday in Munich. Wednesday morning, that was it.

He was shaved and fully dressed when Scardale knocked on the door.

'Top of the morning, Snow. We're nearly there. Any more visitors?'

'No. You look very fresh. Don't tell me you slept?'

'I sleep anywhere. It's a gift. I'm ready for anything, especially breakfast.'

When the train reached Buchs they were the only passengers to get off. The conductor had disappeared.

At Buchs station Snow made arrangements for a taxi to pick him up later. They had breakfast in a *Gasthof* near the station. At the end of the meal Scardale lit another cheap cigar and glared across the table at Snow.

'I still think I ought to come with you.'

'No, you wait here. We'll do it the way we arranged.'

'The way you arranged.'

'That's right. Here's my taxi. I'll see you here in about an hour.'

'It's your funeral.'

'Then it won't be yours.'

It was a beautiful morning. There was very little traffic on the road. A veil of white mist drifted above the Rhine. In the distance loomed the mountains of Liechtenstein. The taxi began the long run over the Rhine bridge.

Snow watched the vast river flowing away below him. Then he looked ahead. The rooftops of Vaduz huddled at the base of the mountain wall. Perched on a hillside above the town Snow could see the Prince's castle, almost like a toy out of the shop in Nuremberg. He had arrived at Vaduz, the key to Josef Bernstein.

·　·　·　·　·

It was dark inside the registration office. Snow sat at a table, surrounded with company records, writing figures in his notebook. When he had written the last figure he put his pen back in his pocket and sat looking at the opposite wall.

Bernstein's philosophy about starting each new day afresh, making an adventure of life, came into his mind. He pushed the thought away from him.

He was at the end of the line. There could be no doubt about the figures. Perhaps it was what he had expected for days now, but he still found it difficult to grasp. He closed his notebook, stood up and turned to go. As he did so a woman came through the doorway.

'Good morning, Mme Savigny.' Snow spoke very quietly.

'You know, then?' Her face was white.

'Yes.'

'But do you realize what it means? In a few months, even in a few weeks, Mr Bernstein will have solved the problem. It's only temporary . . . it would be pointless to . . . Mr Bernstein is a genius.'

'Where is he now?'

'Mr Snow, perhaps we can help you . . .'

'Bernstein would know better than to try that. Where is he?'

'It will serve no useful purpose if you . . .'

'Where is Mr Bernstein now?' Snow spoke very deliberately.

'You want to see him?'

'Yes. At once.'

'He is in Milan. At the Cavalieri. He flew there from Vienna. You will see him before . . . ?'

'Good-bye, Mme Savigny.'

Snow walked out of the building and back to his waiting taxi.

The mist above the Rhine had dissolved now. It was another brilliant day. The river seemed immense in the clear light. The taxi drove back over the bridge.

As it approached Buchs Snow told the driver to take him to the Post Office. Once inside he asked the clerk to obtain Slope's number. There was a short wait. Then the call came through.

'Is that you, Slope? Snow here.'

'Where are you calling from?'

'Buchs. It's the nearest Swiss town to Vaduz. I've just come from there.'

'Anything interesting?'

'You gave me a list of companies. You said there must be assets distributed among them worth £500 million as backing for the combine. Is that right?'

'Yes.' Slope's voice sounded serious.

'You're quite sure of what you told me. You didn't miss out any companies?'

'No, all the companies are on that list.'

'Then you'll be interested to know that the total assets of those companies add up to something less than £30 million.'

'Snow, did you say thirty million? I was talking about five hundred million.'

'I said only thirty million.'

'My God.'

There was a long pause.

'Slope, are you still there?'

'Yes, I am. I wish I wasn't.'

'What does it all mean?

'One of the biggest financial crashes in history. That's all. If Bernstein isn't sound, no one is. The repercussions will be enormous . . .'

'You can get someone over from Zürich to check my figures. I think you ought to.'

'I've already got someone in Sargans waiting for me to call them. I had a nasty idea I might need them. I'll have to report this information, Snow. I can't sit on a thing like this.'

'That's up to you. I've got to go now. I'll see you in London. Maybe quite soon. Good-bye.'

Snow walked out into the sunlight. It was pure warmth, the start of a glorious day. He climbed into the taxi and directed the driver to the *Gasthof*.

Scardale was waiting outside in the street, an expression of annoyance on his face.

'You took long enough.'

'We've got to hurry, Scardale. We've just time to catch the train to Zürich.'

'We're going back home?'

'Not yet. I must be in Milan this afternoon. We shall do it easily. The Ticino Express leaves Zürich for Milan at 12.35 p.m. It gets into Milan at 4.30 p.m. Hurry up!'

Scardale picked up his bag and got into the taxi. As it moved off he turned to Snow.

'What did you find out at Vaduz?'

'Everything. I know now why Roberts was murdered. And there's little doubt he was murdered.'

'Why was he murdered?'

'He stumbled on something. Don't let's talk about it now. I want to make sure we catch that train to Zürich. I think we've arrived. Yes, there's the station. After you. Hurry up!'

17
North – South

The Ticino Express swept out of Zürich Hauptbahnhof into the afternoon sunshine. It picked up speed, following the bends of the curving track, moving faster every second.

The railway avenue ran between tall blocks of modern flats. Beyond them on the left were occasional glimpses of the Zürich See, rectangles of blue lake glittering with sun flashes.

Inside the dining-car the air was heavy and hot. At the tables passengers in shirt-sleeves drained glasses of beer, called for new bottles and ordered cold lunches.

Snow sat in his corner seat looking down the car. It was barely a quarter full. Single travellers had a table for four to themselves. They were mostly businessmen, Italian and Swiss, as accustomed to the Zürich-Milan shuttle service as suburban commuters.

Hardly anyone glanced out of the windows. Instinctively they knew where they were. They occupied themselves reading reports, skimming through newspapers, making calculations in notebooks.

Scardale sat opposite Snow, absorbed in thought, gazing towards the serving bar, a glass of beer near his hand.

A man entered the coach from the far end facing Snow. He sat down in the corner at the last table and looked out of the window intently. Dr Zimmermann had arrived.

Snow watched him from a distance of a dozen tables but Zimmermann never once looked in his direction. The stewardess walked up to his table. He gave his order without consulting the menu, almost without glancing up. When she had gone he continued gazing steadily out of the window on his side of the train, as though quite unconscious of his surroundings.

'What time do we reach Milan?' Scardale spoke automatically.

'According to the timetable, 4.35 p.m. We should be there on the dot. These T.E.E.'s go straight through regardless.'

'Are you going to see Bernstein?'

'As soon as we arrive.'

'If he's still there.'

'I think he's waiting for me.'

Scardale drank some beer and swilled the remains round in his glass.

'I find that hard to swallow. What makes you think so?'

'Mme Savigny will have told him I'm on the way. From Vaduz.'

'What did you find out there? I'd like to know.'

'Read tomorrow's papers.'

Lunch arrived, served by a slim stewardess, very smart in her pale blue uniform, rather like an air hostess. A dark round steak, French fried potatoes and cold salad for Snow. Scardale had ordered veal escalope and boiled potatoes, without salad.

'Another whisky, please. No ice.' Snow smiled at the girl.

'Bring me another beer. And see it's cold this time.' A pointed glare from Scardale.

They ate in silence. Scardale crushed a roll in his large hand, separated it into pieces and consumed his meal

212

rapidly. Across the table Snow was enjoying himself, looking out at the countryside, glancing down the train, sipping his whisky, slicing into his steak.

'Do we know any more about what happened to Roberts?' asked Scardale.

'We do now. I know exactly what happened to him. More important still, I know why.'

'Well, you'd better tell me. That's what I came out here for.'

Scardale had finished his escalope. He refused anything else, dismissing the stewardess with a shake of his head.

'Plenty of time, Scardale. You'll be in at the kill.'

'Who's going to get killed?'

'A figure of speech. Cheer up, Scardale. Anyone would think you only had an hour to live.'

Snow was in the best of humours. He ate the last of his steak, wiped his mouth with a napkin and waved gaily down the coach to Dr Zimmermann. There was no response, not even a sign of recognition.

An electric atmosphere seemed to pervade the dining-car. The heat was building up, the air-conditioning losing the battle. Passengers mopped their foreheads, stirred in their chairs, called for more beer and looked hopefully at their watches. Only Snow and the coolly efficient steward-esses remained unaffected by the temperature. The slim girl came over to their table.

'I'll have coffee now,' said Snow. 'You'd better have some too, Scardale. Make you feel better. You look all tensed up. All this travelling, I expect. Tiring if you're not used to it.'

'I don't want coffee. There's nothing wrong with me except I want to hear about Roberts. Withholding evidence isn't exactly what I expected from you, Snow.'

'Evidence of what, Scardale?' Snow was in his most

jocular mood. 'You really are out of sorts. And such a marvellous day! Incidentally, this train we're on is the most luxurious of all the T.E.E.'s. I think it's the latest model. Power-operated blinds . . .'

Snow touched a switch. Inside the double-glassed window a green Venetian blind began to creep downwards.

'They move at a touch of a finger . . .'

He pressed the switch again. The blind froze in mid-air, half-way down the window. At another touch of the switch the blind slid upward again.

Snow rambled on.

'Then there's the air-conditioning. Not that it seems a hundred per cent effective. Still, you can't have everything! On top of all that, we have a first-rate chef to cook our lunch. The life of a lord, Scardale! Just like Bernstein.'

'To listen to you talking anyone would think you were on holiday.'

'Well, in a way I am. Don't take things so seriously! Relax and enjoy the peace of it all. By the way, have you noticed that little man at the end table?'

Scardale turned round slowly and gazed along the coach.

'You mean the chap in the corner by himself?'

'Yes. Have you noticed him before?'

'No. Why?'

'Nothing, except he's been following us half-way across Europe. Probably a coincidence. These things do happen. Good, here's my coffee.'

They sat again in silence. Snow drank a second cup of coffee, then a third. The express curved round the shore of Lake Lucerne, a sheet of water like blue glass. In the distance a steamer crossed the lake, leaving behind it a rippled wave.

The train was moving upward now at high speed, climbing steadily all the time, devouring the mileage with ease, as though entering its natural habitat, the great gorge of the Gotthard.

On both sides the mountain walls began to close in, nearer and nearer to the railway track, shutting out the brilliant sunlight, plunging the canyon in dark shadow. It was a different world, drawing close to the massive Alpine range by the historic north–south route. There was a feeling of approaching climax.

The dining-car was still stuffy, even though the direct heat had gone. Snow looked out at the shadows. He glanced upwards. The mountains were enormous, seeming to stretch vertically to heaven, looming over the train, almost giving the impression they might topple down on the line at any moment. As he peered up at one peaked giant he saw in the distance another jagged summit appearing, even higher. He looked across the table.

'Have you ever done this trip before, Scardale?'

'No. Gloomy, isn't it?'

'It's one of the most fantastic train journeys in the world. Right through the heart of the Alps. We're coming to the Gotthard Tunnel soon. Only twenty minutes inside it and you emerge into the Latin world. This side it's all *Gasthöfe*, steep-roofed timber houses, a Teutonic atmosphere. Then on the other side. . . . You'll see.'

'How much longer, then?'

Scardale was half-asleep, his long body sprawled out, ankles crossed.

'About a couple of hours to Milan. I think we're nearly at Göschenen. That's at the entrance to the tunnel. We don't stop till we reach Lugano. And that's only a two-minute halt.'

'Wake me up when we get there.'

Scardale closed his eyes and slumped in his chair.

The express went on climbing, higher and higher, at the same steady speed. The gorge was very narrow now. On the right-hand side the mountain wall almost seemed to be inside the train. Snow peered along the window. He could see a network of overhead traction wires, the approach to a station. *Göschenen*. He stood up.

'Might as well spend the tunnel in the toilet.'

He was talking to himself. Scardale was huddled in sleep, his arms folded across his chest.

Snow started to walk along the dining-car. As he reached the end the express entered the tunnel. There was a continuous roar of immense horsepower penned inside the Alps. The train lights were already on.

As he opened the door he paused to speak to the man in the corner.

'Good afternoon, Dr Zimmermann.'

No reply. Slowly Zimmermann turned his head and looked up at Snow. He opened his mouth and closed it again without speaking, gazing at Snow, a strange expression on his face.

Snow nodded, slid aside the door, walked out and let it close automatically behind him. The roar was even louder now, an assault on the ear-drums. The area at the end of the coach was spacious. There was an open luggage compartment along one wall and beside it a large alcove with a hanging rail for coats. He walked along to the lavatory, went inside and locked the door.

It was more like a toilet in a de-luxe hotel with plenty of room to move around in. To one side was a wide washbasin with a huge mirror behind it. He decided not to hurry.

Taking off his jacket and tie, he rolled up his shirtsleeves, had a leisurely wash, dried himself and dressed again. Yes, he had plenty of time. There was nothing to see while the express was thundering through the Alps. He cleaned off some soap from the plastic top beside the basin. The room encouraged neatness. He had just finished and was putting out his hand to unbolt the door when he paused.

He had heard nothing but the sullen roar of the train, but he felt something was wrong. He looked at his watch There was another seven or eight minutes inside the tunnel. He listened, his ear pressed against the door. It was impossible to hear anything above the sound of the train. But he was perfectly sure he was right. He had a distinct sense of imminent danger.

He glanced round the little room. No mirror faced the door. He took his Smith and Wesson out of his pocket and swiftly calculated distances. Then he picked up the wet soap and ran it across the floor immediately in front of the door. Dropping the soap back in the bowl he dried his hands, picked up the gun again and took up a position to the side of the door. It was still quite dark outside the window. He leant forward and drew back the bolt with his left hand. Then he turned the handle and pulled the door inwards at a normal pace.

A figure came through the open door in a rush, hand extended, knife pushed forward in a vicious thrust at the point where Snow's stomach should have been. Feet slithered on the soaped floor. A shoulder thudded against the wall as the attacker recovered balance.

Snow's gun hand flailed downwards with tremendous force, aimed at the wrist gripping the knife. The gun-barrel missed the wrist and only just caught the outstretched thumb, but the knife clattered to the floor.

An iron fist crashed into the side of Snow's neck. He reeled back against the rear wall as the attacker slammed

217

the door shut. The man came forward and Snow swung his gun hand again, feeling it scrape down the side of jaw-bone. A savage kick smashed into Snow's shin. He doubled over, feeling sick, but his hand still held on to the revolver. The side of a hand struck the back of his neck, driving him down towards the floor. He made a supreme effort and rammed his head forward with all his remaining strength. It drove into a stomach. He felt a slither of feet and his opponent landed on the floor, almost between Snow's legs. Fingers wrapped themselves round Snow's gun hand and began to twist. Other fingers jabbed to-wards Snow's eyes. He stifled the instinct to drop the gun, to try and pull away from the forked fingers. Instead he dropped his head and rammed it forward into a face. He felt a head crack back against the door. With a sudden movement Snow tore his hand loose, brought up his gun and held it pointed, the muzzle almost touching a glaring eye. His trigger finger tightened. The eye wobbled crazily.

'One move and you're dead, Scardale.'

'You wouldn't dare . . . it would be murder.'

'With a knife on the floor plastered with your finger-prints? You must be off your rocker. A clear case of self-defence, Mr Zenith.'

'You wouldn't shoot . . .'

'You've got just five seconds to tell me who you really are before I pull this trigger. Don't think about it. . . . Quick.'

'Heinz Dietrich.'

'Well, you're the best fake Englishman I've ever met. Not quite good enough, though. You're Zenith, of course?'

The gun muzzle was still within an inch of Scardale's face. The eye wobbled erratically.

'Yes.'

Snow straightened up slowly and stepped back to the outer wall. Scardale was still sitting on the floor, his back to the door, his legs stretched out in front of him. He made a move to get up. Snow jabbed the gun forward.

'Not yet. Stay where you are. You must have spent some time in England?'

'Only six months, but it was long enough. Most of it in pubs. The best place to study English.'

'A short course, Zenith, a short course. Too short.'

'How did you spot me?'

'Your manner partly. Not quite right for a C.I.D. inspector. Then there were a few phrases you used, or misused, the odd colloquialism you didn't grasp. And that business on the paddle-steamer. If you'd been genuine you'd have reported I was missing as soon as you found my bags on the boat. But you didn't, otherwise you'd have told me at the Astoria so the police could stop looking for me. You didn't report it because you'd moved the bags yourself, after you tipped me into the Danube.'

'Pure guesswork.'

'Except for the button.'

'What button?'

'The one missing off your jacket cuff. It's identical with one I picked up in the lobby of the tower at Schloss Ludwig. Ironical, isn't it? You tore off one of my own jacket buttons and left it under the umbrella stand to suggest a struggle when I was supposed to have murdered Bibi. Then you go and lose one of your own buttons in the lobby. You killed her yourself, of course?'

'Yes. And with a bit of luck you'd have been held by the police for her murder. I still can't understand why you weren't. On the way back to Munich I phoned the desk clerk at the Schloss from a call box and told him I'd heard screams on Floor 7. I even took off her tights to suggest . . .'

He stopped speaking suddenly when he saw the expression on Snow's face.

'Well, for one thing, Zenith, her body was discovered in an abandoned car by the roadside half-way to Munich. Why did you have her taken there? You couldn't have done that yourself because you drove back to Munich ahead of me.'

'I didn't. I left the body in the lobby of your suite.' Zenith looked genuinely amazed.

'What part of Germany do you come from, Dietrich?'

'Altona. It's a suburb of Hamburg.'

'I know it. And I suppose you chose the name Zenith when you were establishing your reputation as a professional killer?'

'*Ja.*'

Dietrich's relapse into German gave Snow a slight shock. He wondered why confidence was creeping back into the assassin's manner.

'I take it you also killed Roberts?'

'Yes, that's right. An excellent example of German organization.'

There was almost a trace of arrogance now.

'Well, get up on your feet. Very slowly. Your next mistake will be your last. I could shoot you down like a mad dog without even thinking about it.'

Snow stepped back against the wall. He watched Dietrich climb slowly to his feet, avoiding the slippery area.

As he did so the train roar suddenly faded. Daylight appeared outside the window. They were out of the tunnel, passing through Airolo station.

'Turn round, Zenith, and face the wall with your hands

flat against it. Any movement at all and I shall pull the trigger.'

Snow patted Zenith's clothes. There were no other weapons. Snow was not surprised. The organizer of a killer gang was unlikely to risk incriminating himself by carrying round an armoury.

'All right, you can turn round now. Stand up against the door.'

Zenith turned round to face Snow.

'You won't be able to prove a thing.'

'You are off your rocker. Now we know you're Zenith the police can track your movements. I think we can get you for the murder of Bibi Decker on circumstantial evidence alone.'

'Did you have a good time with her?'

Snow froze. He must be careful not to allow Zenith to throw him off balance.

'Dietrich, put your hands behind the back of your neck.' He spoke quite casually.

Zenith lifted his hands and clasped them behind his neck. As he did so Snow took a step forward and swung the gun through the air. It caught Zenith on the side of the jaw in the same place as the previous blow. He squealed with pain, slipped and crashed to the floor.

Snow gazed bleakly down at him.

'Get up. And be careful what you say from now on. You may not get off the train alive.'

Dietrich climbed painfully to his feet. He looked at Snow with an expression of hate. His manner still held a trace of his old confidence. Snow again wondered why.

'Dietrich, I suppose those two cars in the square at Munich were driven by your own people. They never intended to hit you?'

'That's right. It was to convince you I was genuine just in case you still had doubts.'

'And the notebook in your suitcase? Left deliberately for me to find?'

'Like I said, an excellent example of German organization.'

Snow lifted his revolver a little higher. He spoke very slowly.

'Dietrich, we're going back to the dining-car now. If you want to try something you can, but don't forget what happened to Volga and Strauss.'

'What did happen to them?' Dietrich glared at Snow.

'They were too keen to make it look like an accident. Now open the door and walk out very slowly.'

Dietrich turned round and reached for the handle. As he twisted it he rattled it. Then he pulled the door open very carefully, walked out and stood still as Snow came behind him, stepping over the soapy floor.

Snow was half-way through the door when he realized the sound of wheels hammering on rails was louder than he would have expected. He walked out quickly as Dietrich turned towards the dining-car.

Someone had opened the coach door, which explained the terrible wheel roar. At the foot of the steps yawned eternity, a landscape moving past so rapidly that it was little more than a flashing blur.

Out of the corner of his eye Snow caught sight of a man standing inside the coat alcove. His arm was raised and he was holding a bottle by the neck like a club. Snow suddenly slashed his gun sideways, catching Zimmermann a ferocious blow across the bridge of his nose. He vaguely saw Zimmermann staggering backwards.

As the gun barrel struck Zimmermann, Dietrich spun

round, his hand reaching for the gun. Snow's lifted knee caught him full in the groin, a vicious blow.

Dietrich lurched backwards, struggling to find his balance as he tilted towards the open coach door. The express was just crossing a deep gorge. Dietrich wobbled desperately on the brink, a ludicrous expression on his face, half crouched forward, trying to straighten himself up.

His left foot missed the top step. His hand shot out to grasp the edge of the door. Then he was falling over backwards, screaming, clawing at the air. He catapulted out of sight.

Keeping his gun trained on Zimmermann, Snow stepped to the open doorway and looked down. The express was racing over a sheer drop down the side of a precipice. Dietrich must have fallen at least three hundred feet on to the scattered boulders below.

Snow shut the door and looked at Zimmermann. The little man was crouched down inside the coat alcove, his hands pressed over his nose.

'Come along, Zimmermann. We'll sit down in the dining-car.'

Opening the door, he watched Zimmermann stagger inside and collapse into his old corner seat. He closed the door and sat down opposite him. The dining-car was almost empty and there was no sign of the stewardesses.

Beyond the window the sun blazed down. More cloud-scraper mountains towered above the far side of the gorge, mountains like gods. The train was following vast curves as it wound its way steadily downward, dropping all the time, away from the main Alpine range. It was an incredibly rapid descent.

Immediately below the train lay the valley floor. Here and there they passed a village, Italian-looking although they were still in Switzerland. There were *ristoranti* instead of *Gasthöfe*, pink-washed houses with flat roofs instead of the steep-roofed wooden homes of the Teutonic north. The train had entered the Latin world.

Snow leaned across the table and started talking.

'Of course, you were the decoy, Zimmermann, all the way.'

'I do not understand.'

'Yes, you do. Your job was to make sure I spotted you right from the beginning, to distract my attention from Zenith. It was what they call in military terms a diversion. Then there seemed to be a chance of getting rid of me in Nuremberg. It didn't work so you had to start popping up again. It had the added advantage that if anything went wrong, as it did on the paddle steamer, I'd still suspect you and never think of Scardale-Zenith.'

'I have nothing to say.'

Zimmermann made the effort. He managed to speak with a show of dignity, although his finger-nails were digging into the table-cloth.

'Then in that case when I hand you over to the Italian police in Milan you'll be charged with the murder of Bibi Decker.'

'But I have never killed anyone in my life. Zenith . . .'

'Your only chance is to make a full statement. I happen to know one of the Milanese police chiefs. When the train stops at Lugano I shall send him a wire to meet the train at Milano Centrale. You will certainly be arrested. It is only a question of what the charge will be. You have your life in your own hands.'

'I have never killed anyone. I beseech you . . .' The little man's face had dissolved into terror.

'Frankly, I believe you. But until you have made a full statement I'm holding an attempted murder charge in reserve.'

224

'Attempted murder? But . . .'

'Yes, the attempted murder of myself. I was meant to go out of that coach door – which you opened. Ah, here's the stewardess. We'd both like some coffee. . . . My friend? Oh, he's all right. He bumped into something while the train was in the tunnel. He's feeling much better now.'

Snow waited until the stewardess had gone back to the kitchen. Then he got up from the table.

'Zimmermann. I'm going to collect Scardale's knife from the toilet. I'll be back in a moment. Don't go away, will you? There's nowhere to go.'

18
Ticker-Tape

Snow walked outside the terminus of Milano Centrale, put his bags down on the kerb and mopped his forehead.

The sunlight had vanished. Overhead storm clouds were assembling like an army massing for battle, pressing down, squeezing the airless air. The temperature was almost unbearable and the sky had a yellowish tinge. Snow was bathed in a slow perspiration. He felt dehydrated.

The via Pisani stretched away from him towards a cluster of skyscrapers in the distance. To his right rose the immense white shape of the Pirelli building, its end tapered like the prow of a concrete liner. A hot wind was whipping up stale summer dust and sweeping it along the via.

Waving to a taxi, Snow picked up his bags. As it stopped he opened the rear door and stepped inside. He gave his directions in Italian.

'The Cavalieri. Let's try and get there alive.'

'Si, si.'

The engine roared and the taxi leapt forward, cutting round a corner in the path of an oncoming tram, accelerating and hurtling down the via Pisani in a series of mad swinging lurches. Snow gritted his teeth and looked out of the window at the dust-infested afternoon. There was a jolting halt for traffic lights. The taxi waited in line with other traffic, snorting and straining at the leash. The lights began to change and the wave of vehicles surged forward. The last lap at Le Mans.

In front of the Cavalieri Snow stepped out, paid the driver and turned away with a feeling of relief that no bones were broken.

Inside the entrance hall he walked over to the reception desk. A crowd of men were huddled together in one corner, talking excitedly, waving their hands, turning to speak to new arrivals.

'What's going on over there?' asked Snow.

'The ticker-tape machine, *signore*. There is bad news from London. I am not sure but they say . . .'

'Watch my bags. I'll be back in a minute.'

Snow walked over to the growing crowd and shouldered his way through with smiles and apologies. A man grabbed his arm.

'Have you heard? It cannot be true. Extraordinary! You are from London?'

Snow pushed his way forward. The machine was chattering away, spooling out lengths of printed tape non-stop, as though in a frenzy. Fat Italian businessmen in dark suits grabbed handfuls as the tape unwound, showed torn pieces to their neighbours. It was almost like a free fight, a babble of voices rattling away at machine-gun speed. Complete chaos.

When he reached the machine Snow bent down and picked up strips from the floor. He tried to read them. It was a disjointed message, thereby seeming more dramatic.

Collapse on London Stock Exchange . . . Rumours started at noon . . . Paris Bourse falls . . . Panic in Frankfurt . . . Wall Street opens lower.

Stuffing the tape into his pocket, Snow started to elbow his way out of the mob. He neared the edge of the crowd and gave one last thrust. The bodies closed in behind him, sealing the circle again.

The crowd was growing every minute. Taxis arrived at the entrance, people rushed in through the doors, hurrying across to join the crowd. Snow went back to the reception desk.

'That machine. It belongs to the hotel?'

'Signor Bernstein arranged for it to be installed once. He always stays with us when he is in Milan. It keeps him in touch. What is the latest news?'

'Never mind. I have come to see Mr Bernstein. Is he in? My name is Snow.'

'Signor Snow? He is waiting to see you. He said you would probably arrive on the Ticino. We sent a car to . . .'

'Never mind. Just announce me. And keep my bags for the moment. No, I won't be staying.'

The clerk picked up the phone and spoke into it rapidly. He put it down and beamed at Snow.

'Gino will show you up. Signor Bernstein is ready to see you.'

'I'll have a quick wash first. This infernal heat. Over there? Tell Mr Bernstein I'll be up in a minute.'

19
Foul Champagne

Bernstein stood looking out of a great bay window, hands in his jacket pockets. He stood there for some time, not saying a word, gazing out into the world. Then he turned round and faced Snow, a mocking smile on his face.

'It was good of you to come, Snow. I wanted us to have a little talk. . . . Are you a student of human nature? . . . But of course you are. A superintendent of police when you were thirty . . .'

Snow looked up, surprised. The man appeared to know everything.

'Well, Snow, you are going to learn a lot more about people during the next few days. I can tell you exactly what's going to happen. All those people who have fattened on me for years, the great bankers, the financiers, the ministers of finance in half a dozen governments, the new industrial aristocrats . . . men who would fly a thousand miles to attend my receptions . . . the *élite* of nations: they won't be able to run fast enough to dissociate themselves from me. . . . You'll see it, Snow. You'll see it all . . . the mad stampede to get away from Bernstein . . . like people fleeing a great liner which is sinking. It will be an illuminating spectacle. Even more illuminating than the Stagenwand!'

Bernstein laughed shortly, picked up his holder, carefully inserted a cigarette and lit it, his hand quite steady. Even now, in the very path of the avalanche, Bernstein's iron self-control impressed Snow. He almost gained the impression that Bernstein viewed it all as though from a distance, a cynical spectator of events which no longer concerned him.

'Do you blame them?' asked Snow, abruptly.

An amused wave of the holder, a hint of the old sparkle.

'Blame them? I could only blame them if I respected them. You mustn't think this is a sudden revelation, Snow. I have always known what they were like: pathetic, the lot of them . . . jackals, to the last man. They trailed after me because I achieved things they didn't even dare contemplate, these giants of money. . . . Now they will try to pretend they never even knew me. The ship is sinking . . . abandon it . . . every man for himself. . . . This is the law of human nature.'

'You must have known the risks you were facing.'

Bernstein began walking up and down the room, flourishing the holder with buoyant gestures.

'Of course I did. But *they* didn't, the jackals . . . they should have done. That is why they occupy the positions they do . . . so they can estimate a risk. But can they? No! The simplest housewife can decide better where to buy her week-end meat than they can where to place the next million.'

'Someone must have been suspicious of you, surely?'

'Oh, yes. In the beginning they all were. I was the man from the back of beyond. My hardest job was making the first thousand dollars. That was really difficult. But once I really succeeded everything came true. . . . All the doors were open . . . "Mr Bernstein, the man who can make you ten per cent" . . . these shrewd money men used to come running . . . they would do anything just to get an appointment with me . . .'

Bernstein's eyes were ablaze now as he recalled his

amazing life, almost as though he were about to start all over again.

'How exactly did you do it?'

Bernstein walked over to a cocktail cabinet and poured himself a glass of champagne. He glanced at Snow, his eyebrow raised, but Snow shook his head. He lifted the glass in salute, drank half its contents, and started prowling round the room.

'How did I do it? Very simple really. I offered to make ten per cent on any sum – millions if available. They were. I believe in myself and these people believe in me. It's all a question of confidence. Everything is. You wouldn't dare put a foot in the street if you hadn't confidence you'd reach the other side safely. . . . So they handed over the money to me and I paid ten per cent interest every year, on the dot. An American bank once lost confidence in me, so I delayed the interest payment six weeks. They pressed me hard and I paid them back their ten million dollars plus a million in interest. Then they begged me to reinvest the money, but I refused. The news travelled round the grapevine. No one else questioned me again.'

'Yes, but how did you manage in the beginning. Was there always a deficit?'

'Of course not. That's of very recent origin. I made the ten per cent by streamlining business, which is usually run very inefficiently. . . . I created trusts, then international trusts. Monopolies, if you like. The Americans love them. They pretend not to, but that's window-dressing. Individual companies do this sort of thing all the time: buy up the competition and then put up the price of the thing they're selling. People have to pay. There's nowhere else to buy from. . . . The difference is I did this on a vast scale . . . buying up whole industries across a continent . . . a matter of calculation . . . and vision.'

231

'Yes, but what went wrong?'

'I reached a point where I couldn't create monopolies fast enough to support the amount of money pouring in for me to invest . . . at ten per cent, of course . . . so I had to adopt other methods . . . temporarily, I thought.'

'What other methods?'

'I paid them back their interest out of their own money. A bank which had loaned me a million pounds expected £100,000 interest at the end of each year, so I paid them. After three years there was only £700,000 left. . . . They didn't know this, of course . . . a question of confidence, as I said. . . . Hence the situation at Vaduz. Mme Savigny phoned and told me you had been there.'

'I calculated almost five hundred million had disappeared. Is that so, Bernstein?'

'Yes, but it's a good deal more than that. It's not all down in books. I carry a lot in my head. Safer than keeping ledgers.'

Snow pulled out the crumpled tape and dropped it on Bernstein's desk.

'You've heard the news over the ticker-tape?'

'Oh, yes. It's been coming through for several hours. I suppose you phoned London from Vaduz?'

'Actually, from Buchs.'

Bernstein nodded as he lit another cigarette.

'I expected you'd do that.'

The phone rang. Bernstein picked it up, listened for a moment, said a few words and put it down again. He looked at Snow.

'The Süddeutsche Bank has just failed. Almost a riot outside the doors this afternoon. Poor old Sternberg, he'll be like a jelly – he always was, of course.'

Snow stood up and walked over until he was standing very close to Bernstein. His face was grim.

'Bernstein, I want to know about Roberts. I want to know now.'

'He found out – about the deficit. The first man to do so. You asked me if anyone suspected. Roberts did. And he went on digging until he discovered the truth. As an accountant he was brilliant. In fact, he started all this.'

'How do you mean?'

'I hired him simply to prove that the Checkers Group had to be merged with Ikolon. Nothing to it, really, but some of the directors didn't agree and I prefer to prove a point rather than act like a dictator. . . . At the end of my first meeting with Roberts he asked me to leave a file containing certain information. I put my hand into my briefcase and gave it to him. Then I dashed off. . . . When I look back, it was very funny the way it happened.'

'I still don't follow you.'

Bernstein smiled sadly and pulled a face.

'I handed him the wrong file. It was as cruelly simple as that. You see, I was feeling unwell that morning and the one I gave Roberts contained a list of assets in certain companies. Alongside them was another list I'd written in, showing what the real assets were, which were only a fraction of what they should have been. . . . Most accountants wouldn't have appreciated their significance, but Roberts did.'

'He said something to you?'

'No, not then. When I reached my hotel I found out what had happened. I rushed back, gave him the right file and took the other one away. There was nothing in his manner to show that he had spotted anything, but then he was a quiet man.'

'When did you realize he suspected something?'

'He turned up in Frankfurt and started asking me questions. I very quickly saw that the names and figures in the

233

first file had told him what to look for, and he had looked. When he left, I half thought I had satisfied him, but I had him followed anyway. Instead of going back to London he took a plane to Zürich. He ended up in Vaduz, like you did. Then I realized he knew the truth. . . . He was going to report his findings to the authorities. He actually phoned me from Zürich before he flew home.'

'Go on, what happened then?' persisted Snow. They were standing very close to each other, face to face.

'I made a very bad mistake. I told Sternberg about it . . . not the whole thing, of course. He had no idea about Vaduz. I said this man Roberts had found out certain secret information . . . international connexions we wanted kept quiet, or we might find future operations more difficult. I should have handled it myself. . . . I see that now.'

'What did Sternberg do?' demanded Snow.

'I expected him to come to an arrangement with Roberts. Perhaps he tried to. I shall never know. If he did then Roberts must have refused. Sternberg then made a very big mistake. He panicked: he got in touch with Zenith and asked him to deal with Roberts – a crazy thing to do.'

'How on earth would a man like Sternberg know a man like Zenith?' Snow's tone of voice growled disbelief.

'I don't know. I don't think he did. I asked him at the Munich reception what he had done. He was very vague. I gathered he spoke to someone who knew someone who spoke to Zenith . . . these things are apparently never expressed openly . . . just a nod, a few words, a hint, a mention of a sum of money. Just like a business deal . . . complete madness. . . . I've even wondered if there were some ghastly mistake . . . if Sternberg didn't intend it to go as far as it did. . . . It could happen, I suppose.'

Bernstein didn't sound very convinced.

'So you knew Roberts had been murdered all along?'

'No.' Vehemently. 'Not until I talked with Sternberg at the Sacher after I got back from that awful drive to the border. I was appalled . . . I could have killed him.'

Bernstein stopped, embarrassed at his choice of words. Then he started talking again, as though desperately eager to convince Snow.

'I'd had a previous talk with Sternberg at the Munich reception. He told me Zenith was on to you . . . which is why I warned you as you left the Mozart.'

'You could have called off Zenith – or Sternberg could.'

'No, we couldn't. That was the horrible thing about it. Sternberg was already getting frightened. He had passed a message to Zenith from Munich that there must be no more violence, but Zenith wouldn't listen. He thought you had found something out about Roberts' death, so he insisted on protecting himself. Sternberg said he was in Zenith's hands. . . . What a position! You let in these gangs and they take over.'

Snow stood thinking for a moment. He was beginning to believe Bernstein, simply because it all seemed likely. The two men were still standing within inches of each other, as though engaged in a secret discussion in a public place.

'One thing doesn't make sense, Bernstein. I was followed from the moment I left London. So before you ever saw me I was being watched. That doesn't fit in, does it?'

'Yes, it does. Zenith was always very thorough. I gather he had been running this murder gang very successfully for a long time. Mainly because even after an episode he took care to watch out for trouble later. They were watching that Australian woman's flat and you were seen there. They found out you were an ex-policeman. That did it.

From then on they never let you out of their sight. When you came to see me they were convinced you were dangerous.'

Snow went back to his chair. He watched Bernstein take a sip of champagne and sit down behind his desk.

'Snow, you've got to track down Zenith.'

'I've already done so. Zenith is dead. He fell out of the Ticino Express when it was crossing a gorge, rather like one of his own accidents.'

Bernstein took the holder out of his mouth.

'Fell out?'

'Let's leave it at that. He killed Bibi. What I can't fathom is how she came to be found in a car half-way to Munich.'

'Joachim drove her there. On my instructions.'

It was Snow's turn to look surprised. He gazed blankly at Bernstein.

'Joachim? I don't understand.'

'When I reached Vienna there was an urgent message for me to phone Joachim at once. He's the receptionist at the Schloss Ludwig. He told me he had found Bibi's body in the lobby of your suite. I immediately realized it was an attempt on the part of Zenith to implicate you in a murder charge. Joachim had left the body where he found it while he waited for me to phone. I told him to take Bibi's body down in the lift, get it into a car and to leave it at the roadside well away from the Schloss.'

'You were taking a risk, weren't you? Could you trust Joachim to do all that for you?'

'No risk at all. I once financed the escape of Joachim's parents out of East Germany. He has a sense of gratitude. I've often noticed that the smaller people can be more decent. It's the big ones you have to watch. They appear to think that power excludes morality – or even decency.'

Bernstein opened a cigarette-box on his desk, looked inside and closed it again with a wry smile.

'That's really serious. I'm out of cigarettes!'

'Here you are.'

Snow offered his case, took one himself, lit them both and went back to his chair.

'You are telling me, then, Bernstein, that Roberts was murdered by Zenith?'

'Yes, he dealt with it himself.'

'I shall want that in writing. Now.'

Bernstein picked up his holder, paused and then put it down again without smoking. Opening a drawer, he took out some photographs and pushed them across the desk.

'I can do better than that. There's your evidence that Roberts was murdered.'

Snow picked up the prints and examined them. They were an amazing series of pictures. They showed a block of flats, taken from high up on the opposite side of the street. A few were enlargements of a window area only.

He began to arrange them in a certain sequence, like a collection of film stills. They showed a man looking out of an open window, quite clearly it was Roberts. He was gazing towards the camera . . . leaning out . . . further out . . . falling. And behind him, in the last pictures, as he was falling, another man stood framed in the open window, his arms outstretched. It was Scardale-Zenith-Dietrich.

Bernstein put his hand down into the drawer again and came up with a flat aluminium canister. He pushed it over the desk to Snow.

'Those prints are stills from a 16-mm. film. The complete film shows the whole horrible business from start to finish.'

'Why was the film taken?'

'A stroke of luck. It was taken from the house opposite by one of Zenith's own men who stayed on afterwards to watch the place. Zenith didn't know the film was being taken, of course. The other man knew Sternberg had hired Zenith. He got the idea of selling the film to Sternberg for a large sum of money. Then if Zenith turned awkward Sternberg could use the film to neutralize Zenith by threatening to send the film to the police anonymously.'

Snow frowned. 'But Sternberg could have used this film to keep Zenith in line. Why didn't he?'

Bernstein smiled bitterly. He picked up the holder and started fiddling with it.

'Because by then Sternberg was scared stiff of Zenith. He thought that if Zenith knew he had this film he might kill him. I told you, Sternberg is a jelly.'

'So you took the film off Sternberg?'

Bernstein laughed shortly, without humour.

'No trouble at all. Sternberg was only too glad to give it to me. That took the responsibility off him and put it on me. Pity I didn't get it earlier – I'd have used it. I didn't know of its existence until last Tuesday afternoon in Vienna.'

'You took a terrible risk in not telling me this when we were heading for the Czech border.'

'I didn't know then that Zenith had murdered Roberts. I only suspected it. I've never even met Zenith so I couldn't identify him. I thought it would sound like a fable I'd made up . . . after all, a murder gang . . .'

'Bibi never said anything to you about Zenith, then?'

Bernstein looked bewildered. He put the holder back in the ashtray.

'No. Did she know about him?'

'She'd heard a rumour. Nothing more. One last ques-

238

tion, Bernstein. What made you take the film off Sternberg?'

'I had started thinking about Roberts' wife quite a lot
by then. I don't really know exactly why I took it. In a
way perhaps I anticipated this meeting between us. I have
a talent for predicting the future.'

Snow stood up slowly, as though reluctant to leave. He
picked up the canister and put it inside his pocket with the
prints.

'You realize, Bernstein, I shall have to tell the British
police where I got this film from, and all you have told
me?'

'Yes, of course. Not that you could ever link me with it
in a court of law.'

'You might be right there.'

'Although I am completely responsible.'

Bernstein said the words very quietly and stood up
behind his desk. They shook hands. Snow turned to go,
but Bernstein was speaking again.

'Snow, would you come back here in an hour's time?
I have something else to show you. Further evidence. I
shall have it ready by then. You have brought down the
pack of cards so it is only fair you should be in at the
death.'

'You brought the card house down yourself, I'm afraid.
You should have suffocated me with indifference when I
turned up. Seeing me, talking to me, that was what did
the damage.'

'Yes, but I didn't know how much you knew. I thought
it safer to keep you in sight. A great mistake, I admit. But
I have always preferred to meet danger half-way.'

'All right, Bernstein. I'll be back in an hour.'

Snow walked over to the door. Then he stopped, looking back at Bernstein's desk. The cigarette-holder lay in

the ashtray. Inside it was a half-smoked cigarette which had burnt itself out. Nearby stood Bernstein's champagne glass. Snow felt he had to say something.

'You haven't finished your champagne.'

Bernstein smiled slightly.

'It tastes foul.'

20

A Dead Cigarette

The reception hall of the Cavalieri was empty when Snow returned an hour later. The crowd in the corner had gone. The ticker-tape machine was muttering away quietly to itself, a streamer of paper snaking down slowly into the overflowing bin by its side. Snow shook his head at the receptionist and walked straight over to the lift.

At the second floor he stepped out into a deserted corridor. He glanced at his watch. It was 7.30 p.m. He walked along to Bernstein's suite and pressed the bell. There was no answer. He pressed the bell again. Still no answer.

He tried the door. It was unlocked. Opening it quietly he walked into an ante-room and closed the door behind him. The room had a sound-proof atmosphere. He sat down on a chair and lit a cigarette.

For several minutes he listened to the silence, absorbing the feeling of emptiness, as though the suite had been vacated long ago. At one moment he almost fell asleep.

Then he stubbed his cigarette in an ashtray, stood up and listened again. An idea began to grow that no one was coming.

His feet made no sound as he walked across the thick carpet to the door leading to the room where he had left Bernstein. He listened again, opened the door slowly and walked inside.

Bernstein was lying across his desk, his head to one side, his right hand close to his head, a pistol slipping through the fingers. The side of his head where the bullet had entered was an unpleasant sight.

Snow walked round the back of the desk and looked down at him. From that angle Bernstein gave the impression he had fallen asleep. Bending over him, Snow felt his pulse and checked the artery in his neck. Bernstein was dead.

Putting his hands in his jacket pockets, Snow stood quite still for a moment, as though in memory. He recalled Bernstein's voice, full of vitality, talking away nineteen to the dozen. The stillness of the room seemed unnatural. He said something to himself which sounded like '. . . cruel farce.'

As he looked down at the desk he noticed the champagne glass was still half-full. The holder lay in the ashtray where he had last seen it, containing the dead cigarette. Since he had left the room an hour before Bernstein had neither smoked nor drunk any of his beloved champagne.

A long white envelope lay on the desk. Snow picked it up. Written on the front in neat handwriting were the words *Private. For John Snow.* In the bottom right-hand corner was a signature, *Josef Bernstein.*

He opened the envelope and took out a piece of folded notepaper. The letter, very brief, was written by hand.

Please convey my deepest regrets to Mrs Roberts. I should like her to know that I knew nothing of what was going to happen. Had I known I could never have countenanced it. It is all too late now, mud under the wheels of history. Good-bye.

Imre Esterhay
PS. You might like to know that I was born within sight of the Carpathians, the grimmest mountains in the world. Not that it matters any more.

Snow put the letter back inside the envelope and tucked the envelope in his pocket. Walking over to a small table he picked up a telephone directory and found a number. Then he lifted the phone and asked the hotel switchboard to get the number. He walked slowly round the room until the phone rang.

'Police? Please put me through . . . Giordano . . . I know him personally. . . . Is that you, Dante? Snow here again. I'm in Room 79, the Cavalieri . . . you'd better come over right away . . . yes, yourself. . . . Bernstein has shot himself . . . yes, dead. . . . I've phoned the news to a press agency . . . quite wrong, I know . . . but it will save your people trouble, deciding when to release the news. . . . Blame me . . . I mean it . . . *arrivederci*.'

He looked up another number and again asked the hotel operator to get it. When the phone rang Snow picked it up and began talking rapidly.

'Exchange Telegraph? . . . Listen carefully . . . switch on your recording machine if you've got one . . . I'm speaking from Room 79, the Cavalieri. . . . Josef Bernstein has just been found shot dead . . . yes, dead . . . yes, Josef Bernstein, the international financier. . . . There's only one, you know. Suicide? You'd better ask the police. . . . That's all. No, my name is of no importance.'

He put the phone down and looked across at the desk. He felt certain Bernstein would have wanted the news announced at the earliest possible moment. Now it was out of his hands. He could stand aside and watch the fall of the avalanche.

21
The Last Train

The taxi hurtled up the via leading to Milano Centrale as though escaping from the police. There was hardly any other traffic as the solitary taxi raced through the night.

Snow looked out of the window. The Pirelli building was flood-lit, soaring up into the blue darkness. It reminded him of a mountain on the Austrian-German border, hundreds of miles away to the north-east beyond the Alpine range. Perhaps the searchlights on the Stagenwand would be switched off for ever, like the life of Josef Bernstein.

Swinging round a corner, the taxi braked to a halt in front of the station. Snow stepped out, paid the driver, took a last look at the white skyscraper and walked inside the station.

He rode up to the top terrace on an aluminium escalator and walked into the vast concourse. The stale air of a long hot day filled the terminus.

Passengers milled about in the concourse, scurrying backwards and forwards like disturbed ants. Alongside the platforms giant trains waited patiently, ready to start their trans-continental journeys.

With a bag in each hand, Snow walked past the platform barriers. He checked the departure board. The night train to Calais, departing 2200 hours, was waiting at Platform 11.

He started trudging alongside the endless train. He felt

he was walking to Calais. At long last he saw the coaches marked *Wagon-Lits*. He climbed aboard. There were plenty of empty sleeping compartments. He went inside one, manhandled his bags up to the rack, and sat down on the bed while he paid the ticket inspector. Then, in spite of the heat, he firmly closed the door and locked it. He was alone again.

Waves of fatigue swept over him. He was almost giddy with exhaustion. It was the inevitable reaction. There was no need to worry any more, no one to creep into his compartment with lethal weapons. It was all over, time to give way.

He sat quite motionless until suddenly the express began to move north. Again there was no warning, just instant movement. He listened to the rumble of wheels, felt the shudder as the coach crossed the points outside Centrale. Then the only sound was a steady thud-thud as the train gathered speed, heading across the Po plain towards the Swiss border.

With an effort he stood up and opened the window. Taking off his top clothes, he washed at the corner basin. When he had dried himself he took out a cigarette, looked at it, put it back inside his case, switched off the light and lay down on the bed.

After an hour he realized sleep was impossible. He could hardly move but his mind was racing round like a cog-wheel out of control.

The train stopped at Lugano for several minutes and then resumed its long journey. After a steady climb into the hills above Lake Maggiore there was a sudden change. The train began to plunge downhill rapidly, lurching round curves, swaying from side to side. Snow knew it was the beginning of the long slide to the Ticino valley.

He sat up, lifted the blind and peered out. The plain lay

far below, a terrifying drop at night. Away in the distance, hundreds of feet down, he could see the lights of Bellinzona, like a tiara crowning a whole town. The lights began to blur and dance before his eyes.

As he pulled down the blind he wondered whether Mrs Roberts was still up. Then he lay back on his pillow and fell fast asleep.

22
Tail-Sting

Mrs Roberts looked at him with puzzled eyes.

'But, Mr Snow, I expected you to keep in touch as you found things out.'

'Just exactly what do you mean by that?'

Snow was sitting in the same chair he had occupied when he first met her. It was almost the same time of day, but this time the light was on when he arrived. His elbow touched the same polished table by his side. The same reflection of the overhead lampshade was mirrored in its gleaming surface.

She frowned, her eyes dark and staring.

'You should have phoned to tell me what was happening. I tried to reach you but it was impossible.'

'You could hardly have helped. In any case your husband's name is cleared now beyond any doubt.'

'Yes, but it's too late now. Bernstein is dead.'

'Too late for what, Mrs Roberts?'

'With this information in my hands about the money missing from Vaduz I could have done something. Have you any idea, Mr Snow, what Bernstein would have paid for my silence?'

'How much would you have suggested?' Snow's voice was very quiet, almost matter of fact.

'A quarter of a million, at least.'

'A quarter of a million? Pounds, marks, francs or dollars?'

'Pounds, of course.'

'Are you really saying that if I had phoned you from Vaduz you would have asked me to blackmail Bernstein?'

'No, of course not. You wouldn't have done it. I'm quite sure of that. I would have caught the first plane to Milan myself. I would have demanded the money from Bernstein. I am quite capable of it.'

'I believe you.'

Snow's face was expressionless.

'Now the chance has gone for ever.' Mrs Roberts's face was tense with exasperation.

Snow leaned forward in his chair. He spoke gently.

'I was under the impression you wished to clear your husband's name at all costs. For the sake of your two children, you said.'

'That is quite right.'

'But part of your attempted deal with Bernstein would have been a promise of silence on your part. Remember, you say you were going to ask him for money. And a quarter of a million too. Rather a large sum, isn't it?'

'He had millions, hadn't he? He would have paid a large sum to avoid exposure. I'm sure I could have made him see it my way.'

'You are talking of blackmail, Mrs Roberts. Blackmail is a crime.'

Her face expressed indignation. She sat up very straight.

'And so is murder. He was responsible for the death of my husband. Nothing can bring David back now. I have to look after myself and the children. I could at least have made him pay. Only a large sum would hurt a man like that. I think he was married to money.'

Snow was again startled at her perception. She had never even met the man, yet she hit the nail on the head.

'Mrs Roberts, you talk about looking after yourself, but I thought you said you were well off?'

'And so I am, compared to many people. But a quarter of a million! Think of what I could have done for the children with that.'

Her eyes were huge with the immensity of the thought. She held her hands clasped in her lap, the knuckles white under the pressure of her grip.

Snow stood up, still outwardly unmoved. He picked up the film canister and photographs and put them back in his pocket.

'I shall hand these over to the police. I intend to see your husband is fully exonerated from the suicide verdict. We shall also do something about Mrs Warner. You must excuse me now, but I must go.'

Mrs Roberts stood up, her hands by her sides. She was calmer now.

'You'll send me a bill for your expenses. I posted off a cheque for your fee to your flat. You'll find it waiting for you. I expect you to add any further fee to your bill.'

Snow made no reply. He stood for a moment looking at her. Perhaps the shock of her husband's death and the ordeal which followed had unbalanced her. He didn't think so, but it was just possible.

'Was it a very difficult investigation, Mr Snow?'

'In places. I must go now. No, don't bother. I can let myself out.'

He walked across the room. She followed him, opened the door and stood holding the handle.

'I want to say I am very grateful, Mr Snow. I hope you won't feel too badly about me. Will you come and see me some time?'

The extraordinary thing was she sounded as though she

meant it. She held out her hand as she said good-bye. It seemed very small and fragile as he shook it briefly.

Picking up his bags he went down the stairs. As he walked across the lower landing and down the next flight he could see her out of the corner of his eye, standing at the door, watching him until he disappeared from view.

Outside in the street a taxi was passing. He hailed it, gave the address of his flat and climbed inside. He could hardly keep his eyes open. On the train he had woken up again at Basle and found it impossible to get any more sleep. The Dover ferry had been delayed several hours at Calais, waiting for a storm in the Channel to subside. He had had enough.

As the taxi drove through the night streets of London his thoughts jostled each other in a confused way. He found fragments of Bernstein's conversation on the road to the border drifting back into his mind.

'The wife of that accountant could probably do with some money, a lot of money.'

Bernstein and Mrs Roberts. They had never met but how well they had guessed each other's character. Snow sighed to himself. The only thing he knew about people was that he never really knew anything about them.

He glanced out of the window. The taxi was moving down a narrow street very slowly, crawling behind a line of traffic. Standing against a wall was a row of newspaper placards, their messages printed in huge letters.

Wall Street Panic.

Run on the Dollar.

Shares Collapse.

SLUMP?

As the taxi began to move more quickly he closed his eyes and fell asleep.